I0663876

The Museum of Lies

J. Timothy Hunt

Clink Street

Published by Clink Street Publishing 2024

Copyright © 2024

First edition.

ISBN:
978-1-915785-43-5 - paperback
978-1-915785-44-2 - ebook

NEW YORK POST

A MUSEUM OF UNNATURAL HISTORY

Mummified human remains found in Upper West Side condo

by Calvin Crestwood
Wednesday, April 21, 2015
Last Updated: 12:37 p.m.

In what police are calling "the most bizarre case in recent memory," the mummified remains of an unidentified male were discovered in a "museum-like" Upper West Side condominium.

Shortly after 3 p.m. yesterday, the superintendent of 264 W. 81st St, Jorge Ortega, entered a 4th floor apartment after downstairs neighbors complained of water leaking from the unit above.

Ortega telephoned 911 after finding the desiccated body of an adult male lying face-up on the floor in the middle of the studio apartment. Odder still was the room itself. Police Detective Olga Watson described it as "an old-fashioned cabinet of curiosities – like something out of a Victorian horror novel."

Two walls of the room had floor-to-ceiling mahogany display cases containing a large number of eccentric oddities. Among the artfully arranged items were the skeleton of a cat, a jar of ipecac, a Polynesian grass skirt, surgical scalpels, a 1950s vintage rubber enema kit, a rotary-dial analog phone, a cracked motorcycle helmet, voodoo dolls, a copy of the 1960 children's book *The Boy Who Fooled the Giant*, and a 1977 copy of *The Joy of Gay Sex*.

The focal point of the apartment, however, was an articulated anatomical skeleton fashioned from the bones of a human cadaver.

Flanking the skeleton was a "shrine" to 1970s pop star Karen Carpenter and a wall of framed photos and documents including an animation cel of Pebbles Flintstone, and two RIAA certified records: a platinum record for Kitty Belle Crawford's 1975 novelty hit "Lookey, Lookey" and a gold record for Senator Marla Wylie's early career pop classic "My Karma Ran Over My Dogma."

Police estimate that the body of the man found on the floor could have been there for months, or even years. A large, industrial air purifier and dehumidifier – most likely meant to preserve the curious collection – in effect "mummified" the dead body, making the time or date of death difficult to determine. A leak in the dehumidifier's drain hose was the cause of the downstairs neighbor's complaint.

Only one tenant in the building can recall ever seeing someone come and go from the apartment. Patty de Palma, a longtime building resident, recalled "a thin, white-haired gentleman" who would occasionally nod to her as they passed in the hallway.

According to city records, the condo was purchased by R.B. Welch in 1993. The identity of the body in the apartment is unknown, but is described as a white male, 5'4" tall, possibly 40 to 70 years old. No identification was found on the body or in the apartment. Police are searching for friends or relatives of Welch to determine if he is the deceased.

Anyone with information about R.B. Welch is requested to contact Detective Watson at the 33rd precinct at 212-793-3745 ext 32.

CHAPTER ONE

1983

There are only three places in Taos, New Mexico, where you can buy Boston cream doughnuts: Smith's Grocery store, which is nearest my artist's studio; the Safeway about a half mile south down Paseo del Pueblo Sur; and a little restaurant and bakery called Michael's Kitchen just north of the plaza. I have an ingenious plan mapped out by this, the third week of my poet's residency here. Since it would be unthinkable to just go into one of these places regularly (well, *daily*) and ask for a dozen Boston cream doughnuts, I put myself on a random time-and-location staggered shopping schedule so that no store in Taos will suspect me of being a regular customer.

It's 10:30 in the morning on a Thursday: time to make the half-hour walk to the post office to check general delivery for my mail. Of course I never receive any mail. There is no one on earth who would consider writing to me. The post office is just an excuse to drop into Michael's Kitchen which is located so very conveniently on the next block.

Buying doughnuts is an emotionally wrenching experience. The post office is always a good place to stall a moment and gather my courage before going to the bakery. Sometimes even the post office isn't enough. Often it takes a trip to the post office, a half hour browsing at Radio Shack, *and* a half hour wandering the aisles at Ten Directions Used Bookstore before the obsession for the Boston cream doughnuts outweighs my shame.

Today, however, the post office is enough. The call of the doughnuts is deafening. As I steel my resolve and pull open the screen door to Michael's Kitchen, my heart races in my chest just the way it always does whenever I try to buy a porno magazine. Unfortunately, I can't avoid the humiliation of the salesgirl's glance by shoplifting the doughnuts like I shoplift a *Playgirl*. For some reason, doughnuts in bakeries are kept behind glass like diamond bracelets at Tiffany's.

Michael's Kitchen is a funky joint. The front section is a ramshackle bakery and gift shop dealing in rib-sticking baked goods and rough-hewn souvenirs. It looks more like the lobby of a fishing lodge than a restaurant. This is the area you have to wait in before a very hairy man – a walking time capsule of the psychedelic sixties – shows you to your seat in the shellacked plywood booths of the dining room.

But I never come to Michael's Kitchen for lunch. As always, I'm here for the bakery case. Today there is someone behind the cash register I don't recognize, the oldest teenager I have ever seen. The deep labial lines around her mouth and the streaks of gray through her blond pigtails belie her intended illusion that she is some sort of college freshman. Anyway, I don't know the old coed and she doesn't seem to recognize me. Good. My time-staggered schedule is working. She has no clue I have been at this very counter just yesterday afternoon at 4:37 p.m.

"Hi," she says, and that look briefly shoots across her face. That look people get when their impulse to gasp or gawk is squelched to be replaced with strained politeness. "Can I help you?"

"Um, I don't know," I say, feigning indecision, trying to breathe slowly, act casually. "Um, um, I, uh … Those look interesting. What are they?"

"Bear claws."

"Oh. Yes. And these?"

"Boston cream."

"Uh … give me one of the Boston cream."

She grabs a square of wax paper from a pop-up box on the counter and takes the first chocolate-covered, cream-filled doughnut out of the display case.

"Wait," I say. "Why don't you make it a dozen? They'll keep won't they? I'll put them in the freezer and it'll save me coming back here for a couple of months."

She doesn't reply. She just assembles a bakery box and fills it up with thirteen doughnuts. A baker's dozen. I take the money out of my wallet way too soon. The ten-dollar bill I hand her is damp with the sweat from my hands. I notice that from the moment after she says hi until the moment the screen door slams behind my ass on the way out, she never once makes eye contact with me.

Out on the sidewalk. Free. Mission accomplished. I instantly wish I were back home, or had a car, a bicycle, anything, anything to shorten the long walk home from Michael's Kitchen. I'm not in the best of shape these days and the sidewalks of Taos are a pedestrian's nightmare, narrow, rolling walkways with lots of little steps to climb on the steep uphills or precarious sloping runs on the sharp downhills. "No," I think to myself, "I couldn't use a bike here. I could never make it up and down these streets. Besides, there's too much traffic and too many damned tourists hogging the sidewalk."

Just as I'm thinking this, an obnoxious family of five is huddled in front of a gift shop window, completely blocking my way. Cars parked close to the curb and standstill traffic in the street make it impossible for me to get by the loud family any other way than right through their midst.

"Excuse me," I say with just the slightest edge to my voice to indicate my annoyance with the rudeness of their taking up the whole walk. I squeeze by them, hugging the bakery box close to my chest, trying to keep the guilty smell of fresh baked goods from their detection.

I hear the mother mumble to her husband, "Well, if he wasn't so damned fat, there'd be *plenty* of room for him to get by."

My heart gives a sharp thud. One of the children makes rhythmic farty sounds with his lips in sync with my footfalls while another child tries to suppress a giggle. I ignore them, or rather try to give the impression that I am ignoring them, and walk on down the sidewalk.

I'm not that fat, I say to myself, tightening my stomach muscles, walking just a little taller to make myself feel thinner. I'll do a few sit-ups when I get home. Or maybe I'll go jogging out on the back roads toward Cañon. That way, if I have to stop and walk every so often, no one will see me. God, it's getting hot. I'm really starting to sweat. I can't go jogging in this heat. I'll wait till this evening when it cools down. I want one of these doughnuts now.

As I walk along, I break the thin red twine on the box and reach inside for a Boston cream. The heat of the day is making the chocolate run and my fingers get all brown and sticky. I don't care. I take a large bite out of the side of the doughnut, practically inhaling it. The second bite is more of a normal-sized bite as I suck and draw most of the inner well of custard into my mouth.

The chocolate is running down the side of my hand. I can feel its stickiness on my upper lip and a rivulet of chocolate running down my chin. I don't have a napkin with me so I get one of those squares of wax paper from the box and try to use a clean section of it to wipe my face.

I don't know if I got it all. I check my reflection in an appliance store window for any embarrassing traces of chocolate. The corners of my mouth and the tip of my chin are stained dark brown. I lick my thumb and start to erase the remaining spots on my face. The plate glass window is slightly bowed out like a funhouse mirror. It makes my head look chinless and neckless, a perfectly round globe sitting atop my shoulders. I look quickly away from my reflection in the glass and turn down the side street on the way to my dark, cool adobe house.

I'm an artist at the Wurlitzer Foundation, an artist colony for people in the creative arts – painters, writers, and composers (as opposed to interpretive artists like actors, singers and dancers). I don't know where in the hell interpretive artists go to work on their craft. They probably do summer stock in Cleveland or something. Anyway, I'm a poet. Or at least that's what I tell people I am, as I'm the one who believes it the least of all.

The Wurlitzer Foundation is just a group of ten little adobe houses that old Mrs. Helene Wurlitzer, the juke box and organ heiress, bought up around her rambling New Mexican home. Before she died, she set up a foundation granting free rent and utilities in these little houses to artists from around the world.

I'm more amazed than anybody that I was chosen to spend my summer here, as most of my fellow inmates have frighteningly impressive resumes while I basically have no resume at all. I call myself a poet when the truth is I wrote a silly poem when I was fifteen and, by sheer happenstance, a country singer turned it into a top-ten hit. That was back in 1974, almost a decade ago, and I haven't published a thing since. I'm just "The Guy Who Wrote That Dumb Song." It's depressing.

I stumble, sweaty and gasping, up onto the porch of my house and sit myself down on an old wooden straight-backed chair. The shade of the porch and the coolness of the adobe walls help to revive me. Out in the yard, black-and-white magpies caw fiercely and peck at one another in a bird duel. I nonchalantly look around to see if any neighbors are watching or if any pedestrians are apt to come walking by. There's no one around. Just me and the birds.

And so I begin.

The third doughnut out of the box is always the best one. That's the doughnut I can enjoy because it's the first one I actually pay any attention to. Doughnuts One and Two are only there to be inhaled, shoved desperately into my mouth to relieve the mania that caused me to buy them in the first place. Doughnuts One and Two are the dirty, illicit ones. Just like *Playgirl*, they're porno.

Doughnut Three is the one out of the whole dozen that tastes most like a doughnut. It's the one I spend the most time with, feeling the contrasts of textures in my mouth: the oily cake, the sticky chocolate, the satiny custard. Doughnut Number Three is the best moment of the day for me. The one Zen moment when I'm truly living in the present, awake to my senses, alive.

Then my day changes.

Doughnuts Four, Five, Six, Seven, Eight, Nine, Ten, Eleven, Twelve, and Thirteen are the doughnuts of obsession. They are when my work truly begins. I know after Doughnut Three that I've had enough and I should close the box, but I don't do it. I know there will be no rest for me until the last doughnut is consumed.

If I should rally my willpower and place a half-dozen doughnuts away on a high shelf, or under the kitchen sink in back of the bottle of Drano and the box of Brillo Pads, even if I should wrap the leftovers tightly in plastic wrap and place them in the freezer telling myself they're there for long-term storage, they call to me from their hiding places as cruel and incessant as *The Tell-Tale Heart*. They keep me from reading books, from scribbling at my poems, from sitting in a chair, from sleeping at night.

So now I've given up the hollow sham of willpower and found that life is so much easier if I just buckle down and eat the entire thirteen in one sitting. I stuff myself until my stomach is queasy from the sugar and is as ready for popping as a birthday balloon.

I only get as far as Doughnut Eight before I see some movement down the long rutted dirt driveway that connects all the artist casitas. Marla Wylie is walking toward me. I nimbly close the doughnut box and stash it on the ground behind my chair and wipe my mouth. She hasn't seen me yet. I need to find something innocuous to be discovered doing before she arrives. What? I remember that my notebook and ballpoint pen are on the table just inside the screen door. I get up and nip inside the house, grab them and sit back down on my porch chair. I'll make her think I've been writing a poem.

She's getting closer. I can hear her footsteps. Marla clearly sees me now. She waves. I pretend to be shaken out of my poetic reverie by her approach and allow a convincingly realistic wave of recognition to wash over my face. I wave back. Marla starts talking to me long before she actually gets up to my house.

"I'm just on my way back from a church flea market. Wait till you see what I bought. Well, I guess you already see it right now 'cause I'm wearing it. Isn't it great? Five bucks."

She arrives on my porch and turns around to model the bright red baseball jacket she is wearing. Across the shoulder blades is embroidered "Taos Fire Department" in yellow cotton braid. A cartoon of a Dalmatian puppy drooling longingly at a golden fire plug is centered on the back. It's a camp masterpiece and I'm wildly jealous over her find. Although I note that Marla is roughly the same build as a prepubescent little leaguer, had I been the one to make the find there's no way I could have ever fit into it. This makes me doubly jealous so I pretend to be politely interested but unimpressed.

"It's beautiful," I say. "It should clean up very nicely."

"It is clean," she says, bluntly unaware of my envious little dig. "Couldn't be cleaner. I came by this morning to see if you wanted to go with me, but you weren't around."

"I walked to the post office."

"So I went by myself and ran into Karma at the Taco Tia."

"What is that? A Buddhist country song?"

"No, Karma Minkowitz. In house number four. The one we hardly ever see? Not the house. Karma. She's like this hermit. Paints portraits of people in food. You know, olive pits for nostrils and bananas for eyebrows, stuff like that. Well, I ran into her at the Taco Tia and guess what she was doing?"

"Gerald Ford in chimichangas?"

"Working behind the counter!" Marla exclaims.

"So?"

"We're not supposed to hold jobs while we're here. Didn't you read that weird rule sheet on the inside of your front door?"

Actually, I had glanced at the foundation's list of rules the day I moved in. It said things like guns, overnight trips, guests and jobs were forbidden. Since the concept of me having a job was even more farfetched than the thought of me owning a gun, I pretty much ignored it all. These were rules for people who were definitely not me.

Marla continues on. "Well, of course I'm not going to say anything to anybody about Karma. I don't want to get her in trouble. But Jesus God it pisses me off 'cause I know that if I did anything like that, I'd be thrown out of here in a minisecond."

"Millisecond," I correct her.

"It really freaked me out when I saw all the rules and stuff they've got here. No gardens, no pets, no friends, no phones. I'm afraid to fart the wrong way for fear of getting evicted."

"Well, I'm sure they just didn't come up with this stuff out of thin air," I say. "Some people must have been really out of line at one time."

"We got this place in Seattle I go to, The Zenporium, where they don't even have rules because nobody ever breaks them."

This little vacation from logic amuses me. "Wow," I say. "Maybe if we get rid of driver's licenses, there'd be no more car wrecks."

"You know what I mean." Marla says, scowling. "I knew you'd say something really sarcastic like that."

"What's the matter? Don't they have sarcasm in Seattle?"

"No," she says. Only she says it with such unintended irony that I burst out laughing.

Marla apparently doesn't appreciate being laughed at. She fixes upon me a look of regal disdain and says, "Wipe your face."

I stop laughing, stunned. My hands immediately fly toward my mouth, wiping furiously. She turns and walks away.

I hoist myself off my chair and rush inside the house to look at my face in the bathroom mirror. My heart starts pounding again in rage and humiliation. Not only do I have chocolate smeared on my chin, but I've also got it on the underside of my nose, my cheekbone, and all over the front of my shirt.

I turn on the faucet and start splashing water on my face. I must have looked ridiculous out there! I sat there talking to Marla looking like a pig and had the nerve to make fun of *her*. I desperately want to call her back, to apologize, to win back her sympathy before she starts going door to door telling everybody about how that fat pig, Cary Scott, treated her like an idiot.

As I take off my shirt and start scrubbing off the chocolate stains under the running tap, I realize I'm not really sorry I was condescending to Marla. I'm only really sorry I looked foolish while I was doing it. I'm a terrible person. I deserve to be humiliated. In a way, we had both run into Karma today.

Fucking chocolate! It's not coming out of my shirt. Now every time I wear it, there's going to be this stain, this Boston cream doughnut stain, that's going to remind me and Marla (and everyone she tells) about what a pig I am.

I look up from my washing into the mirror. I take a really hard look at myself, shirtless. The rolls of fat on my chest make me look like I have breasts. I draw in my stomach muscles. It doesn't help. I still look fat. I raise my chin an inch and stand a little taller, as if to convince myself that I'm not really overweight, it just looks that way because I've got bad posture. It makes no difference to my double chin, to my rounded cheeks, to my lack of neck. For the first time ever, I notice that even my earlobes are overweight.

I'm enormous. I'm disgusting. I want to take a sharp knife and carve away all the fat parts of me. I want emergency liposuction. I've had enough. That's it, brother – I'm going to lose weight. I'm going to go on a diet. No, I'm going to go on a fast. I'm never going to eat again. No, that's not good, I can't not eat. I'll become a vegetarian. I'll just eat steamed vegetables. I won't even have milk or milk products. Unless I go on Slim-Fast, then I'll have to have some milk. And potatoes are a vegetable. I can have those, and if I mash them, I'll have to put a little milk in there, too.

These thoughts come flying through me as I stand before the mirror. In less than thirty seconds I have decided that the only way to fight the humiliation of Marla telling everyone what a fat pig I am is to get thin. And get thin fast.

I'll go jogging today. Well … later. It's too hot right now. First I'll walk over to Smith's Grocery and stock up on stuff to make me thin. Vegetables. Slim-Fast. I'm going to go right now. The sooner I get the things I need, the sooner I'll get thin.

I throw my chocolate-stained shirt into the waste basket and go into my bedroom to find something else to wear. I choose an oversized white Abba t-shirt and pull it on over my head. I leave the shirt untucked to disguise my body shape as much as possible. I go into the kitchen and start purging the cabinets and the refrigerator of anything fattening. Crackers, cookies, chips, ice cream, jack cheese, sour cream, butter, Crisco. Out they all go. I tumble all these evil parcels into a couple of brown paper grocery sacks and march determinedly toward the front door.

As I pass by the chair on the front porch, I see the box with the five remaining Boston cream doughnuts tucked between the two back legs. I reach down and retrieve the box, shoving it resolutely into my bags of groceries to be discarded, then I'm on my way. Smith's Grocery is only a ten minute walk from my casita, down at the end of Los Pandos Road where it meets Paseo del Pueblo. The Indian Cliffs Motel is at this intersection, too. As I walk by the side of the motel, I see an open green metal dumpster and fling my sacks of fatty foods into it. They're gone. They're out of my life. I'm free.

I cross the busy Paseo when the light changes and go across the parking lot to the grocery store.

Smith's is a large chain of Mormon-owned grocery stores. One half of the store is devoted to groceries, the other half (decidedly un-Mormonly) sells drugstore items and liquor. I extract a wire shopping cart from the tangle by the front door and push my way directly to the produce department.

Mounds of leafy kale, broccoli, spinach, and red leaf lettuce line an entire wall and glisten with cold mist. The whole display is very sumptuous but about as appetizing as a well-tended English garden. If I bought these vegetables I wouldn't have a clue how to prepare them. Jicama? What is that? Pyramids of fruit are in the bins in the center of the aisle. Fourteen kinds of apples, tangelos, grapefruits, plums, and peaches are all perfectly stacked for inspection.

But I don't like grapefruit. Apples aren't in season so they probably taste mushy and the plums and peaches are hard as rocks. I put a plastic bag of oranges and a bunch of green grapes in my cart. The grapes I keep on the child's seat by the handlebar so I can snack on them as I shop. I have no idea what else I should buy. Maybe if I find the Slim-Fast, there'll be an insert or something in the package that will tell me what else I'm supposed to eat.

Slyly putting a grape into my mouth like a conjuring trick, I push my cart over to the pharmaceutical aisles. I go past disposable diapers, depilatories, and douches before I find diet aids. There are a lot of products to choose from: Metracal, Nutrament, Dexatrim – and a familiar candy box from my childhood that says "Lose Weight the Ayds Way!" I wonder if this new disease everyone's freaking out about will hurt sales. Some perverse part of me hopes it does.

I find the canisters of Slim-Fast toward the middle of the aisle, just where the merchandise segues into digestive remedies. As I reach for the Slim-Fast, I catch sight of a tiny bottle on a nearby shelf. Although it resembles a bottle of iodine, the label says "ipecac." Of course I know what ipecac is. It's to make you throw up.

Back home in California I saw an item on the news that some drug stores had to take ipecac off the shelves and put it behind the pharmacy counter because teenage girls were buying lots of it and becoming bulimic. I remember kicking myself at the time for not knowing about ipecac sooner because there were many times I'd love to just vomit myself empty after going on a binge. A spoon down my throat didn't seem to do anything for me because I guess I don't have much of a gag reflex. Ipecac seemed like an ideal answer for me, but by the time I first heard about it, it was unavailable.

I take the bottle off the shelf and read the label. Emetic. Even the word is comforting. Hopeful. I'm feeling the greasy weight of the eight doughnuts inside me and I long to emit. I want this bottle. I'm afraid of it, but I want it. The thought of vomiting brings up all sorts of unpleasant memories of childhood illnesses and bouts of stomach flu. Surely the stuff in this bottle won't make me feel sick. It'll just flush out my stomach. One quick spoonful and – blech! It's over. I'll still have to go on a diet, but if I cheat, I can just undo the damage with a teaspoon of ipecac and a quick trip to the loo.

Dulcolax. The little box of laxative tablets near the ipecac steals my attention next. You know, the less time the food I put inside me stays inside me, the fewer calories I'll absorb. If I can force food out of one end of me, why not both ends? I'll rush the food through me like a freight train. I'll never be hungry and I'll lose tons. Tons!

I add Dulcolax to the ipecac and fruit in my cart. I get a can of chocolate Slim-Fast and a plastic gallon jug of whole milk, a box of Sweet 'n Low, instant mashed potatoes, margarine, five boxes of sugar-free vanilla instant pudding, a plastic measuring tumbler with a lid (for mixing the Slim-Fast and the pudding), a box of fruit-sweetened cream sandwich cookies (only fifty calories a cookie), and a large bag of frozen burritos (why not?).

There is now more food in my grocery cart than there was in all the bags of food I threw out of my kitchen. But that was bad food, I tell myself, and this is good food. I have so many items that I'm not ashamed to go through the checkout stand. Surely the sheer quantity of products I pile onto the conveyor belt will keep little Kevin, the post-pubescent Mormon cashier, from being able to focus on any one item, or, for that matter, me.

Of course it's a little daunting when I see that I have to shell out forty-five dollars and I have to lug three very heavy sacks of groceries home on foot. Milk sure weighs a ton when you buy it by the gallon. Add to that the five-pound bag of oranges and another pound of (slightly nibbled) grapes and I ruefully note I'm in for a very long, arduous, walk.

It takes about twice as long for me to get home as it took me to get to the store, since I have to put down my bags and rest every fifty yards or so. I'm exhausted. That's it then. No jogging for me today. I've had my exercise. I put away my new food in my kitchen cabinets and take the ipecac and Dulcolax reverentially into the bathroom.

I'm feeling a little hungry again. That must mean the doughnuts are out of my stomach now, so I can't think of any better time than the present to send them on their way. I pry open the Dulcolax box and take two tablets. As the tiny pills slip down my throat, I feel awash with satisfaction that at least the doughnut pig-out I did today won't make me any fatter. I'll be free of the damned things inside me as soon as the pills kick in. The Dulcolax pills are really small, though. They can't be very powerful. I take another two just for safe measure.

My stomach gurgles a little. It's crying out for something sweet. I go back into the kitchen and get the canister of Slim-Fast. I measure a heaping scoop of powder into my plastic measuring tumbler and fill it up with ten ounces of milk.

Ten ounces? That's nothing. That's hardly any milk at all. The picture on the can shows an enormous frothy chocolate milk shake in a deep fluted stemmed glass. There's a lot more than ten ounces in the glass on the picture, so I fill the tumbler to the top, snap on the lid and shake furiously until my arm gets tired. About twenty seconds. I pry the lid off the tumbler and take a big swig.

Ugh. It's so weak. Not thick and frosty like they promised at all. Well, I *did* add a lot more milk than they said to, so I should add more powder, too, to get the right proportions. More powder goes in the tumbler, more shaking, tasting. That's better.

God, I'm starving. I drink the whole diet shake in about five swallows. "A satisfying shake!" it says on the label. Well, hardly. Weak, gritty chocolate milk is more like it. Still, it is kind of good.

I dust the brown powder off the Slim-Fast Diet Plan booklet and read it. A shake for breakfast, one for lunch, a shake in the afternoon for a snack, followed by a sensible dinner. So it's three o'clock in the afternoon and I've only had one shake. I am way behind in my diet plan. Dinner will be in a couple of hours and I'm still two shakes behind.

Still feeling hungry and realizing it's my duty, I mix myself another proper-sized (proper for me that is) shake and retire to the cool darkness of the living room. I know I'm here to write poetry, but I can't work today. I can't. If I wrote anything, it would just be garbage and I'd have to throw it away anyway, so it would just be wasted effort. I'll work tomorrow. I'll play one of my subliminal inspiration tapes when I go to bed tonight and I'll wake up bursting with inspiration.

Normally, I'd turn on the TV at a time like this, but we're not allowed TVs at the Wurlitzer. I've started reading *Madame Bovary* this week, so I grab my shiny Penguin edition and crack back the spine so it stays open to the page I'm on. I sip this tumbler of Slim-Fast slower as I read with thinly veiled condescension about how shallow and self-destructive Emma Bovary is.

After only two pages, the second Slim-Fast shake is gone. I wait until I get to the end of the chapter before I get up and go back to the kitchen to have my obligatory third shake. This is a great diet plan. I'm not nearly as hungry as I was a little while ago.

I go back to the living room and have my third tumbler of shake and another chapter of Flaubert. Then it's 4:35. If I want to have dinner at five, I'd better start thawing out those burritos now. I lay *Madame Bovary* face down on the sofa and go back out to the kitchen.

The burritos in the plastic freezer sack are tightly welded together with frost. It takes a lot of elbow grease using a fork for a chisel and a bottle of ketchup for a hammer to whack a chunk of them free. There are four burritos in the chunk. Well, that'll have to do, I guess. I can't break them into a smaller chunk. I turn on the oven, place the burritos on an iron skillet and slip them in at 375°. Then it's back to *Madame Bovary* in the living room.

As I start to read chapter seven, my intestines start to rumble a little bit. What is that? The flu? Food poisoning? Oh, yes: the Dulcolax. I'd almost forgotten. I don't have to go to the bathroom yet, but I'm starting to get the feeling I'm going to have to go sometime in the near future. Good. That makes me feel great. That means those doughnuts are on their way out.

I don't quite get through another five pages of my book before the smell of the burritos starts driving me crazy. I want them and I want them now. I toss the book aside and go check on my meal in the oven. The outsides of the burrito chunk are getting nice and hot, but the core is still a solid block of ice. I try chipping away at them again and succeed in breaking the burritos apart into two sections. Back everything goes into the oven.

I have to eat something. Oranges. I grab three oranges, peel them and eat them while standing in the kitchen waiting for the burritos. They still aren't cooking fast enough. I decide to make some instant sugar-free vanilla pudding to have for dessert later in the evening, so I put the pudding powder along with eight ounces of milk into my measured tumbler and shake like mad. I shake and I shake.

Jesus. What is it about diet foods and shaking?

Finally the pudding is mixed fairly well and is setting up a little. I pop the top off the tumbler and start to pour the pudding into a bowl to put in the refrigerator to set completely. Let me just take a little taste of it here first, though. Oh, it's delicious. I take a bigger swig of the thick ecru liquid, sweet with aspartame. It reminds me of the filling in the Boston cream doughnuts.

Before I know it, I've finished off the pudding mixture.

Since that was to have been dessert for the evening, I mix up another batch to replace it, this time dutifully getting it all the way into a serving bowl and into the refrigerator uneaten.

The burritos still aren't ready yet. I open the cookie box and have a fifty-calorie fruit-sweetened cookie. Then another. No, I shouldn't eat these. I should snack on oranges. I peel and eat three more oranges, and still the fucking burritos won't cook!

Losing patience, I take them out of the oven and dump them on a plate. I'll eat around the frozen parts. I don't care. I'm hungry. Covering them in a sea of Ortega medium salsa, I repair with my plate and fork to the living room to continue reading about Emma Bovary.

I always like to read while I eat. Eating is so boring. Eating and shitting. I need some diversion to pass the time. Before I realize it, the burritos are reduced to four narrow pinto bean popsicles.

I am now long past hungry but I'm getting very interested in my book. Emma's now desperately trying to cover all the loans she took out while trying to have an affair.

Just as I need to read while I eat, it is conversely true that I need to eat while I read. I grab from the kitchen the box of diet cookies and the bowl of vanilla pudding from the fridge and barricade myself on the sofa. As my eyes hungrily scan Flaubert's pages, my jaws slowly, unconsciously grind away as I shovel into my mouth cream sandwich cookies dipped in vanilla pudding. I become aware of that old familiar sated feeling, yet I continue to read and eat.

I eat and I eat, robotically pulling cookie after cookie out of the box's plastic inner tray. The pudding disappears in a flash and I realize as I sit there reading that matters are now out of my hands. I will continue to eat these fucking cookies until they are all gone. I cannot be stopped.

As I get toward the end of the box, I put down my book and acknowledge just how uncomfortably full I am. I eat another cookie. Then another. What am I doing? I'm supposed to be on this new diet. I threw out all the food in my house just so I wouldn't do exactly what I'm doing right now.

And what have I eaten since I got home from the store this afternoon? Three double-sized Slim-Fast shakes, a half-dozen oranges, eight serving portions of instant vanilla pudding (four per box), four burritos, a cup of salsa and *forty* vanilla fruit-sweetened cream sandwich cookies. At fifty calories a cookie, that's – two thousand calories of cookies. Add to that three hundred calories per serving of Slim-Fast – one thousand eight hundred calories. And who the fuck knows what the hell was in those burritos? And wait a minute! What about those eight Boston cream doughnuts? The laxative tablets haven't done anything yet! I'm fat. I'm disgusting. I'm stupid. I'm stupid!

I race for the bathroom and fling open the medicine chest. I'll take care of this problem right here, right now. Breaking the seal on the ipecac bottle, I take a careful swig, then I close the bottle quickly and race to lean over the toilet.

Nothing happens.

I make the back of my tongue press down in my throat. I gag and I gag and still, nothing happens.

I sit down on the floor of the bathroom and lean my forehead on the toilet seat. What a loser I am. What a fucking asshole. I'm a pig, a big fat stupid pig lying on a shitty bathroom floor. The damp, mildewed plywood flooring stinks of wood rot and the musky smell of the skunk family that once lived under the house. I hate it here. I want to go back to California.

A wave of nausea sweeps over me. At last!

I get back up on my knees and I retch into the toilet. My stomach heaves in spasms. My lungs feel like they're going to collapse – but still nothing comes out of me. I can't vomit.

I gasp for air, pant hard, and then heave again. Still nothing.

I notice the tears streaming down my face before I realize that I'm crying. Another nauseous wave, another heave producing nothing more than some phlegm.

I want to die.

I reach up to the edge of the sink and grab my black-handled Gillette Trak II razor. I should slit my fucking wrists, but instead I take the handle and cram it down the back of my throat. The twin safety blades slice into the palm of my hand but I don't care. I just don't care. I gag myself with the razor handle, I gag and gag again, and then I drop the stupid razor into the toilet.

The only thing in the toilet water is some phlegm, the razor and a little cloud of blood dripping from my palm. I bang my forehead on the toilet seat. I cry and I cry like a two-year-old. Then I stop.

Oh, my God. It's kicked in.

Not the ipecac, the Dulcolax.

As I squat there on the floor, my anus uncontrollably relaxes and I soil myself. I clench tight, trying desperately to control my sphincter and frantically tug at my belt. It feels like it takes forever to get my pants down.

My colon gives a hard, painful spasm. Dropping my trousers and my defiled underwear, I spin around and plop down hard on the toilet seat, releasing my bowels as the toilet crashes through the rotten floorboards into the crawlspace a foot below the house.

I'm stunned.

The seat on the toilet is now level with the floor and still I can't stop shitting. I can't believe it. I am shitting into the crawlspace. Then everything becomes funny. I am laughing and crying at the same time.

The only reason I don't kill myself right here and now is simple: the thought of being like this isn't nearly as bad as the thought of being found like this. I imagine what the newspaper headlines would be and the thought makes make me laugh and cry even harder.

The laughter helps. If I can laugh about this, then I can pull myself together. I can.

The nausea stops. I guess I'm just immune to ipecac. It doesn't work for me. With a few more deep breaths, my bowels close, too. I kick off my socks, pants, and shitty underwear. I peel myself out of my Abba shirt, stand up and wipe myself. Flushing a toilet that's gone through the floor seems absurd, so I just close the lid and go to put on some clean clothes.

What am I going to do? I can't go tell the director of the foundation that I'm so fat the toilet went through the floor. And even if I could, what would the repairman make of the diarrhea, the razor, and the blood in the bowl?

I can't face it. I've got to get out. Got to think. I'll walk around a bit and think.

It's around eight in the evening. Newly twilight. The evening is cool and breezeless, scented with sage and lilac. Walking around in my abject misery, I should be thinking of a clear plan of action, a way to get out of this humiliating situation. I should be pulling myself together, plotting my escape, but all I can think about are those five damned Boston cream doughnuts that I threw away.

When I'm upset, I want doughnuts, and God knows I'm upset. I deserve some kind of comfort.

Not so coincidentally, I find myself near the Indian Cliffs Motel. There it is: the dumpster I flung all that bad food into. I wonder if it's still in there, the doughnut box.

I have to know. It takes a little effort to get the dumpster lid open and I peer inside. It's full. The motel maids have dumped a lot more stuff in there, but I can still see my trash bags peeking out of the far corner. I look around. There's no one around to see me.

Even if I threw my stuff away on private property, it's still *my* trash, isn't it? My mind is made up even before I realize it. I've got to have those doughnuts back.

The way I hoist my leg up and roll my body into the trash bin isn't pretty. I land in the papery, soapy motel rubbish in a flurry of used Kleenex and Camay wrappers. The "Sanitized for Your Protection" ribbons entwine me like snakes as I flail and grapple for the doughnut box, then suddenly – I've got it. It's mine.

I open it up and see my five doughnuts still unsullied, still pristine throughout their ordeal. I grab one and shove it in my mouth.

Rap rap rap!

There's a tapping. Someone is banging on the dumpster!

"Hey, buddy. Hey you in there!"

A flashlight shines on me and I see two cops staring at me with disdain.

"Um, I uh …"

"Come on, get out of there," one of them says to me.

"Jesus, look at the size of him," the other one says.

I start to fumble for something to say. "See, um, earlier today I was staying at the motel and I threw something valuable away and …" But that's all the explanation I can give before I projectile vomit.

"Jesus!" yells the second cop as he jumps out of the line of fire. "Jesus! Jesus!" he yells again as the vomit keeps spewing out of me.

As if to make the most dreadful possible evening of my life just a little bit worse, the Dulcolax rejoins the ipecac and I once again start to uncontrollably shit as I upchuck.

"Get somebody!" cop number two barks as the first policeman whips out his portable radio.

"Need an ambulance," the first one says. "Indian Cliffs Motel. South Pueblo and Los Pandos. Guy's erupting like a fucking volcano. White male. Obese."

CHAPTER TWO

1963

The day the wind scared the shit out of me, I was out in Grandma's back yard dressed as Satan. I was wearing the Halloween costume Mama made me from a McCall's pattern she got at the dime store. I loved that costume. It was a red cotton jumpsuit that snapped up the back with a high-collared red cape lined in bright yellow fabric. There was a tight-fitting red hood that came down over my forehead in a widow's peak. The hood's side flaps covered my ears and attached under my chin. Stuffed devil horns were sewn on to the top. I was four years old.

It was Mama's idea to dress me up as Satan. The choice didn't seem odd to me because Mama was deeply religious and the devil is in the Bible. She was always talking about the devil to me, or at least saying his name a lot. Saying stuff like "what the devil are you doing?" or "hold still, you little devil," or "goddamn you to hell." Stuff like that. When she told me she was making me a Biblical costume for Halloween, I knew right away I wasn't going to be Jesus. I didn't mind, though. I loved my long, red devil's tail. It was stiff and bouncy because it had a piece of wire from a real southern belle's hoop skirt running through it. And I loved my dramatic cape that caught the air and fanned out the way Loretta Young's dress did every time she came through the door on her TV show.

During all those years in California, I don't remember if the Santana Winds ever stopped blowing. Well, that's what I thought everyone was calling them: the Santana Winds, the winds of Satan. It was no wonder I thought they were the devil's winds. They were hot winds, fierce and dry and scary. I found out later that I got it wrong. I was mishearing it. They were really called the Santa Ana winds because they came out of Santa Ana, not hell. But how could winds come out of an ugly little town? I think Santana made more sense.

So there I was, singing and twirling like TV Loretta out back behind Grandma's house on a day when the Santa Ana winds were blowing harder than usual. The wind was whipping my red cape like a flame. I noticed Grandma's maple tree swaying deeply and groaning in a way I'd never heard before. Standing near the tree, I imagined the vibrations of the sound were going through the soil and humming through the soles of my Thom McAn deck shoes.

Suddenly, I had a terrible vision. The wind was blowing the tree, the tree was making the sound, the sound was vibrating the ground. If it didn't stop, the ground would crack apart and the earth would split wide open, swallowing up me, Grandma and Grandpa, Grandma's house, and the whole wide world.

Terrified, I hugged the tree tight, trying to get it to stop swaying, stop vibrating, but the creaking sound like a wooden ship at sea would not stop. As I hugged the trunk of the tree, I started picturing the low moaning vibrations spreading through my whole body. So I got a little hysterical.

Grandma came outside and found me hugging her maple tree, screaming. She asked me what was wrong.

"The wind! The wind!" was all I could say.

Grandma thought the wind must be hurting my ears, so she took the scarf that was holding her hair in place – a real Chinese silk scarf I saw her buy at the Sav-On drug store – and tied it around my head. The wind buffeted her silver helmet of hair and billowed the skirt of her aquamarine housedress, exposing her Playtex girdle.

"Well, look at you!" she said. "Now you look just like a girl!" and she laughed and laughed. I cried ever harder and yanked at the scarf on my head, trying to pull it off of me. I had a hood over my ears. Why'd she think I needed a scarf?

"Now you leave that on!" she commanded. "It'll help you with the earache. And stop crying! You're crying just like a girl."

Grandma laughed again at that thought. "Cary is a gir-rl!" she taunted. "Cary is a gir-rl! Now you stop that crying, crybaby!" She gave me a swat on the behind.

The sting of her hand knocked the crying right out of me, and the sting of the open safety pin holding the devil's tail onto my butt made Grandma cry out in pain instead. "Dammit!" she cursed and raised her hand to take another swat at me, but I ran into the house. I wanted to find my grandpa. Grandpa would let me cry. And I wanted to keep crying.

Grandma didn't understand. I didn't have an earache. I wasn't crying about my ears. I was crying about something else entirely. She was right about one thing, though. In her scarf I did look like a girl. I looked like a red demon girl crying about the winds of Satan. A devil girl crying about the end of the world.

In 1963 Grandpa was already very sick. Grandma had to put a hospital bed for him in the back bedroom because he had a bad heart. Mama said the doctors told her bad hearts ran in our family, and I misunderstood what she meant. Heck, for the longest time I didn't understand a thing anyone meant when they talked to me. I understood the words, but the meanings to the words were like one of those Godzilla movies where people moved their mouths in one language and something totally different came into your ears. I must've had a disorder or something.

Mama said to me, "Your grandpa's got a bad heart. Doctor said it's hereditary. That means *everybody* in our family's got bad hearts. You, too." Of course I thought she meant that my Mama's side of the family was somehow born evil. Me, too. I knew my grandpa wasn't evil. He didn't have a bad heart. He just happened to have a heart with a disease and a pacemaker to keep it running.

It was an October afternoon and the house was cold and dark. Even in the dead of winter, when day after day of gray dampness made you crave the slightest bit of warmth or light, the inside of Grandma's house was always cool and dim because it saved money. Mama always used to say, "That woman's so tight she takes a shower under a trickle!" Well, I didn't know about that, but I did know Grandma was so tight she didn't always flush the toilet. Water must have been very expensive then.

As I padded down the dark hallway toward the back bedroom, I increased the volume of my crying just for the effect. I wanted to be crying extra hard when I entered the room so that Grandpa would have to try extra hard to make me stop. What I didn't expect was that the very sight of Grandpa, pale and skeletal in his hospital bed, would make me stop crying the second I came in the room.

Grandpa feebly turned his head toward me, looked at me standing in the door and grinned. "Who's that crying?" he said. "Oh, it's just the devil. Well, come on in, ol' devil. Good Lord, what do you got on your head?"

I felt it was okay to start crying again, so I whimpered and rushed to his side, climbing up on the metal bars of his hospital bed so I could cuddle up next to him. "Grandma, Grandma!" was all I could offer in explanation and buried my tearful face in the armpit of his pajamas.

"Has that mean ol' Grandma been after you again?" I looked up at him, nodded, then quickly hid my face against his body. Grandpa chuckled a little which made him cough. "Where's that book of yours?" he asked. I reached over onto the nightstand and grabbed my careworn yellow book from its permanent place. Opening the book to the flyleaf in our well-rehearsed ceremony, he began reading. "This book belongs to Cary Scott." I smiled and snuggled in closer to him. He turned the page. "The Boy Who Fooled the Giant …"

The only story I would ever let him read to me was *The Boy Who Fooled the Giant*. In this story, a boy's parents didn't allow him to do anything because he was so small, so when the king offered a reward to anyone who could get rid of a magical giant, the boy marched straightaway to the giant's castle. The boy astounds the giant by refusing to believe he's really magical. He dares the giant to turn first into a cat, then into a mouse. To prove how powerful he really is, the giant transforms himself from one animal into the other. Unimpressed, the boy scoffs and says the giant couldn't possibly turn himself into a fly. The vain giant laughs at the boy and turns himself into a common housefly – and the boy swats him with a flyswatter.

I loved that story. I also liked that one about David and Goliath they told me in Sunday school. It was good to know small boys could win by being smart when giants were about.

I made Grandpa read *The Boy Who Fooled the Giant* to me every day, sometimes several times a day. I had memorized every word in the book and expected him to faithfully recite my story for me syllable by syllable. No matter how tired or how sickly he must have felt, he never complained or disappointed me when I came to him with my book and I loved him for doing it.

Grandpa was the oldest person I had ever seen. When he could stand up, he was about six feet tall and bone thin. I never saw a picture of him when his hair wasn't pure white or his face wasn't wrinkled and gaunt. The only part of Grandpa that hadn't aged was the color of his eyes. They were still the color of blue popsicles. It was 1963, and Grandpa was fifty-two years old.

As he read to me in the hospital bed, I snuggled up and put my ear next to his pacemaker. The pacemaker fascinated me, that rectangular lump the size of a pack of cigarettes underneath my grandpa's skin. It was there to keep his heart going, although I couldn't figure out exactly how it did that.

I lay with my head against Grandpa's smooth white chest and thought about how different it was from my father's burly chest, which was muscled and covered with curly black hairs. I listened to Grandpa's pacemaker and tried to figure out how it worked. The pacemaker didn't make any noise. All I could hear was the sound of Grandpa's heart beating.

"Grandpa, how do you change the batteries?" I asked him.

He paused a moment and shook his head. "I don't know," he said.

I had another vision. If we couldn't change his batteries, I realized that my grandpa, like a flashlight left on too long, would one day just dim out and die. I made a silent vow to check under him when he fell asleep to see if he had a secret panel in his back.

That's where the D size batteries went in my talking Casper the Friendly Ghost doll, so it seemed reasonable that Grandpa and his pacemaker would work about the same way.

It wasn't long before Grandma found me in the back bedroom. "What're you doing in here?" she growled at me.

"Now, Edna, leave the little fellow alone."

"No, no, now. Come on now," she commanded, clapping her hands and gesturing for me to get down from Grandpa's hospital bed. Grandpa wasn't finished with my story and even if he were, I certainly would rather stay with him than go with her. "Hop to, now!"

"No," I said and pressed myself harder to Grandpa's side.

"Don't you tell me no, young man," she said, then paused and squinted hard at me, trying to see right through the very core of me. "Have you had a B.M. today, Cary?" I didn't answer her, didn't even want to look at her. "*That's* what's wrong with you. You're constipated. Well, come on. You know what we got to do for that."

Yes, I did know what we got to do for that and I certainly didn't want to do it. Grandma opened the top drawer of her burl wood dresser and dug beneath her neat piles of rayon panties. She pulled out the green rubber hose, nozzle and bulb. I started to cry again and held on tight to the metal bars on the side of Grandpa's bed, but she was too strong for me. Grandma deftly pried off my fingers and gathered me up, kicking and screaming into her arms. I called out for my grandpa to help me but he was too frail to move. As Grandma carried me out of the room, the last thing I noticed was that my devil's tail had come off my costume and was lying in the bed next to Grandpa. *The Boy Who Fooled the Giant* lay open on his chest as he stared blankly out the window.

***

We lived in Espada, California, but we called our area of town Elmville. Elmville was once its own town a long time ago, but nearby Espada got too big in the late fifties and just swallowed it up. The neighborhood of Elmville still felt like a small town to us, though, and that's why we liked it. I mean, that's why my family liked it. I was born there. I never really had a say in the matter.

Everybody I heard of in Southern California came from somewhere else. Mama said that Mr. Gustoff, who owned the Phillips 66 station, came from Minnesota where they always had a real white Christmas. Mr. Gustoff always called Mama a "Hot Number." Chuck, the supermarket checker at Safeway who always talked to Grandma, was from Oklahoma. Grandma said he worked his way up to that position and was lucky because he had a wife to support. Being a supermarket checker was a real good job to have, she said. Grandma always bought ground chuck in the meat section, so I assumed he had something personal to do with it. Tony, the barber down at Evans's Barber Shop, didn't have a wife. Daddy liked Tony a lot and asked him a lot of questions every other Sunday when we got our hair cut. Tony was from somewhere called Walla Walla. From the sound of things, it looked like I was the only one around there who was a real Californian.

Everyone but me in my family was from Georgia. When my dad was a little boy, he was best friends with a guy named Arby Welch. Dad and Arby did everything together. They went to school every day together. They walked home every day together. When they grew up and graduated high school they even joined the Army together. They were just about the two best friends anyone had ever seen in Brierfield, Georgia.

My dad was Montgomery Burke Scott, although everybody just called him Burke. Arby Welch's name was really R.B. Welch – which didn't stand for anything. His name was just two letters. When he joined the Army, the government wouldn't accept initials for names on his enlistment papers. Arby told them at the recruitment office that they weren't his initials, they were his whole name, so they told him to make that clear on his form. In the blanks for first and middle name, Arby wrote "R.(only) B.(only) Welch" and they shipped him and my dad off to Korea. That's how it came to be that Arby was forever known to the US

Army as Ronly Bonly Welch. Dad used to bust a gut telling that story. He used to tell a lot of stories about Arby. Good old Arby.

During the war years, Dad and Arby got split up and sent away in different battalions. While they were off fighting in Asia, California fever hit Brierfield and both of their families up and moved out west at the same time. Dad's family got rich in real estate and ended up in Los Angeles, just like the Beverly Hillbillies. Arby's mom and dad and little sister got only as far as the tiny town of Elmville out near the inland city of Espada and stayed just regular hillbillies.

When our country got done with Korea and sent everybody home, Dad drove on out to Elmville to meet up with his best friend again. ("Went to see Arby with my discharge in my hand," Dad would tell me with a wink. I never got the dirty joke until I got older.) Arby wasn't at home when Dad pulled up to the Welch family's yellow bungalow, but his little sister, Juney, was.

The last time Dad had seen little Juney Welch was back in Brierfield when she was just a skinny fourteen-year-old. When Daddy got to Espada, she wasn't skinny no more. And she wasn't fourteen. To Dad's surprise, Juney had blossomed into a high school senior who looked like Suzanne Pleshette.

That's how Juney became my daddy's wife, and then, when I was born, became my mother. That's also how Arby and Dad became real brothers and Arby turned out to be my uncle. Good old Arby.

I loved my uncle Arby about as much as I loved my dad. Arby's face was boyish-handsome and his voice was funny and soft. Soft, like his fine yellow hair that was always falling into his eyes, and funny, like the voices of those people who lived near Lot and Lot's Wife in that filmstrip they kept showing us at Vacation Bible School about the sins of Sodom and Gomorrah.

"Hey, La-aht!" Lot's neighbors would croon seductively from the scratchy old phonograph record that accompanied the filmstrip. "Where are the men who came to stay with you tonight? Bring them out to us that we may knooohw them!" (BONG!) "But Lot went out to them through the doorway and shut the door behind him," growled the narrator, "and said 'Please, my brethren, do not do so wickedly!'" (BONG!) Whenever the record went BONG you were supposed to turn the filmstrip to the next picture.

The first time I saw that filmstrip, I asked Mrs. Rose McDonald, my Bible School teacher, what was so bad about those guys in Sodom? Those Sodom guys in the filmstrip looked and sounded just like my uncle Arby, and he was really nice and I liked him. Mrs. McDonald, who was very fat and red-faced, just glared at me and said, "They were faggots," and left the matter at that.

"What's a faggit?" I asked – and everybody in the Bible School class laughed at me, even though I bet none of them knew what a faggot was either. Anyway, that's what Arby's sweet voice sounded like to me: The Sweet Faggots of Sodom.

Mama and Daddy both had jobs. He was an appliance salesman down at Espada Plaza and she was a secretary at the water department, so until I was old enough to go to school, I had to stay at my grandma's house all day long.

Except for Grandma, I liked staying at Grandma's house just fine. There was a bald patch of ground at the far corner of Grandma's back yard that I called the playhouse even though there was no house there, just dirt and an old tree stump. My toys out at the playhouse were several pieces of a rusted tin tea party set, a hula hoop that I could never master, and several empty food jars and cans. Playing house alone all day, I would be whole families at a time. One second I'd be the tired father, one second the grumpy mother, another second I'd turn around and be Patty Duke, the teenage daughter, then another, I'd be Loretta Young. My favorite thing to do was hold intense, screaming family arguments in which I provided both sides of a husband/wife squabble and ended up throwing the tea set against the tree stump. I was so good at my playacting, Grandma's neighbors would peek at me through their screen doors and wonder if there was a real fight going on.

Sometimes Uncle Arby would come and play with me for a few minutes. He was often just hanging around Grandma's house of a day because, unlike my parents, he didn't have a job.

Grandma always called him a lazybones and told him to get off his fat ass and get to work. I never understood what Grandma meant by that because Uncle Arby always looked pretty skinny to me, and he did do a lot of work every day on his drawings and paintings of men fighting in wars. Uncle Arby was a famous artist. He had one of his war pictures hung up at the Espada Plaza art show on the sidewalk in front of the Barker Company Department Store. They even pinned an honorable mention ribbon right to the bottom corner of the canvas. I was so proud of him.

Now, even though I was only about three or four at the time, I pretty much knew what I liked and disliked in the world of art, and I knew that even if my uncle Arby's picture wasn't entered in the show, I still would have disliked that first prize painting. The picture that won the art show was just a big face of a clown with bubbles in the background. Since I was the kind of kid who hated clowns pretty much since the day I was born, I was the kind of kid who hated that first place picture. Uncle Arby's picture of two shirtless sailors wrestling was a much better painting in my opinion.

Sometimes, out on Grandma's back porch, I'd get to be a model for my uncle, but I didn't care too much for that. Although I could sit and stare for long periods of time, I always felt kind of silly sitting on an upturned bucket while holding a flower or something dumb and precious like that. I wanted him to paint me as one of his wrestling guys.

No. I wanted to paint *him* as one of his wrestling guys.

He'd often let me sit beside him with my own sheet of white paper and my own tin box of watercolor paints. Uncle Arby would never return the favor and sit and model for me, so I always had to try to just imagine what he would look like as Samson in the Bible, Jesus on the cross, or David and Goliath. I wasn't too good at painting. No matter how hard I tried, I could never get a good likeness of Arby. So if my attachment for my uncle was becoming stronger by the day, I didn't think anyone except Arby was catching on. At least Mama and Grandma never figured out that I was painting pictures of my uncle. Looking at my work, they just thought I was gripped by some kind of pre-school religious fervor.

One evening, just for fun, Uncle Arby sat me down on the edge of Grandma's kitchen table, then he turned a dining chair around and handed me his comb. He sat with his back to me and asked me to comb his hair while we watched TV. I scooted up close toward the back of his head, threw my legs over his shoulders, and started combing as we watched a late afternoon rerun of *Mr. Ed* on Grandma's black-and-white Zenith portable that she kept on a rickety stool in the corner of the kitchen.

I ran his black unbreakable Ace comb through his straight blond hair heavily slicked with grease, feeling the sensuous way the teeth of the comb slid along his scalp, leaving rake-marks through his hair, reveling in the smells of bay rum and Brylcreem.

"How'd you like your hair cut, sir?" I asked, doing my best imitation of Tony down at the barber shop.

"Short back and sides, Mr. Barber" Uncle Arby rejoined. Of course I wasn't going to really cut Arby's hair. It was all make-believe, but I never had to tell Arby when I was pretending. He just sort of knew.

I combed his hair straight up so that it stood at attention on the top of his head, like someone had scared him, and used my middle and index fingers as scissors to cut the hair up the back of his neck.

"Hey, you're pretty good at that, Cary. Maybe you should be a barber when you grow up. Mr. Cary's beauty salon!"

"Put your head down, please," I said gravely, although I was glowing at the thought of "Mr. Cary's Beauty Salon," with those big space-age bonnet dryers lined up against the wall and women with magazines shouting gossip to each other as their hair baked.

Then, CRACK! A sharp, smacking sound split the air and Uncle Arby jumped out of the chair, sending me sliding flat on my back across the Formica table top.

Grandma had come into the room and seen me and Arby sitting there watching TV, so she took a hairbrush and hit him hard across the left shoulder. Arby leaped up, sending me flying, and dashed across the room with Grandma in hot pursuit. She didn't say nothing, just started wailing on him with the back of that hairbrush, beating the tarnation out of him. Even though he was a Korean War vet and a good foot taller than Granny, Uncle Arby didn't defend himself. He just curled into a ball, protecting his head from her attack, and let her smash away at his shoulders and back.

I was so stunned by what was happening I couldn't cry. I couldn't even breathe. When she finally stopped hitting my uncle, Grandma stomped back over toward where I was on the table. I recoiled as she reached out for me, but all she really wanted was to grab Arby's comb from out of my hands. Once she got it away from me, she flung the comb across the kitchen, hitting Arby with it on the back of the neck and started to march out the door.

I managed to cry out to her as she was leaving, "What's wrong? What did he do?"

"He was thinking bad thoughts," she said and left. Uncle Arby remained silent, curled up in a ball on the floor by the stove in the far corner of the kitchen.

***

I remember the first day of kindergarten mostly because I didn't get to go. Not that I really wanted to. Uncle Arby was really the only playmate I ever had for my first five years and, judging from those nasty little kids at Sunday school, I wasn't looking forward to being around any more children my age. Still, Uncle Arby hadn't been around much since the incident with Grandma and the hairbrush and Mama told me they'd put me in jail if I didn't go to school, so I steeled myself against the dread of kindergarten.

The weekend before school started, Mama and Daddy had taken me out shopping for school clothes and I thought this was odd. Mama and Daddy didn't do anything together those days except sleep and a lot of times Daddy wasn't even home for them to do that. They bought me Wrangler boy's jeans, sized five slims, a blue plaid shirt, and a brown plaid shirt and a pair of hard-wearing Buster Brown shoes (on sale). I had to admit that if I wasn't look-ing forward to marching into Lincoln Elementary School the next day, I was looking forward to wearing my new clothes.

I didn't start my first day of kindergarten until the afternoon. Mama dropped me off at Grandma's house first thing in the morning and told me not to get my new outfit dirty before she came to pick me up for school at lunchtime. I said I'd try.

I walked into Grandma's house and all the lights were off, which wasn't unusual for cheap old Grandma, but all the drapes were drawn shut, too, so it was even darker and more oppressive than usual inside.

Grandma's cigarette glowed from the vinyl reclining chair in the far corner of the living room. "What're you all dressed up for?" she asked.

"I'm going to school today. Mama's picking me up at lunchtime."

Grandma stared at me from out of the shadows. A little reflection of light off her cat-eye glasses showed me she was nodding slowly. She was thinking. Her cigarette glowed bright for one last drag before she stubbed it out in the floor stand ashtray by her side.

"Well, you better come on, then," she growled as she got up out of the chair. "We gotta get you outta them good clothes before you get 'em all tord to pieces."

"No."

"Don't you argue with me, little man. We're gonna go find you something else to wear and I don't want to hear no backtalk." She grabbed me by the arm and dragged me into my mother's old bedroom down the hallway.

Mama's room looked like it hadn't been touched except for dusting since she was a girl in high school. A picture of Pat Boone was still thumb-tacked to her closet door; a hinged double picture frame sat on the dresser with hand-tinted senior portraits of both Mama and Arby. He looked funnier than she did because his picture was five years older. Mama still pretty much looked the same.

Grandma rummaged through the back of one of Mama's dresser drawers and took out a little girl's dress made out of brown dotted Swiss. It was very ugly and I had no idea what she had in mind to do with it.

"Well?" said Grandma.

I just stared at her.

"Oh, for heaven's sake. Take them good clothes off!"

When I didn't react right away, Grandma lunged at me and started fumbling with the buttons on my shirt. I squirmed and tried to slap at her hands, but Granny reached back and popped me upside the head so hard it made my eyes cross for a minute or two. Whimpering with pain and confusion I let her strip off my shirt and pants and held my arms over my head so she could slip the little brown dress over me.

"There, that's better," she said, buttoning me up the back.

"I don't want to wear this!"

"Hush, or I'm gonna make you go outside and cut your own switch!"

"I want to see Grandpa," I cried and broke free from her grasp, racing for the door.

"I wouldn't do that if I were you," she said bluntly, reaching in the pocket of her housedress for another cigarette. "You want him to see you wearing a girl's dress?"

"I don't want to wear a dress!"

"Well, if you're gonna be a girl, you're gonna have to dress like one from now on."

"I want my grandpa!"

She struck a match and took a deep drag off her Newport menthol. "He can't see you. He's dead."

I looked at her like I didn't know what she meant.

"Go look for yourself," she said and walked out of the room. As I heard her pick up the telephone in the living room and dial the operator to ask for an ambulance, I crept slowly toward the back bedroom to find my grandpa.

Grandma had drawn the drapes next to his hospital bed, too. Grandpa was still, white, and slack-jawed, staring sightlessly at the ceiling. He looked like someone had just let all the air out of him, long white bones draped with thin white skin. I took my book, *The Boy Who Fooled the Giant* and sat with it on the edge of Grandpa's bed. Although I couldn't yet read, this was one story I had memorized, so I sat in the dark, opened up the book and read aloud to my grandpa.

"This book belongs to Cary Scott," I said, turning past the flyleaf. "The Boy Who Fooled the Giant …"

I recited the story to Grandpa about five times through before the ambulance men and Mama came into the bedroom, led by Grandma.

"Here he is," Grandma said, and I wasn't sure if it was me or Grandpa she was referring to.

"What in the world are you wearing?!" Mama exclaimed jerking me off the bed to my feet.

"That's what he runs to put on every day," Granny explained, clucking her tongue and shaking her head sadly. As the ambulance men lifted my grandpa's body onto the stretcher and situated it over the black plastic zippered bag, Grandma paid them no mind.

"Well what do you expect" she said, cocking a disgusted thumb at me, "with that sissy brother of yours and faggot husband hanging around?"

Mama pulled hard on the collar of the little brown dress and popped all of the buttons off the back. Literally ripping the dress from my body, she grabbed me by the right arm and hoisted me a foot off the ground. With her free hand, she spanked me hard in midair.

The ambulance men stared at my spanking for a second, then zipped the black bag shut.

CHAPTER THREE

1967

We sat in Mrs. Clark's second-grade class watching a film called *People of the South Seas*. Even then, in 1967, this Eisenhower-era documentary on Polynesia looked scratched and dated to us. All the men in the movie were brown, blowzy and bare-chested, sturdily saronged down to the tops of their knees. Although dressed this way, they still looked like they came from the fifties, like they'd fit right into an episode of *I Love Lucy*. Even stranger were the South Sea native women who reflected the Hollywood standard of beauty of that time. They had Jane Russell hairdos, cat-eye glasses, formidable multi-colored bras, bare midriffs and skirts cinched right under their rib cages to keep secret that they had belly buttons.

In the movie, we were led through the daily lives of these happy, colorful people. I didn't see what any of this had to do with what was going on in my life in Southern California, so I just let most of the film wash over and past me like a Polynesian breeze.

One brief section of *The People of the South Seas* grabbed me, however, made me sit up and take notice. The camera at one point cut to a shot of men furiously whipping palm fronds on a fence post. A close-up revealed that they had driven long nails into the underside of the wood to make a sharp spike of metal sticking out on top. Beating the palm fronds on this exposed nail, the Polynesians shredded the palm leaves into long, tough fibers that could be woven into mats or ropes – or grass skirts. The next shot on the screen was of hula girls wearing these shredded palm frond skirts, wiggling their hips, and signing away with their hands like the deaf lady on the religious TV programs.

I was mesmerized. Immediately my little brain began calculating. We had two rather short palm trees in the front yard of our house that were always dropping their fronds on our lawn. Wood and nails were easily had in our garage. That was it, I thought, I was going to go home after Cub Scouts that afternoon, and start shredding the palms.

The hands on the round black-and-white Elgin clock above the blackboard crept at a snail's pace all afternoon. The film we saw was followed by math, fifteen minutes of recess, then English. "What is *theee* definite article?" Mrs. Clark kept asking. "What is *ayeee* indefinite article?"

Finally, 3:30 came. English books flew under the hinged lid of the desk. Out came the Cub Scout manual. On went my little blue cap with the yellow piping and out I went through the door.

I knew exactly why I became a Cub Scout. I begged my mother to let me join because I loved the uniform. I was attracted to the yellow and blue neckerchief with the pewter bear-head concho that slid up to hold it in place.

There were other perks to being a Cub Scout in the second grade, too. Being a Cub Scout made me special every Thursday, the day of our den meetings. On Thursdays, I got to wear my uniform to school, and at 3:30, instead of walking straight home, I would stop at another boy's house on Hawthorn Street and would enjoy being a part of someone else's family for an hour. Another family, unlike my own, with an attentive mother and lots of siblings my own age; important things to do with scissors and glue; a book, *The Cub Scout Manual*, that gave the answers to all the mysteries of life from how to use tin snips to how to get a suntan; and an oath of undying loyalty.

"I, Cary Scott," I would pledge at the start of every meeting, "promise to do my best to do my duty, to God and my country, to be square and obey the LAWS OF THE PACK!" We would always recite the oath with rising intensity so that the final couple of words would end up being delivered in a decisive shout.

Neither the handbook nor our den mother explained to us the meaning of this pledge. In 1967, being square was not something many young people strived for, and as for the laws of the pack, "behave" was the only law I ever heard.

"Being haive," as my grandmother put it, was never a problem for me. Momma and Granny made sure I learned how to obey. "Spare the rod and spoil the child," was their pledge, so I learned right from the start that my life was always much easier if I just did anything an adult told me to.

The walk to Gabe Gorman's house was about five minutes quicker than the walk home from school to my own house. Gabe's mom, Mrs. Gorman, always had the back yard set up for us by the time we got there. Mrs. Gorman, fat, redheaded and gregarious, was a new den mother. Our last den mother, Mrs. Buslovich, was always disorganized. She was a den mother because that was the only way she could get her mildly retarded son into the Cub Scouts. When dumb Marky Buslovich proved unable to handle even the simplest Cub Scout rituals, Mrs. B. turned in her notice.

I liked Mrs. Gorman though. She always spent just as much time fussing over us other scouts as she did over Gabe. I suspected Gabe (short for Gabriel) was adopted. His Mediterranean coloring and black wide-set eyes did not make him resemble his large Irish mother in the least. Gabe did take after her, however, in his complete interest and acceptance of everyone, including me. He was one of the few kids in school (and in fact, the only boy) who would speak to me.

Gabe Gorman and I talked together as we walked to his house for the pack meeting.

"Did you ever climb inside the rocket in Laurel Park?" I asked him, referring to a piece of playground equipment, a jungle gym shaped like a space ship.

"Uh huh," he answered. "Someone wrote 'fuck' inside there." That was exactly what I wanted to talk with him about. "You know what fuck means, don't you?" Gabe asked, not daring to look at me.

"No, what?"

"It means something bad," he said. "It's the worst word of all. You're never supposed to say it."

"Fuck?"

"No! Shut up!" Gabe glanced around nervously to see if anyone could have heard me. "Don't ever say that word. It means something awful."

I was cowed. Who in the world, I wondered, would be so evil as to write the worst word of all in the nosecone of the rocket ship where little kids played? And now that I possessed the terrible knowledge of the powerful nature of this word, what was I to do with it? And what would happen to me if I ever said it aloud again?

"Fuck fuck fuck," I said under my breath. It was a magic word now. The worst word of all.

The pack meeting started as usual with the Pledge of Allegiance. It was a relief not to have that retard, Marky Buslovich, there messing up the pledge. When he could remember any of it at all, it was usually wrong. "One nation, invisible, with livery and JUSTICE FOR ALL!"

Next we said the Cub Scout pledge with our index and middle fingers held up, pressed tightly together. We wouldn't be allowed to hold up three fingers until we became Tenderfoot Boy Scouts, and that wouldn't be for another four years. There were seven boys in my Cub Scout den, all of us around eight to ten years old. Timmy McDonald was the largest kid, a big solid boy with a blond crew cut who was kind of dumb about everything except baseball and multiplication tables. He was like a human slide rule, and about as interesting. Wally Montague, with his thick glasses and thick teeth was a compulsive knock-knock joke teller. He was the "personality" of our Cub Scout pack, whereas vacant Paul Blum had no personality whatsoever. The Garfield twins, Jeffery and Geoffrey were radiantly handsome, like little Pat Boones, but were vicious and cruel. There was Gabe Gorman who owned the secret of fuck, and there was me, the smallest scout, the runt cub of the wolf pack, the first link of the food chain.

Our scout meetings were held in Gabe's back yard. After the pledging was done, the Garfield twins pushed Paul Blum to the grass and wrestled him till he was immobilized. I was smart enough and alert enough to avoid the evil twins at all costs. Paul was not, and they knew it. I retreated to a corner of the patio that was shaded with oleander and pretended to study my scout manual.

Soon Mrs. Gorman came through the sliding glass doors with a tray laden with a plastic pitcher of Kool-Aid and a stack of Dixie Cups. She placed the tray on her wooden patio table, pulled back her red hair into an off-kilter ponytail and called the meeting to order. We raced to sit around her, anxious to get hold of the sweet blood-red drink.

"Okay, guys, listen up!" she said while pouring cups of Kool-Aid. "The pack meeting's next Thursday night. Wally, pass that down. What we're supposed to be working on this month is our performing skills, so next Thursday is going to be skits night. Did everyone get Kool-Aid? Paul? Paul, you gotta learn to speak up, honey. Here, pass that down to him. So we gotta think of a skit. Does anybody have any ideas?"

Jeffery's hand shot up. "We could be Rat Patrol and shoot guys in the desert!"

"I get to drive the Jeep! I get to shoot the machine gun!" chimed Geoffrey.

"Well," said Mrs. Gorman thoughtfully, "that's a good idea, but it might be a little complicated. We don't have a lot of time or money to make a machine gun or a Jeep. Let's try and use things we've already got. Does anybody have a really boss prop or a big toy that might be interesting in a skit?"

That really stumped us for a second. Silence fell around the picnic table as we pondered what might be interesting. Finally Wally Montague slowly raised his hand. "I have a toy lawn mower," he said.

Mrs. Gorman's eyes lit up. "Yes! That's wonderful. That should be an easy prop to build a skit around. So now, can anyone think of a story we can act out about the lawn mower?"

"I saw a clown with a toy lawn mower at the circus," Timmy McDonald said. "He chased a little clown around like he was going to mow him down."

The Garfield twins' eyes sprang open. "Yeah!" they exclaimed in unison.

"Good, good" said Mrs. Gorman. "So we need to figure out who is the guy with the lawn mower and who is he chasing."

"I have an idea," I said. Everyone looked my way, surprised because I hardly ever spoke at these meetings.

"What's your idea, Cary?"

"Well, um, what if there's this clown who really likes cutting grass. He likes it so much he cuts all the grass there is to cut and when he's done, he sees a lady clown in a grass skirt and he tries to mow her, too."

Mrs. Gorman threw back her head and laughed. "You're a genius," she said.

I wanted to be cool. I tried not to smile at her approval of my idea, but I wasn't too successful. All the guys were looking at me and one of the corners of my mouth crept up making me look like that lady in church who had the stroke. Mrs. Gorman gave a big sigh then a worried look stole across her eyes. "But where are we going to get a grass skirt?"

"That's easy," I said. "I saw a film at school about how they make them out of palm fronds. I got palm trees at home. I can start making one tonight."

"Then that's settled. Since it's Wally's lawn mower, Wally will be the mowing clown, and Cary will be the lady clown in the grass skirt. Now we just have to figure out parts for you other guys."

For the rest of the meeting, we rehearsed our short skit about the mishaps of the clown with the lawn mower. All the other scouts were given little pratfalls to do as Wally mowed near them, and since we were all clowns and clowns don't talk, we didn't have to learn any lines except stuff like "Woooa!" or "Yikes!"

The climax of the skit was when I hula-ed in from the side of the stage and Wally took a beat to see me and be obsessively drawn to my skirt. He chased me one way across the stage, then we re-entered and he chased me across the other way. That was it. We left the scout meeting feeling pretty excited, laughing about how funny we were and eager to show up at the pack meeting next Thursday to win the prize for best skit.

The thing I was most excited about, though, was that I was going to get to make a grass skirt. I ran all the way home and went directly to one of the short palm trees in our front yard.

In Southern California, we didn't have the kind of palm trees they have in places like Arabia or India, date palms, with long shaggy fronds that droop gracefully and ripple in the wind like a woman's hair. We had the kind of palms with fronds like open hands with fingers spread, as big and round as the fans of Sally Rand, a spiky exclamation of green at the top of every tree.

The stems of the fronds were three feet long and three inches wide with two saw lines of thorns that could really hurt you bad if you weren't real careful. I used extra caution as I broke from the tree a low-hanging frond that was fully developed but only had an inch or two of dead brown tips. I dragged it, holding the stem gingerly between the thorns, through the side door into the garage.

Mama wasn't home from work yet so the garage was empty except for the Maytag washer and Daddy's workbench. I turned on the overhead light and searched through the box of Daddy's tools. I knew where Dad's big saw was, but I didn't want to use it. It was large, unwieldy and rusty. I found a little keyhole saw instead. It looked like it should work just fine.

It took a bit of sweat and perseverance with the saw to separate the stem from the frond, but off it eventually came and I chucked the dangerous stem into the garbage right away.

Now the fun could begin. In the movie, they whipped the frond like a bullwhip over an exposed nail to shred it. I tried to picture myself doing that and couldn't imagine it. There must be some other way to make a frond into a grass skirt. I found a box of ten-penny nails and stuck a nail into the heel of the frond and pulled it along the vein. The green leathery leaf ripped easily. I poked the nail in again and pulled. The feel of the frond splitting was very satisfying. Poke. Pull. Rip.

The garage was silent except for the zipper sound of my nail at work. A white plastic table-top radio sat at the end of the workbench. I thought about turning it on, the way Dad did when he worked in the garage, but I decided I liked the quiet. Besides, listening to the radio would make me think of Dad and I didn't want to think about him.

I remembered the old radio that used to be there on the bench before Dad had to replace it with the white one. He had to get a new one because when I was three I took a screwdriver and completely took the old radio apart. I pulled out every tube and transistor. I unscrewed the knobs and pried all the capacitors out of their soldered beds.

I didn't do it to be destructive. On the contrary, I somehow got it in my head that we needed a little TV in the kitchen just like the one Grandma had over at her house so I was going to make one.

I thought I could take apart the radio and put it back together again as a TV. I didn't realize I couldn't until I got the whole thing apart and started to build the TV. With all the little electronic parts spread out before me it was like awakening from a dream and finding that I'd been sleepwalking. What had made perfect sense the moment before made no sense at all now. I started to cry. I cried for myself out of frustration. I cried for the radio that I couldn't put back together. I cried for the TV that would never get born.

I got up from the mess I made on the garage floor and went into the house. It was a Saturday and Mama had gone shopping at the new thing called a "mall" in San Bernardino and left Dad to look after me. I ran through the side door of the house that led from the garage to the kitchen and into the living room.

"Daddy, Daddy!" I cried.

Daddy and Uncle Arby were on the couch together. They sat up real quickly and Dad ran his fingers across his scalp to straighten his hair. Uncle Arby tucked in his shirt. "What's the matter, Cary?" Dad asked.

"I can't make a TV."

"You can't make a TV? What do you mean?"

"The radio!" I sobbed. "It won't go in a TV."

Dad got up off the couch and let me lead him by the hand out to the garage. "Holy shit," he said as he saw his Magnavox disintegrated on the oily concrete floor. "Cary, what the hell have you—"

His fury was interrupted by the sound of Uncle Arby's laughter. Arby stood in the doorway howling with glee over what I'd done. He scooped me up in his arms and swung me around the garage, kissing me on the neck and on the forehead until I stopped crying and involuntarily started giggling.

"You silly, silly boy!" he chided me. "You can't make a TV from a radio! Silly, silly boy!" And he kissed me some more and made farty sounds with his mouth on the nape of my neck that tickled me and made me giggle harder.

Dad couldn't stay mad with the two of us acting like this, but he couldn't be as happy about what I'd done as Uncle Arby was. "What about my radio?" he whined.

"Don't worry about your radio, Burke. You can have that old white radio of mine. I never use it. Just teach this little boy some sense." Arby rubbed noses with me and hugged me closer.

Dad smiled, too. He looked tenderly at Arby and reached out and touched Arby's cheek. Arby kissed Dad's fingers and I kissed Dad's fingers, too. Daddy pulled his hand back and looked at Arby with surprise and guilt.

Uncle Arby just shrugged and laughed. "Chip off the old block," he said. I had no idea what he meant by that.

Poke. Pull. Rip. The frond was half shredded into long green strings. I looked back up at the white radio again. Maybe I should turn it on. The garage was too lonely and scary there in the silence of the late afternoon. It looked like I was going to think about my dad anyway whether the radio was on or not so I might as well have some noise. I never was very good at getting my brain to stop thinking of something. Every time I told it not to think of something it always thought about it all the more. Maybe, I reasoned, I won't think about stuff if I sing.

"Oh, I went down south to see my Sal, sing Polly Wolly Doodle all the day" I sang, going through the first verse, chorus and second verse before it bored me. I had no idea what "Polly Wolly Doodle" meant, but at least the lyrics weren't quite as creepy as the words to "Puff the Magic Dragon" or "White Rabbit." Kids at school said those songs were really about drugs so I didn't want to sing them anymore.

It occurred to me right then that "Polly Wolly Doodle" might really be something dirty, like curse words. I mean, it certainly sounded like something you wouldn't say in church. The world was funny. Everything always seemed to be about something else. There was a hidden message in everything.

Still, singing seemed like a good idea. Mama always insisted that I sing when I was in the bathtub. As long as I was singing, she figured that I hadn't drowned. Sometimes I'd get interested in something else in the bathtub or start daydreaming and I'd stop singing. Mom's voice would ring out from the kitchen, "Cary! You better keep singing, damn it, or I'm coming in there!" So I'd blurt out "Happy Birthday to You" or "Jingle Bells" or something just to keep my mouth moving.

As I continued to zip my ten-penny nail through the frond, I broke into "Jesus Loves Me" and a whole medley of other Sunday school songs. Now that was music you could pretty much take at face value. I sang loudly so that our next door neighbor, Mrs. Johansson could hear me. If she could hear me singing, it would save her a trip over here to check and see if I were okay.

I was a latchkey kid. That meant that my mom had a job, so I came home to an empty house every day after school. I had my own house key I kept on a chain around my neck. I would let myself in and was supposed to lock all the doors and watch TV until Mama got home at 5:30. She always called to check on me about every half hour and Mrs. Johansson from next door promised Mama that she'd come over every afternoon to check on me. That usually amounted to her coming across to our front door, knocking, and yelling "Are you okay, Cary?" and I'd yell back "Yeah!" from behind the locked door, and she'd leave.

Today was Cub Scout day though, so I didn't have very long to be alone. I finished shredding the last part of the frond then I stood up and held it against my belt to see how it looked. Seemed fine, I thought, but just one frond wasn't going to be nearly enough. It was going to take at least four of them to go around me.

I went out in the front yard and quickly yanked more fronds down. It was a little dangerous to do, since I wasn't supposed to be out of the house until Mom got home from work, but I certainly wasn't going to wait that long. All the same, I hurried to break the fronds down from the tree and scurried to get them back in the garage because she very well could be home any minute.

Mama's car pulled into the driveway just as I got halfway through shredding the second frond. I heard the door of the pink Mercury open and close and heard the click and scuff of her spike-heeled shoes on the driveway. She lifted the wooden garage door and caught sight of me sitting there.

"What are you doing?" she demanded. "You didn't pull those off the trees in the front yard, did you?"

"I had to. It's for a project they're making me do for scouts."

She opened her mouth to yell at me for ruining the trees, but let the air out of her lungs in an exasperated sigh instead. "Well, drag all that stuff out of the way. I gotta pull the car in."

Dutifully, I cleared the way so she could park the car in the garage. She pulled in then closed the garage door behind her. The car engine made little pings as it cooled. Mama dropped her car keys into her purse and turned to go inside the house. She swung back at the last second, shot me a look and asked, "What're you making out of all that trash?"

"I'm making a grass skirt."

"A what?"

"A skirt like a hula dancer wears."

She raised one perfectly arched eyebrow so that it was slightly higher than the other burnt umber crescent she had penciled on her face. She pressed her lips tightly together then turned her back to me. "Come on in and get worshed up in a few minutes," she said as she walked from the garage into the kitchen.

I stared a moment at the pink Mercury, that great ugly car of ours. Why had my parents bought it? They were embarrassed to drive it because it was pink. At least Daddy didn't have to worry about it anymore. The pink car was all hers now, and she loathed it. "Ta-ta-ta-ta-ping-ping-PING!" it sighed as its engine block cooled, as if it knew it was a big embarrassment to the family that we couldn't get rid of.

I could hear the theme to the evening news blaring on the TV in the house. I went back to my work. Poke. Pull. Rip.

***

It had only been a little less than a year ago that Daddy ran away with Uncle Arby. The fact that my father had deserted us, and why he deserted us, was never kept a secret from me, although neither Mama nor Granny had any idea where the men ran off to.

At first I wished they had taken me with them, but then it occurred to me that maybe they joined the Army again and went to Vietnam. I had a deep-seated fear that one day I would have to join the service, too, and fight in a war. I was terrified of the thought of being in a war. I didn't even like being around the boys who tussled on the playground, but Granny said all men had to join the service. If you couldn't show you had gotten an honorable discharge from the service, no one would ever give you a job and you couldn't buy a house.

"You'd have to go on the welfare and live the rest of your life around them Mexicans."

As far as I was concerned that choice was the devil or the deep blue sea. I missed my dad a lot and Uncle Arby even more, but if they had run off to war, it's just as well that they left me behind at home where it was safe.

***

As the days passed, I worked every day on the grass skirt. Once all the fronds were slit into long green spaghetti, I found a roll of gray duct tape and bound them all together using the tape for a belt. To make the ugly tape look a little better, I took a magic marker and drew shells, starfish and mermaids all over it as decoration. It was perfect.

I had all afternoon on the day of my big performance to practice my hula dancing. I danced by myself in the lonely afternoon, the hearth of the gas fireplace as my stage. I put our Don Ho album on the hi-fi and danced to "Tiny Bubbles," making up flowing, languid hand gestures to go with the lyrics.

It was difficult to get my hips to move from side to side, like the ladies did in the film, but I found that a similar effect could be produced by doing a variation on the Twist. In fact, by dancing like a washing machine, I could get my skirt really moving, like a palm grove in a monsoon.

Since I made my skirt almost a week too early, it had started to turn brown and yellow and crackled like autumn oak leaves as I moved. This was distressing, but since the pack meeting was that night, I didn't let it bother me much.

There was a peppery little knock on the front door. "You okay in there?" screeched Mrs. Johansson.

I raced to the door and opened the little brass mail flap with my fingers. "I'm okay!" I called through the slot. All I could see of her was her stomach and noticed she was missing a button from her floral print housedress.

She turned and said, "All right then," and I watched her bottom undulate away. How did ladies walk like that, like they had a pendulum in their butt? I tried swishing my hips that way as I made my way back to the hearth to continue my dance practice.

Mama had called a half hour ago and said she'd be home soon. The pack meeting was at 7:00. That would give us just enough time to eat and get me all fixed up before we had to go. I had it all planned out how I wanted Mom to make me up. I wanted white face, with a big red nose and lips, huge blue circles for eyes, and a big worsher-woman hat like Moms Mabley always wore on TV. If we couldn't find a hat, I knew Mama at least had a big Hawaiian scarf she could tie around my head to hide my hair. A bright colored t-shirt with a couple of oranges for boobs, a pair of shorts under the grass skirt, a big pair of ladies' shoes and voila!: Lady clown hula dancer. The hit of the skit.

I was in my room picking out the perfect t-shirt and shorts to wear when I heard Mama pull the Mercury into the garage. My grass skirt was lying on the bed. It was getting so fragile and dropping strands so easily now, I dared not excite it any further. Next came the sound of the tinkle of keys and the thwump of the kitchen door.

"Cary?" Mama's voice called. There was kind of an echo so I knew she was in the kitchen.

I ran down the hallway to her. "Mama," I said breathlessly, "the pack meeting's tonight. Did you remember the pack meeting's tonight? It's at seven o'clock. We're doing skits, so after dinner, I need you to help me put on some makeup."

She didn't look up at me, but nodded and looked through the stack of junk mail I had laid out for her on the kitchen table. "Go worsh up and set the table," she said. "Did anybody call?"

"No," I said. I knew she meant Daddy, but she didn't say so, so I didn't either.

She ripped the junk mail in halves and quarters and threw it in the trash can. I watched her as she took a pot and ran some water into it, then put it on the stove to boil. She looked over and saw me staring at her.

"Go," she said. So I went.

After dinner, I led her back down the long hallway to her bedroom, a room filled with a cheap blond veneer furniture suite of a double bed, two boxy bed stands, and a dresser with Danish modern drawer pulls. The only other furniture in there was an old vanity from around the 1940s that Mom and Dad had found at a junk store and painted white and screwed new gold knobs on to make it look more elegant.

I sat myself down on the gold wire vanity stool with the white fake-fur cushion and looked at myself in the oval mirror. I wasn't used to sitting here. This is where Mama put on her makeup before going to work, and now it was my turn to have her put makeup on me.

Mama looked down at me, her hands on her hips, and said, "Now what do you want me to do?"

"I have to be a lady clown. I need a white face, a big red mouth, a red nose, and big long lashes."

Mama studied my face in the mirror and laid her hand on my shoulder. "Well, I don't got no white makeup."

I turned and looked at her panicked, imploring. It didn't occur to me that she might not have clown makeup. She had everything else. "But the meeting's in an hour!" I cried. "I gotta go to the meeting dressed like a clown!"

She ran her fingers along the close-cropped hairs along the back of my neck. "Don't worry. We'll think of something." She stroked my neck some more, and pondered a bit. "You know, with the way your hair grows up in the back, if you were a girl, you could wear your hair in a lot of beautiful styles."

She opened a drawer in the vanity and took out a shoebox filled with all sorts of tubes and jars of cosmetics. "Turn around," she said and made me sit so that my back was to the mirror. "I'll make you look beautiful."

I got a knot in the bottom of my stomach. I didn't know why. It felt like I'd eaten a rock.

Mama rooted around and found a small glass bottle filled with thick beige liquid. She put little dabs of the liquid all over my face and then used her fingers to spread it evenly all over my cheeks, nose, forehead, chin, neck and ears. After that she took out what looked like a palette of colors with a little foam brush. She took silvers and blues and painted them on my eyelids and under my brows. To my eyebrows she took a little brown-colored pencil and drew them on, arching them higher, extending them out and down. My mother feathered rouge from a compact over my cheekbones with a soft wide brush with a short little handle, and carefully outlined my eyes with cold black liquid eyeliner.

"You said you wanted red lips, right?"

I nodded and turned to see what I was looking like in the mirror.

She stopped me. "No! Don't look yet. Just sit still."

I turned back around and fidgeted while she found a tube of fire-engine-red lipstick and put it on my lips. "Here, blot your lips like this," she said, handing me a tissue and pressing her mouth open and closed with her lips rolled back over her teeth, looking like an old woman gumming her food. I blotted and she took the tissue from me.

Mama studied my face for a minute more then said, "I know what you need." She opened the top drawer on the other side of the vanity and withdrew a set of false eyelashes in a white plastic case. They were long, spiky starburst crescents of hair, very clown-like I thought, so I patiently submitted to the uncomfortable process of having them glued to my eyes.

"Don't blink," she said, but that made me want to blink all the more.

When at last the eyelash glue had set, she told me that I was almost done. "I need a hat," I said. "I want a big worsher-woman hat."

A gleam stole in my mother's eye. "Oh, I know just the thing," she purred. "Now you sit still and don't look yet. I'll be right back." She bustled out of the room and returned in a flash with a plastic bone. It was part of a toy I had, a motorized dog that would bark and then fetch a plastic bone with a little metal plate that would conveniently stick to his magnetic teeth.

She opened her closet and took down a cylindrical box from the top shelf. Opening the box like a treasure chest, she withdrew a wiglet, a cascade of brown curls which she quickly and deftly attached to the top of my head with bobby pins.

"But I don't want to wear a wig! I'm supposed to be a clown!"

"Hush!" she hissed at me. "This'll be perfect."

She took the plastic bone and a length of magenta hair ribbon and affixed it squarely on top of my head with a big bow, like Pebbles Flintstone. "There!" she cried. "You're beautiful!"

I swiveled around on my stool and caught sight of myself for the first time in the mirror. I couldn't speak. It wasn't me. It was Dorothy Lamour in the mirror. I wasn't a lady clown at all. I was a real lady, a lady as beautiful as a Hollywood star.

"You're gorgeous," she said. "See? This is so much better than being a clown. Everyone's going to love you tonight when they see how beautiful you are."

I was still a little shocked at the way I looked, but I did have to admit I was stunningly beautiful and she was right, the skit would probably be so much better with a glamorous hula girl being chased at the end than a sloppy woman clown.

I turned the rest of my costuming over to my mother's judgment completely. She stuffed one of her bras with a pair of nylon stockings and strapped it on me. This she covered with that Hawaiian scarf I originally intended her to wrap around my head, tying it instead over my new false breasts in a halter top.

Mama did agree that I should wear a pair of shorts, but suggested that I wear hose to make my legs look "finished." A pair of red high-heeled slingbacks on my feet and loads of costume jewelry everywhere else completed the effect.

As she looped strand after strand of glittering necklaces over my head, she kept repeating "Oh you're beautiful. You're so beautiful."

My heart swelled with pride. I even felt bold enough to pick out my own earrings: a dangly pair of clip-ons that looked like Roman coins.

I carefully wrapped my grass skirt around my hips and stood and admired myself in the full-length mirror on the back of the bathroom door. I was a vision. I was ready.

We pulled into the parking lot of the elementary school. It was very close to 7:00, and the lot was overflowing with cars. Mom pulled up to the front of the building and let me out of the car, saying that it would take her a long time to park and she wasn't dressed to go inside anyway, so I should just go on without her. She'd sit in the car and wait for the pack meeting to get over.

"Good luck," she said. She drove off, leaving me alone on the sidewalk in front of the school.

I could hear the monkey house roar of boys from the auditorium as I entered through the double glass doors to the building. My high heels kerchunked and echoed as I walked along the tiled hallway toward the noise of the meeting. It was my plan to just sneak in unobtrusively and stay hidden among the other boys in my den. They should be easy to find in the crowd because they'd all be dressed as clowns.

I came to the entrance of the auditorium and stopped dead in my tracks. I searched the room, scanning with my eyes over and over again. There were no clowns, only a sea of blue uniforms and yellow neckerchiefs. A group of scouts and scoutmasters were gathered by me at the door. They were talking, but took one look at me and fell silent in astonishment. I heard one of them chuckle and my heart started to race. I had to find my den and sit down with them *now*. I was far too conspicuous in this crowd.

Where were they? Where were they sitting? Just then I spotted Mrs. Gorman's red hair way up at the front of the room. The other boys were with her too, but they weren't in costume. They were all wearing their scout uniforms. I hadn't thought of that. I hadn't thought that we'd only put on our costumes right before we got on stage. What was I going to do?

Mrs. Gorman was talking and laughing at something then she turned her head and saw me standing at the back of the auditorium by the door. Her eyes rounded and she stopped laughing. I could see her lips say "Cary?" and all I wanted was to be with her and to have her protect me from this embarrassing predicament, but the only way to get to her was right down the center aisle.

I started to move stealthily down the aisle, keeping my eyes focused on the ground, hoping no one would notice me. As I walked, the noisy room started to become quieter and quieter. By the time I got halfway down the aisle, the whole auditorium was silent. I stopped and looked around. Everyone was staring at me, no one knowing what to say. Suddenly from the far side of the hall, one of the older boys gave a loud, lewd, wolf whistle. The room exploded. Jeers, cheers and catcalls rained down upon me like spitwads.

I ran the rest of the way down the aisle to Mrs. Gorman, my only hope of rescue. I could feel the mascara starting to ooze down my cheeks. The focused derision of the crowd grew and fed upon itself until it was almost impossible to hear Mrs. Gorman's voice as she knelt down to speak to me.

"Cary, honey, didn't your mom tell you about my call? I told your mother yesterday that they got an astronaut to come speak at the meeting tonight. We're going to do skits *next* month."

I stared at her like I couldn't understand English. All I could do was stand there wordlessly and fight for breath. I couldn't believe what she was saying to me. Gabe was standing beside her and nodded. The shocked expression in his eyes told me clearer than language that it was all true.

I turned around and started walking back up the aisle. It was hard to move because the air was thick as oatmeal.

"Cary? Cary, are you going to be okay? Come back here," Mrs. Gorman implored. I didn't answer her. All I could think about was getting out of there. The aisle became a path from a nightmare, one that stretched endlessly toward the horizon.

My flight from the auditorium, my obvious humiliation, turned the Cub Scouts at the pack meeting into gleeful, howling demons. Boys started reaching out to poke at me and snatch at my clothing. A blond kid grabbed at the bone in my hair and ripped it off of my head along with the wiglet. Another boy grabbed at the clasp of my bra between my shoulder blades. The clasp gave way and snapped me hard in the center of my back like a gunshot. I tried running but the hands kept reaching for me, clutching at my false boobs and my disintegrating grass skirt.

I spun around and saw my bone with the magenta ribbon and the brown wiglet of curls go flying through the air. The scouts were playing catch with it. Soaring through the vaulted space of the auditorium it looked like some sort of death kite.

I careened through the assembly room doors and raced down the hallway, losing my mother's red shoes in the process. My feet, covered in nylon stockings, turned the waxed tile floor into a sheet of ice. I went skidding as I rounded a corner and banged my shoulder hard into a dimly lit display case full of trophies. The glass doors on the case impacted in a spider web crack.

Smarting and sobbing, I staggered to the building entrance and emerged into the hot California night. The pink Mercury was parked right before me at the curb and Juney was sitting on the hood waiting for me.

She was laughing. She was laughing hysterically, holding her stomach with one hand while wiping her eyes with the other. As I walked toward her, I could make out what she was saying between her sobs of laughter.

"You're beautiful! You're so beautiful!" she said in a mocking parody of herself at the vanity that evening. "You're both so fucking beautiful," she bellowed with no laughter at all. She lay back on the hood of the car and pounded her fists into the metal. "Fuck!" she cried. "FUCK!"

CHAPTER FOUR

1984

My wieners are boiling on the stove. Two of them. The diet says I can have two along with one slice of unbuttered bread and a half cup of string beans. I read the wrinkled newsprint clipping over again. Yep, that's all I can have. I got this diet from a Penny Shopper flyer I picked up at the bakery. It says it's a sure way to lose twenty pounds in a week. I'd love to lose twenty pounds in a week. I'm not as fat as I was last summer in Taos, but I'm still too big. I want to lose a hundred pounds. I do the math real quick in my head. If I stay on this diet, a hundred pounds is only five weeks from now. No, less. I started this diet two days ago, so it's four weeks and five days to go.

The wieners float and roll languidly in the simmering water. They're nowhere near done and it is torture for me to stand and watch them so I walk away and try to do something else, think of something else, to keep my mind occupied on something besides food. I turn on the television. It's late Saturday afternoon and there's absolutely nothing on that anyone would want to watch: golf, an old rerun of *McMillan and Wife*, a panel discussion about politics on PBS, an old black-and-white pirate movie, stockcar racing, and an impassioned look at the near extinction of the black-footed ferret in Wyoming.

Of course I choose the ferret program. They're going extinct because the only thing a black-footed ferret will eat is a prairie dog, and prairie dogs are getting scarce. I remember the little prairie dog town near my adobe house last summer in Taos. I loved standing in the open field watching them scamper and play in and out of their gopher holes. Now I'll never see them again. When they let me out of St. Francis Hospital after a couple of days, I got right on a bus for the airport at Albuquerque. I didn't even go back to the foundation and pick up my things, I just went back home to Espada with the clothes on my back. I imagine all my stuff ended up in the dumpster with the doughnuts.

I go back and check on the wieners. Hell, they must be done by now. They've plumped. At least I think they've plumped. They look plumper than they did when I put them in the water. I snap off the burner and take a fork to spear the little guys out of the water and onto the plate. I forgot about heating up the string beans, so I quickly open a can, drain it and dump the canned beans into the hot dog water. The water's still at the boiling point. All it takes is a few swishes around with the fork to get them heated up. I sloppily drain the wiener water down the sink preserving as many of the string beans as possible and deposit all the remaining beans on my plate. I know the diet says I can have only a half a cup of string beans, but all the calories are in the wieners, not the beans, so as long as I don't cheat on the meat, I'll still make my hundred pounds in five weeks goal. The hardest thing is only having one slice of white bread with dinner. I choose the biggest piece right from the center of the loaf. I assume ketchup and mustard are unlimited, so I pool them into large red and yellow islands on the side of the plate. I go back over to the couch and eat while I finish watching the show about the black-footed ferrets.

They thought the black-footed ferret was extinct until somebody found eighteen of them a little while ago. The scientists captured all eighteen of them and put them in captivity for their own safety. Now they're trying to breed them back up to sufficient numbers so they can eventually release them into the wild again. The problem with keeping those little fellows in captivity turned out to be the same problem they had in letting them stay in the wild. The ferrets refused to eat anything except prairie dogs. And it wasn't like those researchers had a kitchen-full of prairie dogs to hand them. They assumed that the ferrets, like all other meat-eaters, would eat cat food or canned tuna as long as it was stuck under their noses, but the ferrets absolutely refused to adapt. Prairie dogs were all they recognized as food.

I'm watching the scientists try to feed those cute little weasels while I'm trying to slowly chew my remaining hot dog and I think, "My God, that cat food looks good." And it does. It looks like some sort of Tuscan tuna salad, all oily and flaky. I find myself getting angry at the ferrets. Eat, goddammit! Eat! If I were you, I would. If someone were holding a forkful of food to my lips right now, I'd eat it. And eat it. And eat it.

I'm not even paying attention to what I'm doing. I'm thinking about eating, obsessing about eating, but I'm unconscious to the fact that I actually am, at that moment, eating. I'm completely disconnected from my own fat body. I'm looking hard at the TV screen while teleporting off somewhere in my mind, starving for food, yet not allowing myself to acknowledge the food I'm eating. The sound of my fork clinking and scraping on my plate with the regularity of some Rube Goldbergian timekeeping device starts to speed up, and up, and up. Clink, scrape, bite. Clink scrape bite. Clink-scrape-bite. Clinkscrapebite. As I near the end of my meal, the food goes faster and faster into my mouth. I use the last crust of bread to wipe the traces of mustard and ketchup off the plate, leaving the dish so clean I could probably get away with putting it back on the shelf, unwashed.

The black-footed ferret turns up his nose at the cat food and walks to the other side of his cage. He rolls up into a little ball and goes to sleep.

I look down at my plate. That was it. That was my dinner and it's gone. I'm still starving. I'm torn between going back over to the refrigerator to cram the rest of the raw hotdogs directly into my mouth or just sitting here on the couch and crying. Instead I decide to trust in that ridiculous twenty-minute time delay humans are supposed to have between food entering the stomach and the brain realizing that it's no longer hungry. Why does the body do that? I want to fling my empty plate across the room just to feel the sense of release; I want to scream at God for making people feel hungry after they've eaten; I want to kick God in the nuts for making me fat.

I've got to pull myself together. "It's just food," I tell myself. "What are you getting so worked up over?" Then I do this little self-therapy thing I learned from a pop psychology book I skimmed at the mall. I ask myself, "Do I want to eat because I'm hungry or do I want to eat because I'm upset?" Yeah, I'm upset. I'm upset because I'm hungry.

No, that's not it. I guess I am upset. I'm upset because I feel so useless. I haven't done anything today. I made a vow to start writing again, but it's 4:30 and I haven't done any writing at all today. I haven't written anything in months it seems.

The weird thing is I don't have writer's block. I've never had writer's block. I've got thousands of ideas to write about. Ideas for poems strike me out of the blue all the time, but I can't physically bring myself to sit down and write them. I will do anything to keep myself from having to face a blank piece of paper. Anything. I'll wash dishes that are perfectly clean; I'll jerk off until I start to bleed; I'll walk a mile to buy doughnuts. I just don't want to possibly, maybe, perhaps, inadvertently write a bad poem.

I don't want to find out that I'm living a lie.

Not an hour goes by when I don't allow myself to consider the possibility that I have no talent whatsoever. I'm not a poet. I'm not a writer. Writers write and get published. I haven't published anything in a book or a magazine, ever. Even though I've made more money from my poetry than 99 percent of all the people who call themselves poets, I still feel like I'm traveling with a forged passport. It was a fluke that one little poem I wrote when I was fifteen became a hit song. A fluke. Now I'm this poet, this lyricist, and I haven't a clue what that even means.

No. Stop this. I'm wallowing in self-pity. I'm being negative. If I once wrote a poem that was highly successful, then that means I must be talented. And if I wrote one successful poem, then that means I can write another one, right? Of course. What I need to do is just sit down and write a poem and not care if it's good or bad. Just write a lot of poems. A lot of them. One hundred poems. Good poems, bad poems, whatever. I'll write one hundred poems, then I can look anyone in the eye and say to them, "Yes, my name is Cary Scott and I'm a poet."

Suddenly I envision a loose leaf binder sitting on my book-shelf with a sticker on the spine that says "Cary Scott – One Hundred Poems" and people will see it whenever they come to my apartment and they'll comment on it with admiration and I'll shrug my shoulders and act like it is nothing to me. "Oh, that? That's just my *first* hundred poems." And I'll adjust my black silk bow tie and brush off the sleeve of my tuxedo while admiring my slender waist in the full-length mirror, then I'll say, "Come on, we're going to be late," and we'll go off to the awards banquet together with my black topcoat slung jauntily over my right shoulder.

A commercial for blue dishwashing liquid comes on the TV screen. A glassy-eyed woman runs her finger across a wet white dinner plate until it squeaks. The subtext here is that her dishes are squeaky clean and yours are not. You are inferior to her. I look down at my plate in my lap. An inch of my belly fat is flopping onto the rim, obscuring a portion of the brown floral border. I want to cry. I want to cry because I can't even hurl the plate against the wall to watch the china shatter. I can't because I'm fat Cary Scott who doesn't write poems and whose plates are made of Melmac.

I grab the remote control and change the channel. It's that one or two minutes before the hour when there's nothing on but commercials and it's next to impossible to channel surf. Ever the optimist, I keep flipping around anyway. The flipping keeps me from thinking eating even though it seems every chan-nel has an ad blaring for McDonald's, Burger King or Dunkin' Donuts. Flip flip flip.

As I surf by, I stop when I see two cute guys on the screen. One is blond, one brunette; they sit side by side on chairs. It's a talk show and at first I assume the topic is something like "We're Gay Episcopal Nudists and Want to Be Left Alone!" But it's not. The cute blond guy turns out to be tennis star Svetlana Ivanova and the cute brunette is Jason Hunsacker, her nutritionist. They say he's about forty years old – forty! – but he looks about eighteen. I stop flipping the channel.

Svetlana's on a roll. She's only lost two tennis matches in the last three years. She's achieved dominance in her sport that is almost unparalleled. She's gone from a pudgy Ukranian footnote on the women's tennis circuit to a hard-bodied, invincible lesbian juggernaut. And she says she owes it all to her diet.

Of course when I hear this, my antennae extend.

Jason Hunsacker takes over. He explains what a mess Svetlana was when she came to him: No energy. Not able to concentrate. Low self-esteem. Was going nowhere in her career. Overweight. ("That's me! That's me!" I say to the TV.)

"On a typical day, Svetlana would start with a big breakfast, three eggs, cheese, bacon, lots of coffee. Lunch was fast food, you know, McDonald's, fries, cokes, stuff like that, and then dinner was the classic four food groups kind of thing, a huge slab of meat, lots of potatoes, a teaspoon or so of corn and a glass of milk."

Svetlana shakes her head sadly and stares at the talk show host with a look of "how could I have been so foolish?" in her eyes. "I did not know," she says. "I am athlete. We have been told and told and told to eat the eggs, eat the protein. Meats will make us strong. But I was not strong. I could not run across the court!"

Hunsacker then looks directly into the camera and stares into my eyes. "Ten years ago I was dying," he says. "I had high blood pressure and my serum cholesterol was off the scale. My doctor said I would probably soon have a heart attack and he wanted me to immediately start taking these powerful drugs for the rest of my life." Hunsacker chuckles and then says, "Of course that was back in the early seventies when everything we thought about cardiovascular disease and nutrition was basically wrong. I decided right then and there that I was going to study and devote myself heart and soul to learning about the chemistry of nutrition. I was not going to take any drugs; instead I was going to eat my way back to health."

What did he say? Can I believe my ears?

"Using my program, my blood pressure plummeted and stabilized in a low, healthy range. I lost almost all of my body fat and my doctor says I now have the blood chemistry of a twelve-year-old girl."

Hunsacker's face is angelic, beaming purity and trust. He brushes his shaggy mop of thick brown hair out of his ice-blue eyes. I set my empty dinner plate on the sofa and I get down on the floor so I can kneel closer to the TV.

"The diet's simple," he says. "No fat, no sugar, no salt. Low protein, high carbohydrates, very, very little meat. I mean, do you know what's in a doughnut? Do you know what's in a hot dog? Those things will kill you. You might as well stick them directly in your coronary artery and stop your heart dead."

My hot-dog-filled heart gives a whump of fear upon hearing that. I didn't know food could kill you. I know food makes you unhappy and grossly unattractive, but I didn't know it could get into your blood and stop your heart.

"I go on the program," says Svetlana, "I lose thirty pounds in one month. Of course I am exercising. I am athlete. But on Jason's diet I eat and eat and eat. I never eat so much in my life and I still get thin. I mean look!" Svetlana stands up and lifts up her t-shirt revealing a pair of tiny, rock-hard breasts in a jog bra and a flat, corrugated stomach. The studio audience gives a gasp of surprise then gives her belly a huge ovation.

"Everything we thought about dieting turns out to be wrong," Jason says. "In school, my professors taught me that 3,500 calories equal one pound of body weight. You eat 3,500 more calories and you gain a pound, right? Well the problem is, most people's bodies don't work that way. It's all about metabolism. Some people can eat an additional 3,000 calories a day and not gain an ounce while others can starve themselves on 1,000 a day and not lose any weight at all."

That's me. That's me!

"So metabolism is everything. The foods you put into your body and the amount of physical exercise you get adjusts the basic metabolic rate of your body. Counting calories is worthless. When you go on a low-calorie diet, you put your body into starvation mode and slow your metabolism down making it harder to lose weight. Your body thinks there's a famine and hangs onto its fat for dear life. So the paradox is: if you want to lose weight and lose fat, you've got to eat."

I sit on the floor staring at the television in silent wonder for the rest of the program. I'm immobile, transfixed, all the while Jason Hunsacker is on the screen. The only sound I make is that belabored whooshing noise I tend to make when I breathe through my mouth. Even sitting, I'm always out of breath. Sitting on the floor is especially bad. My stomach gets pressed up against my diaphragm so I can't ever really take a deep breath.

What would it be like to be able to breathe and move without effort? What would it be like to be on a diet that lets me eat as much as I want?

The talk show ends and the sweet, trusting, thin face of Jason Hunsacker is gone. Jason Hunsacker. My new god. My guru.

I push myself over onto my left hip, roll over onto my knees and struggle to get to a standing position. Just the exertion of standing has my heart racing. I'm only twenty-five years old and I feel and act like I'm eighty.

I think about this. I'm five-foot, four-inches tall, small-boned, and somewhere around 275 pounds. Maybe more. I'm not sure how much I weigh because I'm too embarrassed to go into a store and buy a scale. I know, though, that I weighed more in Taos last summer because I could feel it. Back then I couldn't even fit into the fat clothes I wear now.

I look over on the kitchen counter and see my copy of the hot dog diet. Just one hour ago, that stained, wrinkled piece of paper was going to be my savior. I believed its promises. I followed its teachings and now Jason Hunsacker tells me it's all a lie. If I followed that diet for five weeks, I would have starved myself, loathed myself, punished myself and, in the end, I wouldn't have been any different. I wouldn't have been a hundred pounds lighter. I wouldn't have been happy. I still wouldn't have been loved.

I pick up the hot dog diet and slowly rip it in two. Then I keep ripping, ripping. I turn the diet into confetti.

The television is still on. I hear a seductive woman's voice saying, "The Grand-Slam Breakfast: Two hot cakes dripping with butter, two slices of bacon, tender hash browns, and one of our succulent buttermilk biscuits covered in our own country gravy. Only $2.00."

I turn and look at the TV set. All that warm, beckoning food right there before me suddenly makes me feel ill. I imagine the gravy lining the walls of my arteries, the butter sweating through the pores of my liver, the crispy, oily fat on the bacon clogging the main blood vessel to my heart.

I imagine what a heart attack must feel like. I imagine what the suffocating hand of death must feel like. I imagine the size of the coffin I'm going to need. I walk over to the television and turn it off.

I walk over to the front door and slip on my loafers. Even putting on my shoes makes me depressed and angry. It's hard to admit to yourself that you only buy slip-on shoes because bending over to tie laces is just too much effort when you're this fat.

The closest bookstore is seven blocks away. The walk at least will do me good. I've got to have that book. What was it called? Damn. For the life of me I can't remember the name of the diet book. But I do remember Hunsacker. Jason Hunsacker. That's all I need to know.

I'm going right now to pick up the book. I can stop at the grocery store on the way home, too. I've eaten everything I'm supposed to eat for the day on the hot dog diet, but since I'm technically starting a whole new diet program right now, I have a lot of eating to do to catch up with the Hunsacker plan.

***

"Somebody told me you have AIDS," Marla Wylie bluntly says as she walks up to the table.

I don't know how to respond. I haven't seen Marla since that awful, chocolate-smeared day in Taos over a year ago.

"What?"

"There's a rumor going around that you've got AIDS, so I want to know if it's true."

I glance around quickly. There are only about a dozen people at the IHOP, but I bet at least half of them are eavesdropping. No, I guess eavesdropping is not quite the right word since Marla's practically shouting across the restaurant. "Of course I don't have AIDS," I say just as loudly so the people at the other tables can go back to minding their own business. "Sit down, Marla."

She left a message on my machine yesterday saying she was in Los Angeles and wanted to see me at noon at the International House of Pancakes because she needed to talk to me. I wondered what in the world she needed to talk to me about and prayed to God I wouldn't have to order anything to eat. Now I know we aren't here for the pancakes.

"What happened to you?" she asks. "I mean one minute you were this fat little guy sitting on the porch in Taos and the next minute, you're like gone. All we heard was that you had to go to the hospital and now look at you. You look totally different. Of course we all thought you had AIDS. I mean, my God, what else could it have been?"

"I went on a diet," I say.

"Some diet," she says then sits down and orders a double-shot half-caff tall skinny latte from the waitress. The waitress has no idea what she is talking about.

"What is it with you Seattle people and coffee?" I ask.

"We have regular or decaf. That's all," says the waitress.

"Fine, regular, whatever," says Marla.

"Are you really living here now?" I ask.

"Uh huh," she says. "I've been here about a week. I'm sharing this apartment with some guy above a plumbing store in Santa Monica. He's got AIDS, too. He's like covered in these lesions, so I got to thinking of you and looked you up."

"And again – I don't have AIDS, but thanks for the thought."

"Are you sure?"

"Of course I'm sure. How'm I supposed to get AIDS? I've never had sex."

Marla does a funny classic double-take. "Wha?"

"Not once."

"Why not?"

"Oh, come on. Look at me. Who'd want to have sex with someone who looks like me?" As soon as I say it, I want to kick myself. I really don't mean to sound so pathetic and self-pitying. I'm an idiot. An idiot.

"Jee-zus. There's nothing wrong with you. So like how much weight have you lost?"

"I'm not sure. I didn't buy a scale until a couple weeks ago. I guess it's about 120 pounds so far."

"A hundred and twenty pounds in a year and a half? That's a lot," she says.

"No," I correct her, "I only started this diet last March. It's only been about eight months. This is the first diet I've ever been able to stick to because all I do is eat on it. It's really supposed to be for athletes who have to eat a lot, but there's so much food on this plan that I have to eat, after a few weeks I just started getting sick of it. Now I even leave food on my plate and throw stuff away."

Marla looks at me skeptically. "No, really," I say. "But there's a downside to it, too. Yeah, I get to eat a lot, but there's a lot of stuff I can't have. I'm gorging myself on potatoes, pasta and vegetables, but that's about it. Almost everything else is completely off limits. I can't eat butter, egg yolks, cheese, beef, peanut butter, whole milk, sugar, caffeine, shrimp, pork, bacon … Bacon. God, I remember bacon. I used to put it on everything. Now it would be like taking cyanide."

Marla's coffee comes and I ask for some more hot water for my peppermint tea.

"So how much longer are you going to be on this diet?" Marla asks.

I just look at her and then I stammer a bit because I really don't know what to say. "Forever, I guess," I finally admit and it surprises me. I've never conceived of a life where I was not either on or should have been on a diet.

Marla just shakes her head then she asks what happened to me in New Mexico that summer. Why did I just disappear? Why was I in the hospital? What happened to my bathroom?

So I tell her. At first I try to leave some things out, but soon it becomes apparent that everything that happened that day was equally embarrassing, so I just tell her the whole story. And she listens. She doesn't interrupt me once, not even when I tell her about crawling into the dumpster or barfing on the policeman. I expect her to laugh at that part. In fact, I myself giggle self-consciously when I tell her how the cop screamed and backed away from me in disgust.

But Marla doesn't laugh. She looks at me steadily and deeply and her eyes well up. I tell her about the difficulty they had getting me out of the dumpster and onto the stretcher and how it took two cops and two paramedic crews – six people altogether – just to lift me into the ambulance. It was humiliating. They taped large red bags that said "biohazard" around my ass like a big red diaper and attached another bag securely under my chin like a horse's feedbag to contain all the vomit. In the emergency room they couldn't give me any pills or suppositories to stop the vomiting and shitting so they tried to start an IV on me. I was so fat they couldn't find a vein in my arms or hands, so the doctors finally gave up and stuck the needle right into my jugular and administered the solution into my neck.

Marla wipes a tear away and I marvel at this since the only emotion I feel about the whole event is simply embarrassment. Other than that, when I think of it, I'm just numb. It might as well have happened to somebody else.

"So what happened at the foundation after I left?"

"Well, um, they, uh …" Marla stalls for a moment then leans forward and tells me directly, "You might as well know. They had to close your house for two months because they had to do quite a bit of remodeling. I'm sorry, but there you go. Nobody really missed you until two weeks went by, and by then the smell from your house started getting pretty bad. Of course this gave everybody a lot to gossip about. All we knew for sure was that your bathroom collapsed and that they found food hidden all over the house and with the smell of the rotting food and the – the way you left the bathroom, they had to gut the house and fumigate."

I can't say anything. I just bury my face in my hands.

"I'm sorry. I'm sorry," she says. "But you asked."

"I meant what happened to everyone else, not what happened to my house," I say.

"Oh. Not much really. You were pretty much the big topic of conversation for the rest of the summer. Then a couple of months ago we all get a card from Karma Minkowitz – oh, by the way, they did end up kicking her out for working at the Taco Tia – but she sends everybody these postcards with the information about her next art show and she says how she saw you in Griffith Park and how you looked like you had AIDS, so it all kind of fit and that's what we all thought."

"So Karma's doing an art show here?" I ask.

"It's over already and it kind of bombed. I think she's taken the concept of food portraits about as far as it will go. I heard she applied for a Guggenheim. If she gets one I swear I'll kill her. Either that or I'll just join the avant-garde and hop on the no-talent gravy train, too."

"What are you doing now? Are you still composing?"

Marla takes the tin milk pitcher on the table and floods her coffee till it's nearly white. "Stand up," she says.

So I stand up.

Marla howls with laughter. "No! Sit down!" she squeals. "Oh, that was perfect. No, I mean I'm doing stand-up comedy. I've got an act. It was inevitable really, I suppose. You went to one of my performances in Taos, right? I was up there on stage singing one of my new songs and people were like in the back, snickering. God, I was so offended 'cause in Seattle nobody ever laughed at me. They all thought I was like real deep. But one song I did got actual hoots in New Mexico, and then I did a tour through

Texas, Oklahoma, Kansas and Illinois and people were rolling in the aisles because they didn't think I was serious. But I was perfectly serious and I was deeply offended and depressed until I read this one newspaper review of my performance and they said I was some sort of comic genius. So I took some time and processed all the really disturbing information and then said 'well, fine, whatever.'"

"You didn't know you were funny?" I ask. "When I saw you in Taos, I thought you were hysterical and I was embarrassed for you because I didn't think people were laughing enough."

"No."

"Yes. Oh come on. You can't tell me you were actually serious with those songs."

Marla gets a look of indignation on her face which is so comical I still can't tell if she's serious of not. "I was perfectly serious. I thought I was deep."

"Oh, please. You were singing songs like 'My Chakra's Open So Come on In' and 'Your Blue Aura is My Menorah.' And you didn't know it was funny?"

"I thought it was somewhat wry," she says. "I mean I'm not totally brain-dead, but it wasn't a comedy act. The really odd thing is now it is a comedy act, but I can't think of it as comedy. I tried being funny on purpose once and it was a nightmare. I figure I'll just stick to what I'm doing and play it straight because it seems to be working."

"So you're still writing songs like 'Swami River' and 'My Karma Ran Over My Dogma'?"

Marla picks up her napkin to throw it at me, but she pauses then says, "Okay, I know you're making fun of me and everything, but where are you coming up with these song titles? That last one, 'My Karma Ran Over My Dogma,' did you just make that up right now?"

"Well, yeah," I say but I know I'm lying. I heard somebody else saying that quip years ago, only I've forgotten where I heard it.

"Well, I might just steal it," she says. "That's exactly the kind of stuff I need. You know, I wanted to talk to you about this. I want to make a record. I heard your song on the radio last week and I wanted to ask you about it. They were playing it on the oldies station! You didn't really write that song did you? You're not old enough."

I grimace and take a swig of peppermint tea. "I was fifteen years old. God, that awful song. Jesus, that thing just won't go away."

Marla giggles and sings, "Lookey how she comes again! Runnin' past them nekkid men!"

"Stop!" I plead with her. "I swear to you, I did not write the chorus. That was all Kitty Belle's doing."

"How did you end up writing a song with Kitty Belle Crawford anyway?"

"What? You want to know how I broke into the recording industry? You think I might have some clout and connections to help you get a record made? Think again. That was a complete fluke and I wish it'd never happened."

"That's like so easy to say after you've already had a hit record."

"No," I insist, "having a hit record's great if that's what you want. But I didn't want it. In fact I had nothing to do with it. When I started high school, I had to write a poem for homework in English class. It was right in the middle of the streaking craze in the seventies, so I wrote a poem about a streaker and it won a Rotary Club contest. Our community newspaper printed the poem and somehow Kitty Bell Crawford read it. She was doing a show at our county fair. So she comes and visits me in the hospital and asks if she could set my poem to music."

"Why were you in the hospital?"

"Uh ... I don't remember." And then, before Marla has a chance to pursue that thread of the conversation, I continue quickly, "I told her to go ahead – and it became this huge country-western, pop music crossover novelty hit."

"That is so great," says Marla. "Did you make a lot of money?"

"Oh yeah. The money poured in, but at first I saw only $500 of it because the rest had to go into trust until I was twenty-one. At least, I thought having a hit record would make me really popular at school, but it only gave everyone even more reason to torment me. Especially after it became that song everyone loved to hate. I mean, it's really annoying, isn't it? Especially the 'Woo-Woo-Woo!' section. When the streaking fad died, I thought the song would just go away, but it didn't. It's still out there. It's now become immortal as a kind of yardstick of bad song writing."

"Did you ever have any more songs recorded?"

"Shit no! I never wrote another thing. Ever."

"Why not?"

I don't mean to sound angry, but I snap at Marla in spite of myself. "Would you?" I snarl. "Imagine, if you painted a picture that went down in history as the worst picture ever painted, would you paint another one? Even if that one bad painting made you rich?" I take a breath and sit back in my chair. "I mean, I didn't get rich, but I have enough money now that I don't have to get a job. Once I turned twenty-one, I got my money. I spent the last four years bopping around from artist colony to artist colony, eating doughnuts and passing myself off as a poet, only I'm not a poet. I've not written a poem since 1975."

"Well you *are* going to write another poem," says Marla. "And you're going to do it in the next two days."

"What?"

"I'm performing at Chuck-a-Lucks this Friday. I want you to write the words to 'My Karma Ran Over My Dogma' by Wednesday. That'll give me a day and a half or so to put it to music and I'll sing it Friday night."

As Marla stands up and puts on her coat, I say, "I can't write a song in two days."

"You don't have a choice," she says. "And anyway, two days is plenty of time. It's not a book. It's a stupid poem. Three verses and a chorus. It'll take you an hour. I'll call you about getting together on Wednesday. Oh, you know what we'll do? Now that you're like Mr. Health and Fitness, there's a gay gym near where I'm living. We'll go and work out. I've got a guest pass. Go home! Write something!"

And she is gone.

My heart starts racing like it used to whenever I climbed a couple of stairs. In the next two days, I'll have to do two things I haven't done in ten years: write a poem and use a locker room.

I'm not sure which one scares me more.

***

The next day, I do nothing but procrastinate and rack my brain about how in the world I'm going to write this poem. I go to the bookstore and buy new-age books so I can bone up on all that silly jargon. I watch a lot of television because it numbs me and makes me forget what kind of pressure I'm under. I think about getting very drunk or eating doughnuts, but both things are forbidden on my diet.

Finally, after exhausting all my tricks for avoiding work, I sit down with a notepad and I start writing. I actually lose myself in the work. I work for hours, oblivious to the passing time. I work long into the night, coming up with new rhymes and silly turns of phrase that make me laugh. At five o'clock in the morning, I tell myself it's done.

I've written a poem.

It's a dumb poem, but I like it.

My Karma Ran Over My Dogma
by Cary Scott

In my Hot Yoga class with my chakras aligned
Sitting up with a zafu tucked 'neath my behind
I let out an Ohm and I made up my mind
to live a life kinda like Buddha designed.
I'll chuck my possessions, throw open my purse,
Give food to the poor and see hunger reverse,
Read *Desiderata*, rehearse every verse
And be one with the sun and the whole universe.

But my karma ran over my dogma.
In a previous life I was some kind of shit
Now my life's such a mess I'm depressed over it.
My thighs are so fat that my jeans don't quite fit.
My karma ran over my dogma.

So I shake out my tension and empty my brain,
Envision my sphincter's a free-flowing drain,
And wash negativity from me like rain,
And think to myself who am I to complain?
I'm healthy. I'm blessed with two eyes and two feet.
I take high colonics. I don't eat red meat.
I have sex with protection, avoid NutraSweet,
And keep my bowels neat with a treat made from wheat.

But my karma ran over my dogma.
In ancient Judea I must've been bad
Or as little Caligula, murderous mad,
'Cause I just had the worst haircut I've ever had.
My karma ran over my dogma.

When life throws a curve you don't think you deserve
You might find you don't wanna ascend to Nirvana

So the yoga's all over, I pull on my jeans
And write out the check. I reflect what it means
To live a life free of deep Tantric ravines
And cook bean cuisines from small press magazines.
Still, you're hurled to the world and find it's your lot
To work off those karmic debt payments you've got.
You deserve to be strangled! Or spit on! Or shot!
'Cause you were bad *then* – even though *now* you're not.

My karma ran over my dogma.
It's reincarnation's perverse little curse.
You could live out your life as a celibate nurse

And come back as a dog, or a hedgehog – or worse.
My karma ran over my dogma.

It's a silly piece of work, but it's perfect for Marla's needs. More importantly, by writing this poem, I've confronted a huge fear. I would feel really great about myself, except now I'm starting to obsess about the other big phobia I have to confront. It's Wednesday morning and I'm supposed to face the terror of a gym locker room.

No. I can't go to a gym again. I just can't.

Marla will have to take no for an answer this time.

CHAPTER FIVE

1971

The Thursday before classes started at Dirk Falchion Junior High, Mama took me to what our family considered the most elegant department store in town, the Adams Company at the Espada Plaza. We went to the back corner of the first floor, the boys' department, to buy school clothes.

I had never been in the Adams Company before because Mama refused to shop there. From looking at Adams's sumptuous ads for eveningwear and ladies' undergarments in the Espada Sun-Mirror, she was certain that it was a store frequented by only the wealthy. "It's shameful the prices they charge," she'd say. "I can get the same things for half the price at Bargain Save."

Even at the age of twelve, I knew that wasn't true. I could tell good clothes from cheap clothes even if Mama couldn't. All the kids at school could tell, too. They all knew which parents shopped at the Adams Company and which parents dressed their kids in crap from swap meets, bargain shops, and thrift stores. They could tell clothes that were sewn at home from better clothes made in factories. The kids at school weren't stupid. And they weren't kind.

That's why I was particularly thrilled in Mama's sudden change of heart. I was going to have school clothes from the Adams Company this year. The junior high kids wouldn't have anything to tease me about. It was a great omen of a wonderful year to come.

The Adams Company was an old department store, elegant in its heyday but greatly in need of redecoration by the early seventies. The counters were of glass and blond wood veneer that must have been chic in the late 1940s. The mannequins – stiff-postured, glassy-eyed dummies – were hardly any newer. With their World War II heads and out-of-date hairstyles they looked distinctly uncomfortable wearing the mod fashions of 1971. Even the boy mannequins in the children's department with their chiseled crew-cuts and lantern-jawed grins looked earnest and middle aged.

The Adams Company sales floor was not carpeted. The floors were worn brown linoleum that reeked of strong chemical cleansers mixed with liquid floor wax. From the boys' department I could see the wooden escalators and hear their rhythmic paddle-clack sound. Watching the escalators, I imagined they could grab at shoppers' shoelaces and suck them into the machinery like a great wooden dragon sucking up spaghetti.

And this was the place Mama said only rich people shopped at? For the first time in my life, I began to suspect that perhaps the Adams Company might not be the most elegant store in town.

I soon found out that the reason we came to the Adams Company was because it was the official distributor of gym uniforms worn at Falchion Junior High. Mama fished out of her purse the letter the school had sent which ordered her to buy me the following gym outfit: red shorts, a reversible red-on-one-side-gray-on-the-other t-shirt, white socks, tennis shoes (our choice), and an athletic supporter.

I asked Mama if I could see the letter and she handed it to me as she inspected a stack of striped cotton shirts marked down 30 percent. "An athletic supporter," the letter said. I kept rereading the phrase. An athletic supporter. What could it be? Since I was terrible at anything athletic, I was not eager to find out.

Mama and I found the display table with the official Falchion gym wear piled high on it. We selected my shirt and shorts, size small, and grabbed a plastic bag of three tube socks and headed for the counter. As the gray-haired saleswoman was ringing our purchases up, Mama said to her, "Oh, and he'll need a jock."

The saleswoman nodded, reached underneath the counter and took out a stack of small red cardboard boxes that said "Bike."

"What size?" she asked, apparently rhetorically, since I was standing right in front of her, all four-foot eleven, ninety-five pounds of me.

"Small," said Mama and the lady added one of the red boxes to our pile and our bill.

Of course it had not escaped my attention that we had not picked out any nice new junior high clothes to go with my gym wear. It was looking ever more likely that we would be heading for the rumpled bins at Bargain Save before the day was out. To my great relief, however, we left the Adams Company and drove to Stevenson's, a smaller department store that sold basic, no-nonsense clothes at prices Mama considered reasonable.

She was in a fairly good mood that day, too, so I was glad I had not said one word of complaint when we left the Adams Company relatively empty-handed. I know Mama. Had I shown any attitude or emotion whatsoever of feeling deprived, she would have perversely taken me straight to the thrift store. Since I said nothing and felt nothing, I was to be rewarded with a modest amount of well-made, unremarkable new clothes, and that was fine with me. My goal in school this year was to be as unremarkable as possible.

The car radio was on and Mama was singing along to a new top-40 hit by a group called The Jelly-Belles. "Up in the air / That is where / We'll fly so high and free!" sang Mama. "Right by my side / I'll be your guide / and keep you com-pan-eee!"

What an awful song, I thought. It's just an airline commercial stretched out to three minutes. And those saccharin lyrics: "The skies cannot disguise the way / My eyes are filled with love / Above the trees, the seas, the bees / We'll coo like turtle doves." Could anything be worse? Still, Mama seemed to be enjoying it. Again, I said nothing as I looked out the car window and watched the buildings glide by down Tucker Avenue.

At Stevenson's, we bought a set of school clothes that were more or less an exact replica of the same clothes I had been wearing for the last ten years. I got three pairs of school jeans – not proper Levi's denims, but rather colored Wrangler denim pants, one each in light blue, dark green, and brown. They were all "slims," tiny little pants with inseams bigger than their waist sizes. To go with the pants, Mama bought me five nearly identical short-sleeved cotton dress shirts, all of them plaid, and each of them in a combination of hues that more or less matched all three of the pants.

"Now you've got a wardrobe," she said.

I said thank you and nothing more.

On the way out of Stevenson's, Mama was still humming that airplane commercial under her breath. Two shops down from Stevenson's was Crazy Jones Record Shack, a cramped little storefront operation that sold 45s, candy, and cigarettes. Instead of going to the car, Mama led me to Crazy Jones, a place we had never been.

Inside the door was just a counter and room for only about five or six people to stand. A pair of teenage girls in hip-huggers and tube tops stood and gaped at the hand-lettered list of the August 1971 top ten singles in Southern California scrawled on the wall behind the counter. The Jelly-Belles were number one, of course.

An obese, balding man in a lime-green Catalina Island t-shirt came out from a back room and asked us if we needed help. Must be Crazy Jones, I thought.

Mama said, "My son wants a copy of that song, 'Up in the Air.'"

The two teenage girls heard Mama and looked over at me. One whispered to the other and they snickered in a way that was derogatory and cruel and pointedly aimed at me.

I said to Crazy Jones, "I don't want the record. She wants the record. I hate that song."

Mama stopped breathing for a moment, then calmly took two dollars out of her wallet and handed the money to Crazy Jones with a little titter. "Oh, kids. What're we ever going to do with them?" she said kittenishly. We got our copy of the airline jingle and left the store.

We walked in silence about twenty paces into the parking lot. Mama then suddenly turned and slapped me hard across the face.

"Don't you ever – EVER – embarrass me in public again!" she screamed at me.

I didn't cry. I couldn't cry. All I could do was stand there and realize that I had wanted to slap her, too, and say the same thing.

***

That night, in the privacy of my bedroom, I contemplated the pile of new clothes I had laid out on my bed. I opened the red Bike box and took out a white elastic thing that sort of looked like underwear and sort of didn't. First, I took my desk chair and propped it against the bedroom door so Mama couldn't burst in and surprise me, then I removed all my clothes and tried the athletic supporter on.

I put it on backward at first, the little pouch covering my butt, since that seemed more logical to me for some reason. I couldn't wear this thing and have my butt hanging out, could I? Still, it didn't feel quite right – and certainly didn't look quite right as I modeled it in the mirror, especially since my penis was rock-hard and sticking straight out.

"Mr. Tall" I called it back then. I had noticed sometime before that my wiener would sometimes change shape as I dried it off after taking a bath. It would go from Mr. Small to Mr. Tall. I thought it was interesting, but honestly didn't think any more of it than that. I had also recently become aware of four black hairs that had spouted around the top of my wiener. Those were mildly interesting, too, and quite forgettable.

I stepped out of the jock and turned it around and had a little difficulty getting Mr. Tall into the pouch, but still this arrangement seemed preferable to the pouch-in-the-back version. I tried on the red shorts and the reversible t-shirt, wearing it first red-side out, then trying it on gray-side out. I liked the red side much better.

"Look at me," I said as I admired myself in the mirror. "I'm ready for P.E."

***

Junior high turned out to be a huge, unfamiliar place filled with foreign sights, acrid smells and exotic rituals. Unlike the small neighborhood grammar school I had attended for the past seven years, Dirk Falchion was a large, sprawling campus of a school with thousands of students.

The main building, built in the 1930s, was three-stories tall with Depression-Era murals depicting Spanish colonial life during California's mission period. There were wide stone staircases only for walking up and staircases only for walking down. Butcher-paper banners covered in blue and orange poster paint welcomed us to a new school year and said thing like "Go Rapiers!" or had unfamiliar words like varsity or intramural splashed over crude representations of basketball hoops and football goal posts.

I was totally lost in this new universe, desperately looking for something familiar, like a face from one of the kids in my sixth-grade class or a library or a water fountain. I was also desperately looking for my locker.

As if being thrown into this strange planet of adolescence wasn't disconcerting enough, I also had to deal with the responsibility as well as the anxiety of having to remember a locker combination. My registration papers had my new locker number and combo on them and I had feverishly drilled the three-number sequence 29-07-17 until it had lost all sense or meaning for me.

Just in case I should ever blank and forget the code, I had dreamed up an ingenious, uncrackable cryptogram that I could write down in plain sight of anyone and they would never know that they were looking at my locker combo – namely, one is A, two is B, three is C, etc., with zero and oh being the same thing (that's what made it uncrackable). My combination 29-07-17 translated to the futuristic-sounding "BIOGAG."

I wrote BIOGAG on the front of my Wilson Rodeo notebook, taped BIOGAG to the front of my Charlie Brown pencil box and even inked BIOGAG on the white sidewalls of my Keds.

The seventh-grade lockers turned out to be on the third floor – the most inconvenient location in the school – and my particular locker was at the most remote and lonely end.

As I walked up to my locker, I saw Gabe Gorman and two other boys standing by their open lockers, talking. I hadn't seen Gabe all summer long and was a little surprised to see the change that had come over him. He was still a handsome boy, but he seemed more handsome now. He was bigger for one thing and his body had somehow more definition under his t-shirt than before. A sort of dark shadow had appeared over his upper lip and he stood differently, too.

I said, "Hi, Gabe," as I walked past and Gabe gave me a quick flash of friendly recognition that quickly faded into something else, something colder. He closed his locker and walked away with the other two boys. As they got to the end of the hallway, their laughter echoed off the linoleum.

I looked down at the piece of tape on the Peanuts pencil case I was holding and read my secret code. BIOGAG. I started to turn the dial on my locker and then froze for a second.

B is for two, but does I stand for one or nine?

***

The boys' gym locker room at Dirk Falchion was dim and damp, with rows of ancient forest-green lockers that had rusty hinges and bent or missing clothes hooks. I chose a locker in the rear of the room on the left as I went in the door. Bobby Harvey chose a locker nearby as did a few other boys I didn't know.

I knew Bobby from my elementary school. We had gone through all seven years at Lincoln School together and I didn't like him, or rather I was afraid of him because he was generally considered to be a "bad" kid so I was always careful to keep my distance. Bobby seemed all right that day, though.

I got dressed in my new gym clothes feeling rather proud and excited that I figured out the jock thing pretty well, since all the other guys around me ended up putting theirs on with the pouch in front, too.

Once dressed, we all filed out onto the blacktop behind the locker room where all the outdoor basketball courts were. Our gym teacher, Coach Hernandez, was a gargantuan human being whose olive skin, drooping mustache and butternut-squash physique made him resemble a kind of Mexican walrus. He sternly ordered us to line up alphabetically into one long row for something he called jock inspection.

Jock inspection turned out to be a bizarre, yet strangely appealing ritual in which each one of us in turn were ordered to pull the waistband of our shorts open in the front so Coach Hernandez could look down our pants and assure himself that we were all indeed wearing an athletic supporter.

After everyone was inspected, he gave us a stern lecture about surprise jock checks being something we could count on at any moment, so we better always wear one when we were out on the field. Some sort of terrible, painful injury that I could not fathom would be the result of not having proper "protection." I accepted this as mysterious truth even though in a jockstrap I didn't feel overly protected from anything.

The other vital point he stressed to us in our orientation speech was that it was imperative that every boy take a shower after class. There were to be no exceptions and Coach Hernandez would personally monitor every one of us in the showers to make absolutely certain that we didn't go to our next class with body odor.

I had taken a peek at the long shower stall at the other end of the locker room right after I got suited up that afternoon. It looked like taking a shower there was going to be fun. The boys' showers at Dirk Falchion resembled a car wash. It was more or less a tiled passageway with spray heads sticking out from the walls. A portal at one end of the shower stall was marked "IN" and another at the far side was labeled "OUT." Apparently the drill was you walked in one end and emerged out the other, clean.

A towel room with a Dutch door was next to the shower exit and Coach Hernandez's office was, in turn, next to that.

After Hernandez's shower lecture, he divided us up into teams – reds and grays – and sent us out to play soccer, a game I hadn't the foggiest idea of what the rules were. Luckily, I was chosen to be a red so I didn't have to take off my shirt and reverse it to the gray side, the side I didn't particularly care for.

We played soccer for about a half hour and I sort of figured out that if you ran around a lot and tried to kick the ball now and then, that was about all there was to it.

Coach Hernandez blew his whistle and marched us back into the locker room for those mandatory showers. Good, I thought. I'm looking forward to this. I found my locker again and was happy that not only did I remember my locker number, but I also managed to remember my gym padlock combination (45-04-12, or DEODAB).

Since I didn't wish to be the first one into the showers, I dawdled a bit, taking my time undressing. I watched as the other boys, one by one, got naked and started marching single-file toward the IN door of the showers.

I finished stripping off and carefully locked the padlock on my locker because who knew what Bobby Harvey might decide to do. I joined the line of naked boys feeling quite excited about the whole event. I wasn't feeling at all self-conscious about being nude because no one was paying any particular attention to me at all. In fact, the other boys were going out of their way not to look at me.

As it turned out, I was absolutely right in comparing the Dirk Falchion boys' showers to a car wash. Once inside, no one stopped walking. They just kept moving one at a time through the warm spray until they emerged lightly hosed off out the other end. Some boys ran through, yelling so that their voices pinged and echoed off the tiles. Others strutted and walked with their arms outstretched so that the water jets would wash out their armpits. Me, I just walked through at a modest clip with my arms at my side and tried not to get my hair too wet.

Coming out the OUT door, Coach Hernandez at the Dutch door handed me a clean white towel. I didn't know why, but he looked at my naked body and gave me a definite look of disapproval. I assumed he could tell I wasn't athletic or something and there wasn't much I could do about that. I took the towel and went all the way back across the locker room to where my things were.

As I walked back to my locker, I noticed that a hush was falling over the room. I had no idea why. At my locker, I said DEODAB to myself, unlocked my combo, and dried myself off before getting dressed. Mr. Tall was back again, so it was a little more bother getting my underwear back on, but other than that, things were going just fine. Bobby Harvey and the other boys around me were acting weird, though. They kept making these odd faces and seemed to be in an awful hurry to get dressed and get out. I didn't want to miss anything, so I hurried too, although I was sure we still had plenty of time before our next period.

I left the locker room and started walking to my next class.

I didn't get far.

Bobby Harvey and a knot of tough-looking kids blocked my way and surrounded me. None of them said anything; they just stood there, smirking.

Bobby leaned in close to me and said with quiet, malicious glee: "Hey there, boner boy."

The other boys guffawed when they heard this. "Boner boy! That's a good one," a tall kid said.

"Boner boy, boner boy," repeated Bobby, and he kept saying the words boner boy over again, each repetition delighting himself and his mob increasingly until they were all chanting it at the tops of their voices.

They terrified me, but I still didn't quite know what they were going on about. Having carried the boner boy chant for what seemed an eternity, the pack of boys turned and walked away. Not one of them had laid a hand on me, but what they did next was worse than any beating.

"Hey!" Bobby shouted to the passing students. "Cary Scott got a boner in the showers!"

The boys spread out and started tapping anyone, everyone on the shoulders, telling them about me in the gym showers, and even turning and pointing me out to all these kids who had no idea who I was.

Girls mostly giggled and blushed. Boys, however, when informed wanted to know exactly who I was. "Hey faggot!" they'd yell. "Nice going, faggot!"

Of course I wasn't an idiot and realized immediately that Mr. Tall probably was the boner, but so what? It never occurred to me that perhaps Mr. Tall might be a bad thing. Mr. Tall was just something that happened, especially when something made me excited. I couldn't control it, could I? I had never tried. "Of course I'll try now," I vowed. Mr. Tall would never return again if I could help it.

That resolution, however, was no help at all with my present problem at hand. My next class was geography, all the way across the school. My only hope, I figured, would be to get inside a classroom and keep under the watchful eye of adult supervision. They wouldn't dare torment me in front of a teacher, would they?

Would they?

Luck was not with me at all that day. Most of Bobby Harvey's gang turned out to also be in my geography class. By the time I got there, they had spread the word to everyone in the room. Stares, smirks, and muted whispers of boner boy greeted me as I walked in.

It was the first day of class and I didn't know where to sit. I wanted to grab a desk in the back of the room so I could hide, but Bobby's friends were back there. The only place left to sit was also the most conspicuous one: front row center. My only choice was to be the center of attention.

The geography teacher came in the room and wrote his name, Jerome P. Blatchfeld, on the chalkboard. Mr. Blatchfeld was tall and gaunt with a dollop of frizzy white hair on top of his head. He wore high-waist green polyester pants and a pale green shirt. If Coach Hernandez resembled a butternut squash, then this guy looked like an upside-down spring onion.

Mr. Blatchfeld turned to face the room and in a dry monotone said, "I'm Mr. Blatchfeld and this is seventh-grade geography. In just a moment – and by that I do not mean momentarily, which means 'for a moment' not 'in a moment;' people always misuse that word – in just a moment, or soon, I will be handing out the textbook for this course. The book is entitled *Western Civilizations, Third Edition*. Do not mark your name in these books. Do not deface them in any manner as they have to be used again next year and probably for many years to come. You will be expected to cover these books with a handmade, brown paper book cover which you are to decorate with an appropriate geographical theme. The book covers will be graded. They will be marked on creativity as well as functionality."

Mr. Blatchfeld pulled down a world map on a spring-roller shade over the chalkboard. "We are going to begin this quarter," he said, "by studying the major metropolitan centers of the western world, meaning we will start with Vienna and just keep going left until we hit the surprisingly complex city of Perth, Australia. In between, you will be expected to learn the population densities, major industries, and major monuments or buildings of each city."

Mr. Blatchfeld paused and squinted at us. "Just as a matter of curiosity, can anyone here name the tallest building in the world? And by that I do not mean the tallest freestanding structure, like the Eiffel Tower which is not a building, or just a massive structure like the pyramids, again also not buildings, per se. What I want to know is, where is the tallest building?"

"There's a large erection in this room," said a voice from the back row.

The class erupted into gales of laughter, peppered with shouts of Cary Fairy.

Mr. Blatchfeld's brow furrowed and he said, "I don't understand. What are you talking about?"

So in front of the whole class, Bobby Harvey told him.

***

After school, I bolted home, not even stopping at my locker. I took the long way, staying as much as possible on busy major streets to avoid the possibility of being accosted in a deserted area.

Once my house was in sight, I started sprinting for the front door. As I ran, I fumbled for the key on the chain around my neck so it would be in my hand and ready to unlock the door as soon as I reached it. It was the slamming and the locking of the door behind me that offered me the first clear signal it was finally okay to cry.

In fact, I fully expected to burst into tears as soon as I was safe and alone, but for some reason I didn't cry. I didn't do anything. I sat down on the floor of the entry hallway with my back up against the front door and hugged my knees up close to my chest. In the dim silence of the entry hallway, I listened to the buzz of the electric clock in the nearby kitchen.

What had happened? How was it possible to be so stupid? My first day in a new school. I started the day with such hope and now all I had to look forward to was three years of misery until I got the chance to humiliate myself in front of a whole new group of people in high school.

As I sat there, I wondered if I had been followed home by the boys. I wondered if they knew where I lived. I turned around and poked open the brass mail flap in the door with my finger and peeked outside

The phone rang. It was time for Mama's check-in to make sure I made it home from school okay. Since I started junior high, it was no longer necessary to have Mrs. Johansson from next door come over to check on me in the late afternoons. This was good because, over the summer, Mrs. Johansson had died.

I went into the kitchen and answered the phone on the fifth ring.

"What's the matter?" Mama said very sharply. "Why didn't you answer the phone?"

"I just walked in," I lied. "It takes longer to walk home now."

"So how was your first day?"

"Fine," I lied again but that lie was okay. The way she asked the question made it perfectly clear she wasn't interested in knowing anything.

"Well don't mess up the house," she said. "I'll be home at 5:30."

I hung up the phone and looked at the kitchen clock. Four o'clock. Mama wouldn't be home for an hour and a half and I was starving.

In the refrigerator, among other things, was a plastic tub of Cool Whip and a bowl of butterscotch pudding. The Cool Whip was brand new and unopened. I pried the lid off and hesitated before sticking my finger into the cold, white dairy-free whipped cream substitute. If Mama saw a finger-swipe through the new Cool Whip, she'd kill me.

I was about to snap the plastic top back onto the container when I realized the inside of the lid had lots of Cool Whip stuck to it. I got a butter knife and scraped the inside of the lid clean and greedily inhaled the tablespoon or so of whipped topping I harvested.

I put the lid back on the Cool Whip and then took it off again to see if Mama would be able to tell that I'd snuck a little taste. To my relief, my small theft was completely undetectable.

In fact, snapping the lid on the tub made more Cool Whip cling to the inside of the lid. I scraped off this new dab of cream, ate it, then put the lid back on, took it off and ate the Cool Whip on the inside of the lid again. I kept doing this until the level of the Cool Whip in the tub stopped reaching the lid and I had to give up.

I put the Cool Whip back in the refrigerator and went into the living room to watch television.

An independent station showed reruns of *Batman* every afternoon, but I never liked watching it unless Julie Newmar was on as Catwoman. Not Eartha Kitt. Not Lee Merriweather. Just Julie Newmar. That day's episode, however, featured the repulsive Frank Gorshin as the Riddler, so I changed the channel.

The 3:30 movie was well into a severely edited version of *Fathom* starring Raquel Welch. Raquel, wearing only a tiny lime-green bikini, was piloting a speedboat to escape from some sort of international intrigue. I liked Raquel, and this was normally the sort of bombshell heroine stuff I loved to watch, but I couldn't get interested in the movie.

All I could think about was the Cool Whip.

Maybe if I tried the lid thing one more time.

I went back to the refrigerator and took the top off the Cool Whip again. It was clean. In a flash of inspiration, I took the butter knife I had been using and carefully ran it around the inside perimeter of the tub with the blade flat to the sides. This left the top of the cream completely unmarked but when I withdrew the knife, it had lovely gobs of Cool Whip sticking all over it.

This was very exciting. It was just like finding the key to a chest of treasure. And if I could do this trick with Cool Whip, then I would be able to do the same thing with any food in a bowl.

Naturally, the next object of my desire was the bowl of butterscotch pudding. The pudding lent itself beautifully to the knife trick because the skin on the top of the pudding fell back and covered any tell-tale tracks of the knife. Pudding was also thicker and stickier than Cool Whip, so I got to eat more of it.

I stayed in front of the open refrigerator, experimenting with each and every item to see how much I could take without Mama knowing.

Actually, for most things it wasn't a problem at all. I drank milk and juice right out of the cartons. Ketchup I sucked out of the bottle with impunity. Mustard and mayonnaise could be eaten with a spoon, defiantly and greedily because Mama never paid attention to the state of our condiments.

I got into a grazing rhythm. I wanted everything in the refrigerator. Mama wouldn't miss an olive. Or two. Or three. Mama wouldn't miss one slice of Wonder Bread or one big spoonful of sweet pickle relish.

I drank barbecue sauce. I drank Worcestershire sauce and washed them both down with apple juice. I stole a piece of cheddar. A dill pickle. A pat of butter.

I wasn't hungry any longer. In fact, I was making myself a little sick, but I didn't stop eating. I opened up a Tupperware container of leftover macaroni and ate almost half of what was there.

I slurped Kraft Thousand Island dressing out of the bottle. Then drank some Catalina. Then drank some Green Goddess.

Oh, I was definitely making myself ill. Nothing could stop me though. Nothing, that is, except for the sound of Mama's car pulling into the garage.

I slammed the refrigerator shut and ran with my knife and spoon to the living room where I placed myself in a casual, TV-watching pose on the couch and tucked the cutlery, the instruments of my guilt, under the cushions.

I just had time to wipe my mouth with my hands before Mama came into the room. She didn't say anything to me. She just dropped her purse onto the recliner and kicked off her work shoes before going back into the kitchen to start dinner.

A moment later, Mama came back into the living room.

"Who's been in the refrigerator?" she asked.

"I don't know," I said.

CHAPTER SIX

1990

The International Ballroom of the Beverly Hilton is so large I can't figure out how the roof stays up. There is not a single structural column to interrupt the expanse of a thousand burgundy chairs set in rows. The chairs are arranged in a fan-shaped half-circle configuration, radiating outward from a raised platform with a podium at the center of the far wall. Soothing new-age music fills the air along with the pleasant henhouse conversational cluck of a thousand fat women.

To be fair, not all the people in the room are fat or even female. There are quite a few women who are so thin they look like parking meters wearing clothing. There is even a sizable contingent of ladies who are not sizable in any way, just painfully average.

Men, however, are very hard to find. Other than me, I can count only about five other guys at this event and all of them are rotund. One man is so morbidly obese that he has to use two canes to walk and two chairs to sit down. I estimate that he's only about twenty-five-years old.

The majority of the people in the ballroom, however, are women in the 180-280 pound range. We have all come for an intensive two-day workshop with Jennifer Blume, the author of a half-dozen books on eating disorders. It is certainly no surprise to see the long row of tables by the exits, groaning under the weight of the stacks of Jennifer Blume books, cassettes, mugs, and t-shirts for sale and the feeding frenzy of ladies trying to snap up as many of these items as they can physically cart away.

The clackety-clack of the credit card imprinters is so regular it sounds like a train is going by.

There is no question that I'll buy a few things, too, but I'll wait until later when the crowd has died down.

I stumbled upon Jennifer Blume a couple of months ago while I was watching public access television, of all things. One of those dreadful amateur talk show hosts had somehow managed to snag Jennifer as a guest and, since there were no other guests on the program, Jennifer took the opportunity to turn her half hour of cable time into her own personal infomercial.

It was mere chance that I happened to be flipping by that station just as Jennifer said the words "never go on a diet again." I had just reaffirmed my allegiance to Jason Hunsacker for about the fiftieth time in the last six years and begun another cycle of extreme dieting. Now Jennifer was telling me that no diet ever works and the only way to not be fat is to recognize that food has become something other than food for me.

Boy did that ring a bell.

I watched the entire program intently, completely amazed at how a stranger on television could know all about my struggles with dieting, my twisted relationship with food, my belief systems, and my crazy little inner monologues.

But I didn't do what I usually do once the program was over. I didn't go and buy her book. The things she said on TV were too scary, too radical. Never go on a diet again? She might as well have said never blink your eyelids again.

Still, she had tempted me. Thinking about my body in one way or another consumed all my time. What would my life be like if I put all that energy into something else?

When I saw the ad in the newspaper for Jennifer Blume's workshop, I clipped it out and stared at it for two weeks before finally calling for reservations.

I know why I hesitated. I'm a man – and an eating disorder is a woman's thing. I needed no more proof of this than a cursory glance around the room. This confirms it: I must be a hopeless fag.

The workshop wasn't due to start for another fifteen minutes, so I selected a chair in the middle of a row, halfway back. Hopefully, when all the ladies take their seats, I'll blend into the crowd and no one will pay much attention to me.

I also want to be well away from the front or the aisles in case there's any sort of audience participation element to the workshop. I hate audience participation.

I always carry a book with me wherever I go so I can avoid looking like someone who is sitting alone because he is lonely (i.e., a loser) and instead give off the impression that I'm a guy sitting alone because I'm an avid reader (i.e., an interesting guy to know). I realize that having my nose in a book all the time makes me even more unapproachable than just looking lonely, but it keeps my brain numb and distracted, and I'm not much good at small talk anyway.

I sit casually in my chair reading a book by P.G. Wodehouse and try not to make eye contact with anyone.

A soothing female voice comes over the loudspeaker and instructs those who are still milling about to take their seats so our weekend with Jennifer Blume can begin.

I am soon packed in tightly with the ladies. To my right is a lesbian couple dressed for softball. I know they're a gay couple because they're holding hands and they're dressed alike, with pink triangle earrings and matching wedding bands. They're also quite overweight.

To my left is a waif of a girl with a shaggy brown haircut, a large t-shirt, and baggy jeans. If I'm hiding in my book, then she's hiding in her clothes.

The new-age music reaches an improbable crescendo just by having the volume increased and the female announcer says, "Maternal Voice Books in association with the Omega Life Center is proud to present the author of seven books, including *Eating Our Hearts Out* and *A Clean Plate for Mommy*, the internationally celebrated author and lecturer, Jennifer Blume!"

The room erupts into a deafening roar as Jennifer mounts the dais. She takes a moment to soak in the applause, and in fact does her best to keep it washing over her for as long as possible by nodding, smiling and extending her arms in an attempt to embrace the applause. The applause, the cheering, quickly turns into a full-scale standing ovation, and Jennifer is clearly thrilled with it.

Before hearing her speak, it's easy to see why she's so popular. For one thing, she's lovely; one of those fifty-and-fabulous ladies who has kept her natural good looks without resorting to surgery. Her tall, gamine frame and shoulder-length cascade of thick brown hair gives her an appearance not unlike Mrs. Peel on the Avengers.

The applause eventually dies down and we in the audience resume our seats. Jennifer keeps nodding and smiling. After a moment of silence, she gives a delicious exhale into the microphone, the obvious conclusion to a deep cleansing breath.

She says, "Thank you so much. That felt so good. A standing ovation. Have you ever had a standing ovation? In your entire lifetime, have you ever stood in front of a crowd of strangers and let them cheer for you, just for you?

"'Well, I'm not you, Jenny,' you're saying. 'I'm not special like you.' Well, you are. You are special. Each and every one of you here. And you deserve a standing ovation, too. But you have to first realize that you do truly deserve it, and then you have to ask for it.

"This weekend, as we go through our workshop together, if you feel the need for a standing ovation, I want you to just get up on your chair and we'll drop whatever we're doing and we will give you that standing ovation."

Immediately a middle-aged woman scampers up on her seat and Jennifer leads us in a rousing standing ovation for this brave, beautiful lady. No sooner than our ovation starts to die, two more eager souls stand atop their seats and we cheer them, too. In fact, we keep on giving standing ovations for the next half hour – long after the entire exercise has lost its novelty or poignancy.

I start to hear moans of exasperation from the women around me after the tenth or the eleventh ovation when the next needy soul gathers the courage to ask for our approval. It's funny how unconditional love and approval can turn into annoyance after only a dozen standing ovations.

We finally get to the point where it becomes obvious to even the most insensitive person in the room that the mob would probably kill the next person to stand on her chair.

Back in control once more, Jennifer instructs us to find the folder of workshop materials that has been placed underneath each of our seats. Along with the expected photocopied lists of inspirational thoughts and promotional materials for Jennifer's merchandise, there are also five sheets of notebook paper.

"I want you to take out a sheet of paper," Jennifer says, "and right now I want you to write 'If I were a food, I would be:' at the top of the page. Now I want you to take fifteen minutes to finish that sentence and write a paragraph explaining it. Go."

Oh, this is really stupid. Still, what am I going to do, sit here and not participate? I look around and see all the women around me already engrossed in their writing assignment. At the very least I have to look as if I'm writing something.

If I were a food, what kind of food would I be? What a dumb question. Who the hell knows? I'm not food. Ever since I was a child it's given me the willies whenever I've seen anthropo-morphized food. The Charlie the Tuna commercials on TV in the sixties always upset me: a fish begging a tuna company to capture him, chop his head off, gut him, cook him, and pack his flesh in a round can. What sick fucking advertising agency thought that up?

I still haven't picked a food yet and the clock is ticking. So I'll bluff it, then. I don't know what kind of food I am, but I do know what kind of food I want. I want cake. A big slice of chocolate cake. No, a whole chocolate cake. I want it because I know I will never have a piece of chocolate cake ever again for the rest of my life.

I start writing and get a few sentences out before Jennifer says: "Time's up! Now I want you to break up into groups of four and I want you to read aloud what you wrote to each other.

You *must* tell your group what you wrote. Don't be shy. Nobody is going to judge you. Just do it."

I wince and remain immobile until I feel a tap on my shoulder. The two women seated behind me ask if the lesbian on my right and I would like to be in their group. "Sure!" says my seatmate and she and I turn our chairs around.

The two women we have joined introduce themselves as Audrey and Christine. The woman who was seated next to me turns out to be named Lois.

"So who wants to go first?" says Audrey. "Because if nobody wants to go first, I'd like to."

Audrey speaks like a chipmunk cheerleader. She is quite attractive with red hair and a slender, yet not skinny, figure. I imagine that she's probably a flight attendant, but I cannot imagine why she's here.

No one objects to Audrey reading first, so she begins.

"If I were a food, I'd be strawberry shortcake. My grandpa used to call me strawberry shortcake because I've got fair skin and red hair. He would also tell me that I was sweet. Sweet enough to eat, so the image of me being strawberry shortcake has stuck with me all these years because I loved my grandpa. And even though sometimes he touched me inappropriately, he was always the one person I loved the most and the person I was closest to."

Audrey puts down her paper and grins broadly at us. "Who's next?" she asks.

"Wait a minute," says Lois. "What do you mean he touched you inappropriately?"

"It was nothing," Audrey assures us. "I'm sure he meant nothing by it."

Lois is not to be deterred. "So give us an example," she demands – and Lois has a way of demanding something in a way that you feel obliged to hand it over.

"Okay," says Audrey with a sigh, "sometimes when he'd give me my bath, Grandpa would clean out my vagina with his fingers."

We stare at her for a moment, not knowing what to say.

Christine finally breaks the silence. "How old were you?"

"Thirteen," says Audrey, "but I don't want to talk about it. Who's next? Christine, you read."

Christine looks at Lois and me and shrugs, then she reads her piece. Christine, it seems, views herself as oatmeal because she's so bland yet hardworking.

Poor Christine. Once I think about it, she reminds me of oatmeal, too. She's lumpy and colorless with brown-gray hair, gray eyes and sallow skin.

Lois goes next and tells us that she's a bag of M&M's – colorful and hard on the outside, soft and sweet on the inside.

"My lover, Patty, says I melt in her mouth and in her hand," Lois says as the punch line for her piece. Audrey giggles and claps her hands, but Christine just looks puzzled and a little embarrassed.

Finally, I have to read my piece. I'm really uncomfortable speaking the words out loud because I just know that Lois is going to pounce on me the minute I'm done.

"If I were a food, I'd be devil's food cake," I read. "That's because I'm sweet and people should like me, but liking me is forbidden. I'm dark and black inside and am quite bad for you if you take me in anything other than small doses. That's because I'm loaded with fat. Fat and sin. They tell me I'm food for the devil, and they must be right, although it was not my choice to bake myself this way. Someone else chose to create me as food for the devil, and now I have to endure an existence that is completely out of my control."

Lois pounces.

"Who told you that you were food for the devil?" she asks.

I pause for a second. "Well … my mother was a religious fanatic and later became kinda psychotic," I say. "Jesus would talk to her and tell her all kinds of things. Apparently Jesus didn't like me because I was different from all the other boys."

"What do you mean?" says Lois.

Even though I know she's a dyke, for some reason I can't tell her and our group that I'm gay. "I got really fat when I was a teenager, around 250 pounds," I say instead, "and I've got to tell you, since I'm not fat now – and since I'm a man – I really don't know if I need to be here at this workshop."

Christine asks: "How much do you weigh now?"

I start to hem and haw. This is really embarrassing. "With all my clothes on? Fully dressed I'm around a hundred twenty pounds."

"And without your clothes?" snaps Lois with demand in her voice.

"One eighteen – but I'm really short and I've got a small bone structure."

"You need to be here," Lois states with such conviction any further argument is unnecessary.

Jennifer gets up to the microphone and tells us it's time to move on because we've got so much to cover in so short a time. My God, what does she have in mind next? Rorschach blots?

"Volunteers are going to be coming around to give each one of you a cup," she says. "When you get yours, don't do anything – and above all, don't eat anything. Just hold it until we're all ready."

My mind starts racing to all sorts of possibilities about what the cup could possibly be about. Didn't people at EST weekends back in the seventies have to go for two days without using the bathroom? My God, the cup isn't a urine thing is it? I am definitely not going to pee into a cup for Jennifer Blume.

A woman in round spectacles comes to the end of our aisle and starts passing out paper cups for us to hand down the line. As they go by, I'm relieved to see they're not specimen containers at all. The cups have food in them. When I get my own cup, I look inside and see a raisin, a corn chip, and a Hershey's Kiss.

"Okay, does everyone have a cup?" asks Jennifer. "We're going to do something really dangerous in just a minute. We're going to eat. And we're going to pay attention to our eating and we're going to give ourselves permission to love the feeling of food in our mouth."

I've heard enough. She's going to start doling out the standard, new-agey, Zen crap about feeling your feelings and being where you are.

Of course I feel my feelings. In fact I feel them too much. I wish I could stop feeling my feelings most days, but someone like Jennifer Blume wouldn't know that. Someone like Jennifer Blume is certain that I'm the way I am because I walk through my life unconscious to what's going on, but I'm not. I'm thinking all the time. I'm hyper-aware of everything that's going on around me. That's my problem.

That's also why I've never gone into therapy. I can't imagine some guy sitting there trying to pull all these repressed traumas out of my unconscious. I've not repressed a thing. I am acutely aware of every shitty thing that has ever happened to me from my earliest memory to the present day. I have forgotten nothing and my list of grievances is long and chiseled in stone, like a cenotaph of anger and pain.

"Let's start with the corn chip," says Jennifer. "I know for a fact that each and every one of you has eaten an entire bag of chips in one sitting on at least one occasion, but I'd wager that this has happened more than once. Am I right? And while you ate the bag of chips, you were probably watching television or reading a book or focused on something completely different than the act of eating those chips. It's like you're unconscious and suddenly you come to when you reach the bottom of the bag and you wonder where all those chips went. You go digging around in the bottom of the bag for those last few small little broken chips and you finish by tipping the bag up and letting the salt and the little crumbs roll directly into your mouth. And what's the next thing you do? Right: look for another bag of chips."

Well I've got to hand it to her. She got that scenario pretty much right. Although I have not allowed one single corn chip into my mouth in over three years now, I remember the last time I ate them it was exactly in the way she just described it – except I was eating chips and watching TV and reading a magazine at the same time.

"I want you to imagine the possibility of being the kind of person who can reach into a bag of taco chips, take one, enjoy it, and walk away feeling satisfied."

There is nervous laughter and a low rumble of voices in the room.

"And I can tell what most of you are thinking right now. 'But Jennifer, you don't know me! I can't be trusted! If I have one chip, I'll have the whole bag. There aren't enough corn chips in the whole world to satisfy me.'"

She has a point there, too. I was just thinking something along those very lines.

"So we're going to try a little something right now. When I say go, I want you to take a bite out of your corn chip and hold it for a moment in your mouth. Go."

We all take a bite of our chips and I'm already about four steps ahead of her. She's going to get us to really, really, really taste what a corn chip tastes like and we'll be so moved by the whole experience it will totally change the way we look at food forever or some sort of bullshit like that.

It's interesting on one level though, to have a piece of a fatty, greasy, salty corn chip in my mouth. It's something I haven't allowed myself to do in a very long time and I hope that Jennifer's not going to be feeding us a lot of junk food all weekend because that means I'll have to do a lot of running to work it off.

The one piece of chip in my mouth is worth about ten calories right there. If she makes us eat the other half of the chip, then that'll be twenty calories and since I burn ten calories a minute when I run, these two bites are going to cost me two minutes of hard exercise right there and is that worth it to me, just to taste a corn chip?

"Okay, you can swallow," Jennifer says. "So how was that? Wasn't that something? A corn chip has all these interesting tastes and textures you probably never noticed before. The chip is rough and salty, but after a moment, it sort of melts on your tongue and you get the silky slickness of the oil and you can taste the corn. It's sweet, isn't it? The corn is all sort of buttery and sweet. These are things that you haven't allowed yourself to notice, have you?"

I'm an idiot. I'm an asshole. I was such a smug smarty-pants a second ago when I bit into the chip. I knew exactly what she wanted us to do and I was exactly right about it and I was so smart about it I ended up not doing it. I have no idea whatsoever what the bit of corn chip I just ate tasted like. It was salty and crunchy and that was it. I think. I don't know. I wasn't paying attention.

Give me another chance, Jennifer.

"Okay now, you can all eat the rest of your chips and then we'll move on," she says.

The rest of the ladies in the audience waste no time in cramming the remaining small bit of corn chip into their mouths, give it one chew and swallow it fast. I want to do this right, though. I want to redeem myself.

I slip the chip slowly onto my tongue the way I've seen Catholics accept the host from the blessed hands of a priest and I let its corn goodness dissolve on my tongue and the image of the priest makes me think of the countless Communion Sundays I've endured at our own Baptist church.

Funny, but it had never occurred to me before that the main difference between Catholic and Protestant communions is basically the level of hygiene involved in the service. The Catholics stand in line and have the priest place the body of Christ on their tongues with his bare hands and then give them a sip of the blood of Jesus out of a communal chalice. This was obviously one of the things the Protestants protested, so we choose to remain seated and have our holy flesh delivered to us in our pews on silver platters and our blood served in little whiskey shot glasses.

My God, now that I think about it, what a grotesque ritual it is either way. What must other religions think of us Christians? It's hard to conceive of the Buddhists chowing down on Buddha every week.

"Okay, now I want everybody to look in your cups and take out your raisin and just hold it in your hand for a minute."

What?

Oh, fuck. I'm hopeless. I am absolutely the most stupid, useless person on the planet. My corn chip is gone. I don't even remember swallowing it. This is so frustrating. Why can't I have a simple, stupid brain that can follow instructions?

I take my raisin and hold it in my right hand. Okay, raisin, it's you or me. I don't even like raisins. They're ugly and dry and faintly nasty tasting. This one, in fact, looks like a mouse turd.

"First, really look at this raisin," Jennifer says. "Notice how it's not just black, like you expect, but it's actually got a lot of colors, a lot of iridescences going on there. Roll it around in your fingers. It's sticky, right? It's sticky because of all the concentrated fruit sugar in it. Oh, yeah. When I said that, right away you could almost taste it, right? Am I right? Now notice how squishy it is. Raisins are moist. They're plumper than you think they are. I bet you never took the time to really look at a raisin before, have you?"

She's right. I can't think of a time when I ever really looked at one. Certainly not for this long.

"Now put the raisin in your mouth and keep it there. We're going to hold this raisin in our mouths for two whole minutes, and I'm going to time you. Now, go."

I hesitate for a second because I don't think I really like the taste of raisins. Once it's on my tongue, I'm hit with that familiar, unpleasant grandmother flavor that I'm expecting. The taste of death and decay. I want to spit it out, but I force myself to continue with the exercise. I may have failed corn chips, but I swear I'll pass raisins.

Quite unexpectedly, the raisin in my mouth starts to become sweet. Very, very sweet, like candy. The flavor of the grape that it once was releases slowly, blooms on my tongue like dessert wine – yes, it's the sweet, concentrated grapey flavor of port wine. My saliva feels like it's causing the raisin to plump, to reconstitute. It feels like it's doubled in volume already. The raisin feels huge in my mouth.

"Time's up," says Jennifer.

That was two minutes? That was fast. I swallow and then it occurs to me that for two minutes I was actually present with that raisin and that if I had a bowlful of them in front of me, I probably wouldn't bother reaching for another.

Raisins, however, are not chocolate.

We are just about to start unwrapping our Hershey's Kiss when a woman on the far side of the auditorium stands up on her chair. Everyone in the audience doesn't notice this at the same time, though. The group around her stands up and starts a wave of fat ladies rolling across the ballroom as we rise to give another proper standing ovation. Not surprisingly, this encourages four more copycat chair-standers to seize the opportunity to demand their own standing ovations, too.

Thankfully, this does not go on for as long as the last round of begging for approval and I suspect the uneaten Hershey's Kisses waiting for us has a lot to do with it.

Jennifer takes us through the eating with full attention one more time with our little piece of chocolate. I stay pretty well focused on what is in my mouth and am surprised again at what I discover.

Unlike the raisin which turned out to be even more delicious than expected, the little Hershey's Kiss is actually a disappointment. I didn't expect it to be so dull and waxy, so artificial.

Come to think of it, even during my worst periods of binge eating, long before chocolate became absolutely forbidden under any circumstance, I never really pigged-out on chocolate. Yeah, my absolute favorite food, Boston cream doughnuts, has chocolate on top, but it's the custard filling that I'm really attracted to. And despite what I wrote in the writing exercise this morning, I prefer carrot cake to chocolate cake.

With this one Hershey's Kiss, I'm having a little chocolate epiphany. Here's one thing I can take off my forbidden foods list because it turns out I don't give a shit about the flavor of chocolate in the first place.

After the chocolate is gone, we endure a long, inspirational pep talk from Jennifer and then she has us go back to another writing exercise. Our assignment this time is to write a top-ten list of our beliefs about food. I decide to drop my attitude of smug resistance and slip into my good-boy mode.

I wonder if this is how cults are born.

When Jennifer tells us that our writing time is up, she instructs us to pair up with one other person. "Pick someone new. Don't go back with a person who was in the last group."

The girl sitting to my left and I quickly form a pair. Her name is Rachel and for the first time I get to take a good look at her.

She's thin. Too thin. It's easy not to notice because of the way she dresses and wears her hair. Everything about her is ample and loose – everything, that is, except her. Rachel reeks of anorexia. At her proper weight she would be considered a beautiful young woman. In her present condition, she resembles nothing more than human remains.

My God, I will never get that thin. Of course, it's not even possible. I was so fat for so long it wouldn't be possible without surgery to attain Rachel's skeletal state. Although I've lost almost 200 pounds in the last five years, there are still pockets of fat I cannot get rid of, namely around my gut and between my thighs. I know if I just work a little harder and lose five more pounds, I can get rid of that last bit of flab. Of course that will bring me down to 112 pounds, but like I told Lois, I've got such small bones and I'm so short it's not a problem.

But there's no way I'll ever get as thin as Rachel.

"I noticed you the minute you came in," says Rachel, "and I wanted to talk to you. That's why I sat here."

Oh no. I've seen that look in the eyes of a girl before. Rachel's looking for a husband and I'm the only man in the room under 200 pounds. I'd better tell her right away that I'm gay. The problem is it's not something that naturally pops up during a conversation with a stranger.

"I thought there were going to be more anorexics here at this workshop," she says, "but other than you and me, there's not many."

Anorexics? She's got to be kidding me.

"I'm not anorexic," I say. "I mean, no offense, but I'm one of the fat guys."

"You are?"

"Yeah. My problem is with overeating, not under-eating."

Rachel pauses and looks like she's mentally recalibrating her battle strategy. "So you're bulimic then. You gorge-purge?"

"No, I don't," I tell her. "I mean, yeah, I did ipecac and laxatives and stuff in the past, but I had some really bad experiences. Now I'm just really very strict about what I put into my mouth. Actually, even if I weren't fat, I'd have to be on a strict diet anyway because I'm a marathon runner."

"Really?" she says, clearly impressed. "You've run a whole marathon before?"

"I've done ten of them. Ten in the last three years. I've got two more coming up soon, too."

"How many of them have you finished?"

The question exasperates me, but I try to appear to laugh it off so as not to offend her. "Why does everybody always ask me that? I finished all of them. I finish everything I start. That's just the way I am. Even on my training days, I always do the number of miles on my schedule, even if I'm sick or it's raining. I know me. If I take one day off, then I'll never run again. And I kinda have to be the same way with food. If I don't watch myself, I would totally go nuts and just keep stuffing myself until I exploded. Some days I do slip and I eat something I'm not supposed to, but I don't barf it up or anything now. Now I just figure out how many calories that thing I just ate was worth and I figure out how many miles of running it will take to work it off and I add it to my training schedule for the week. Most of the time now I just see a doughnut and it doesn't even look good to me because I know that equals an hour of exercise and it's not worth it. As it is, I'm going to have to do an extra two miles because of the eating exercise we just did."

I stop talking because Rachel's stony glare tells me to quit babbling.

"You're bulimic," she says. "I don't care if you don't make yourself vomit. Whether you purge with exercise or purge with a finger down your throat it's still purging. It's still bulimia. I did that, too, you know. I was totally hooked on exercise. Totally. It's all I did all day long."

"So are you a runner, too?"

"No, I swam," she says. "I was on the swim team at school and then my dad had me training for the Olympics. It was really bad because swimmers are like totally body conscious to begin with. You know, you spend almost all of your free time in a tight bathing suit with people staring at your body and they're constantly commenting about how you look. You get like hyper-conscious of every extra ounce on your body and your coaches are really fat-phobic. Then when you get to the higher levels of competition, it gets even worse."

"Did you ever make it to the Olympics?"

"No," she says. "I had to go into the hospital for a while. But I'm better now and I'll probably begin swimming again soon. At least that's what my dad would like me to do."

"Don't you want to be a swimmer?"

Rachel shrugs. "Yeah, I guess. I don't know. I'll need to bulk up a bit before I can start again, though. I lost a lot of muscle tone when I was at my worst, but since I've been out of the hospital I've gained ten pounds. Hopefully it won't take me too long to get back in shape."

She just gained ten pounds? I try as hard as I can, but I can't envision Rachel any thinner than she is right now.

"How long have you been out of the hospital?"

"A week," she says.

Jennifer Blume ascends the dais again and purrs into the microphone, "Okay, ladies! Time to move along."

Rachel and I hadn't even started sharing with each other our list of top-ten beliefs about food. Thank God. Rachel probably wrote something really harrowing. I don't think I could take what she had to say.

"Now we've explored our beliefs about food," says Jennifer, "we need to explore our beliefs about ourselves. Compulsive eating isn't about food. It's about control. When you eat compulsively, you feel out of control. You feel helpless to the situation, to the food itself. You feel victimized while you're in the middle of a binge and then afterwards when you're punishing yourself either by purging or dieting or even just calling yourself nasty names, you feel helpless and victimized all over again. But when you look at the situation rationally, you're not helpless. Food is just food. It's inanimate. How can something inanimate have any power over you at all? It can't. It's just food. If you don't eat it, it's not going to humiliate you or beg you or even jump up and attack you. It's just going to sit there and spoil. Big deal. You are not helpless to food. What I'd like to suggest to you is that you're confusing your relationship with food with some other very real relationship in which you feel powerless."

Oh boy. Here it comes. The old "it's not what you're eating, it's what's eating you" school of psychobabble. I really have to hand it to Jennifer, though. She really had me there in the palm of her hand for a while. I had a lot of hopes for this workshop, too. It looked like she was actually going to give me what I came here for: a concrete, step-by-step plan that I could follow daily to help me get food into the proper perspective in my life. Now that she's veering off into the la-la land of second-rate psychotherapy, she's lost me.

"I want you to think about your life and relationships as they are right now. Maybe you feel trapped in a situation you feel you cannot change. Is it with a job, a lover, a parent? Think about this situation or this relationship and notice how you feel. You probably think you should be feeling anxious or trapped or something like that, right? But what are you really feeling? I would imagine that, instead, you're feeling something more like bitter resignation. You can't change this situation, so why bother? You might as well eat."

She's losing me. She's losing me. I hate this crap.

"What we're going to do now is a little visualization exercise. Okay, now I want everybody to sit up straight in your chairs, uncross your legs and put your palms up in your lap. Okay? Is everybody ready? Now I want you to close your eyes and just breathe for a moment."

Jennifer begins talking us through a breathing and relaxation visualization. Her voice gets all legato and fuzzy. She's talking to us the way you'd talk a small child to sleep. I know exactly what she's doing. She is trying to hypnotize us – although she would never call it that. To enhance Jennifer's hypnotic effect, the sound of a distant harp and flute start to swell in the background. There is even the whispery tinkling of wind chimes. It is all way too cheesy, but I close my eyes and listen to Jennifer's voice.

"I want you to think back. Back to a time when you were very young. Back to a specific incident where you felt powerless and afraid. There is no one to help you and ..."

I don't even need to relax or regress. Immediately, my eyes snap open and all the breath escapes out of me like I've just been punched in the gut. I remember sitting on the floor of the entry hallway, my back up against the front door. I remember being terrified. I remember ...

I remember everything.

The memory is so solid, so true, I don't for a moment question if it's real or not. It's real. It really happened and I know it isn't a memory of something casually forgotten. It's a memory I tried very hard to extinguish.

My first feeling is one of intense anger. I had buried this awful thing in the back of my brain a long time ago and now it's back again. Feelings of vulnerability and panic surge in to sweep away the anger as it all comes back to me, every detail. I remember every moment of it.

Or do I? No. I don't remember the end.

I clearly recall sitting on the floor, hugging my knees with my back against the bolted front door. I remember getting the courage to turn around and peek through the mail flap. I remember what I saw and all the things that led up to ...

But what happened after the knock at the door? What happened after I heard his voice?

"Cary? Open up, buddy. I know you're in there."

He called me buddy. I remember ...

No, I won't do this. It took me a long time to forget this. I haven't thought about what happened to me that day in almost twenty years, but now it's back. Thank you very much Jennifer Blume.

My heart is pounding. I feel my eyes welling up and my lips trembling. I can't start crying. I can't. All I want to do is get up and run. The memory of 1969 fills me with panic. Panic and deep shame. I want out of here. I want doughnuts. I want protection. I want to hide. I want to stop feeling.

No. I want to stop feeling lonely. I want to stop running. I want to stop being a victim and the butt of every joke. I want …

Hell, I want one of those fucking standing ovations.

Just for one moment I want people to look at me and not laugh or judge or physically attack me. I would like just thirty seconds of approval. Is that too much to ask?

It takes a great deal of courage, but I rise and step up onto my burgundy stacking chair. Lois is the first one to see me make my move and she shouts, "Yeah!" Beaming and applauding, she stands up, too.

In an instant, all the other women around me are standing and applauding. I close my eyes and soak in the first real sense of unconditional love and approval I've ever felt.

"Excuse me!" Jennifer says over the PA system. "Excuse me! I'm sorry, but we're having quiet time now. This is not an appropriate time to ask for a standing ovation. Sir, please sit down."

Chastened, the women in the audience stop clapping and resume their seats. Their eyes avert from me. Even Lois is so embarrassed she can't look at me.

"God, he must be humiliated," I hear her whisper to her girlfriend.

"Sir!" Jennifer says to me from the podium. "Sir, you have to sit down now so we can finish our meditation. You can ask for approval some other time."

CHAPTER SEVEN

1969

By the age of ten, I had successfully trained myself to have bowel movements only at 3:30 in the afternoon. It was the only time no one would ever see me going into a bathroom to do "that."

I learned early on to hide my bodily functions from the prying eyes of my grandmother, who until her dying day clung to her perverse obsession with my regularity. She even made up a little song about me sitting on the toilet that she would sing repeatedly in my presence and would even warble unabashedly in the presence of others:

> *"I had a little boy,*
> *His name was Cary Scott.*
> *He sits and he grunts on the pot, pot, pot!*
> *I had a little boy,*
> *He had a pretty knee.*
> *He goes to the bathroom to wee, wee, wee!"*

Grandma wasn't much of a poet, but what she lacked in literacy, she made up for in malevolence. Even on the day of her fatal stroke in 1967, she sang my B.M. song five times in repetition out in her back garden while dancing the squatty little jig she specially choreographed just to humiliate me.

It's a terrible thing to make a seven-year-old child feel relieved at the death of a grandparent. Certainly, guilt is not known for its laxative effect, either.

When I became a latchkey child after Grandma dropped dead, I was given the priceless endowment of two private hours of solitude each afternoon from 3:30 until 5:30. During this after-school period, I was to remain locked inside the house and was to see no one, to not answer the door, and to keep away from the stove. I was to answer promptly when Mrs. Johansson came over from next door to see if I was alive and to always answer the telephone by the second ring otherwise Mama would fear the worst when she phoned from work to check in on me.

I happily agreed to all of these rules and followed them to the letter, grateful just to have the freedom to keep myself locked away from the atrocities inflicted on me by family members and other children, and the sanctuary in which to take a shit.

In October of 1969, I was alone at home in the afternoon, sitting on the toilet. I was pretty much done with everything I needed to do, but I lingered on the pot and read a well-thumbed copy of a *Little Lulu* comic book.

Without knowing why, I suddenly sat up straight and dropped the comic on the floor. I don't know if I felt something move or if I was reacting to the silence. At that moment, no birds sang, all dogs stopped barking, and the incessant high-pitched white buzz of the California cicadas ceased. I sat motionless on the toilet for five seconds.

Then the earthquake hit.

I instinctively grabbed onto the toilet seat as the bathroom jiggled side to side. Plastic shampoo bottles tumbled to the floor of the shower stall and tampons and toilet paper fell down upon me from the shelves above my head.

What was I to do? In school we were taught to dive under our desks or stand in a door frame. At the present moment I could do neither. Yes, there was a door only a few feet from me, but even in the face of death, I was unwilling to walk away from an unflushed toilet with my pants around my ankles.

The initial jiggle of the earthquake amplified to a series of rolling waves. Clinging fast to my toilet seat, it felt like I was riding a buoy in an ocean harbor.

Then it stopped.

There were a few moments of complete silence then the normal sounds of the outdoors filtered once again back through the bathroom window. Fearing an aftershock, I quickly wiped myself and flushed. I pulled up my pants and, still in a panic, wondered if I should run outside. Was it safe to be in the house? Could the whole building collapse on me?

The telephone rang and put any thoughts of escaping outside to rest. It was probably Mama calling about the earthquake, I thought. The closest phone to the bathroom was in Mama's bedroom on the nightstand. I ran to answer it before the forbidden third ring.

"Hello?"

"Hey baby, I'm waiting for you. Why don't you bring your juicy little bod over here and give me some love." The caller's voice was low-pitched and sleepy, and he spoke with an odd, growling tone.

"You have the wrong number," I said.

"Isn't this Cindy?"

"No."

"What number did I call?"

"688-9885," I replied.

The caller paused a minute and made a sound like he was stretching to reach for something. He asked me to repeat the number, so I did.

"So what's *your* name?" he asked. He spoke so gently and intimately, I answered him without hesitation.

"Cary."

"Is that a boy's name or a girl's name?"

"A boy's name. My daddy named me after Cary Grant. I guess my mom did, too," I added.

"That's nice," he said. "Cary's a nice name. What's your full name?"

"Cary Scott," I said.

"Cary Scott," he repeated. My name seemed to satisfy him very much. "And how old are you, Cary Scott?"

"Ten."

"Ten years old? Mmmmm. What are you doing right now?"

"Nothing."

"Nothing? Did you just get home from school?"

"Yes."

"So who's with you right now?"

"Nobody."

"Nobody? You're all alone in the house?"

"Uh huh."

"Where are your folks?"

I told him my mother was at work and, when he asked, I told him yes I was always alone every day at this time and that my mother got home at 5:30. I don't know why I told him that stuff, but he seemed genuinely interested in me and I had never had a conversation like this before.

The caller asked me how I was doing in school and if I had a lot of friends. I said I didn't like school because the kids made fun of me and he was very sympathetic.

I told him I should get off the phone.

"No, sit and talk with me for a minute," he said, and he said it like a gentle command so I didn't hang up. I couldn't hang up. He wanted to know more about me. He asked me where I lived. I said Espada. He asked if I knew my address.

"Yes."

"What is it?"

I told him. He asked about my father.

"He ran away," I said. "Mama said he went to San Francisco with my uncle Arby. He's been gone a long time but maybe he'll come back and get me some day."

"So you need a daddy," the caller said.

"Yeah."

"I could be your daddy," he said. "You can talk to me, Cary."

"You're not my dad."

"No, but we could pretend. Where are you right now?"

"In Mama's room."

"Are you sitting on the bed?"

I told him no.

"Why don't you sit on the bed and get comfortable? I'm comfortable right now. I'm very comfortable. Are you sitting on the bed?"

I said, "Yes," but in reality I was only leaning against it. Mama would throw a fit if I messed up her bedspread. Even leaning against the tightly-made bed left a pucker in the spread, but I could probably smooth that out when I got off the phone.

"Stretch out on the bed," he gently commanded. "I want you to be comfortable." Again he said that word comfortable with all four syllables dripping like sweet molasses.

I told him I was lying on the bed even though I remained leaning against it. He asked me if I was wearing shoes. Of course I was wearing shoes: the navy-blue deck shoes from Thom McAn I always wore. He told me to reach down and untie my left shoe. Slowly. He said to ease apart the bow in the shoelace and then slowly, slowly pull my foot out of the shoe. I noticed my heart was starting to beat harder.

"Is your shoe off?"

I said, "Yeah," but I didn't take it off the way he told me. I just slipped out of it without even untying it.

"Now take off the right shoe." He coached me to take off the other shoe the same way – slowly, gently – and when I said with a quiet yes that the shoe was off he gave a soft groan of pleasure.

But my shoe was not off. I was not going to do anything else that he told me. I didn't like the way the conversation had turned. The tone of his voice wasn't scary, but I found it unsettling nonetheless.

"Now your socks," he said. "Take off your socks."

"I want to hang up."

"Don't hang up. Don't hang up the phone, Cary." That command had a bite in it. It scared me. There was no sweet molasses in his voice that time. "I said take off your socks, Cary Scott. That's an order, buddy."

I did nothing. I said nothing. I could hear him breathing.

"Do you have them off?"

"Yes," I lied.

The caller voiced an exhale of pleasure. "Good boy. It feels good, doesn't it? Nice and comfortable. It feels good to have your shoes off. Good to be barefoot and wiggling your toes. I'm wiggling my toes, too, Cary. It feels good. Do you like how it feels, buddy?"

"Yes."

"Good. Good boy. It's hot today, Cary. Poor little fellow, cooped up in that hot house. Take off your shirt, Cary. It's too hot to wear a shirt today."

I wanted to hang up and get away from this guy, but I didn't do it. Why? Why didn't I hang up the phone? I didn't know why. Instead of hanging up, I stood there, motionless, at the edge of Mama's bed with one shoe off and I lied to the man. I told him yes I had taken my shirt off just the way he told me to – slowly, slowly. He liked it when I lied to him. He told me how good I was and sighed with pleasure.

I heard him take a drink of something. He slurped and smacked his lips and turned his attention toward my pants.

He wanted them off.

It was a hot day, he reasoned. How could I be comfortable wearing pants?

"I'm not wearing my pants, Cary," he said. "It's too hot for pants. It's too hot for everything."

My heart pummeled the inside of my chest as he told me he was completely naked and how good it felt. He wanted me to be naked, too. He commanded me to strip off my pants and my underwear and lie naked on my Mama's bed.

And I told him yes, yes I was doing everything he ordered me to do. I didn't do a thing, but I made him believe I was obedient and good. I made him believe I was comfortable. And I made him believe I liked it.

The caller told me we were going to play a little game called follow the leader. "I'll tell you what I'm doing and then I want you to do it, too."

He told me he was holding the telephone receiver in his left hand and with his right index and middle fingers, he softly was touching his own lips.

"Do it, Cary. Do it. Yes. Good boy."

He then led me on a vicarious exploration of his body, part by part, with explicit instruction on how I should be following his lead.

I did not touch myself, but in my mind I could see his nude daddy body stretched out on an orange velvet couch just like the one we used to have in the living room. I didn't know what the caller looked like, but in my mind he looked just like that picture of my dad taken at Newport Beach, the one photo of my dad that remained in the house only because I stole it and kept it Scotch-taped to the underside of my sock drawer.

"Touch it, Cary. Grab hold of it. It feels so good. Yeah."

The caller described all the things he was doing to his own wiener. He called it his dick, his cock. He was breathing hard. I was, too, because I was scared. Scared of this situation, scared of being caught, scared of all the new feelings rushing through me.

The caller changed the game. Follow the leader became let's pretend.

"Let's pretend we're in the same room," he said. "You're the one who's working my cock, up and down, with those soft little hands. Yeah, Cary. Take my cock. Take it. Come down close to it and kiss it. Taste it. That's it, Cary. Suck my cock, buddy. Take it all in your mouth."

I wanted to throw up. "I'm hanging up!" I said.

"No!" he barked at me. "Stay on the line! That's an order! I thought you were a good boy, Cary. A good boy wouldn't hang up the phone. A good boy would stay on the phone and suck his daddy's cock. You're gonna have to be punished now, Cary. I'm gonna have to take the phone cord and tie your little hands behind your back. Tie you up real tight. Oh, yeah. Then I'm gonna have to roll your naked little body over and paddle that bad butt of yours. Oh, yeah, Cary. Spank you real good. Then while your ass is still hot from the spanking, I'm gonna spread those red little cheeks and fuck that sweet ass of yours, Cary. Yeah, I'm gonna fuck you, buddy. Yeah, buddy. Yeah. Oh, yeah!"

He let go a series of short, explosive cries and then was silent and panting for a moment. I was so terrified I felt cast in concrete. I couldn't move. I couldn't talk.

"That was great, stud," the caller said. "You're the best. Cary Scott, 688-9885. Ten years old. Damn! Same time tomorrow, buddy." And he hung up.

I stood there on the edge of Mama's bed with one shoe off and listened to the phone make that "off the hook" pulsing quack. Same time tomorrow, he said. He was going to call me back at the same time tomorrow. What was I going to do? He knew my phone number.

In that flash of a second, the gravity of the situation really hit home. Not only did he know my phone number, but he knew my first name, my last name, my age, my address, and he knew that I was in the house, alone, every day from 3:30 to 5:30.

I was stupid. I was so stupid! I was stupid and scared. And I was in serious danger.

The worst part was that I couldn't tell anyone about it. If Mama found out what I told the caller, she would murder me. She would want to make us change our phone, change our house, change our names. She would tell me I had just ruined our family.

The telephone rang again. I hesitated but picked it up on the second ring just as I'd been instructed to do. It was a good thing I did.

"You okay?" said Mama in that way of hers that made it clear she only wanted me to say yes and end the conversation.

"Yes, ma'am," I answered.

"I called a minute ago and got a busy signal," she said. "Who was on the phone?"

"It was a wrong number."

"Well all right then."

"Mama?"

"What?"

"That earthquake was really big," I said.

"Earthquake?" she said. "There wasn't no earthquake. What are you talking about?"

"But Mama …"

"What'd I tell you about making up stories? I'll be home at 5:30. That house better not be messed up."

Mama's work was only a short drive from home. How could she have missed a giant earthquake? When I hung up the phone,

I looked back in the bathroom and saw the contents of our shelves tumbled out upon the floor. In Mama's bedroom, her perfume bottles on the vanity had all tipped over and the three Styrofoam heads heavy with wiglets had tumbled off the closet shelf.

As I roamed around the house, picking up all the items that had fallen down, I began to wonder: *was* there an earthquake?

***

The next day at school, I couldn't concentrate on anything. All I could think about was that guy calling my house again. And I knew I'd have to answer the phone, because if by chance it were Mama calling instead of the guy, I'd get in serious trouble.

In class we were doing multiplication speed drills which I found difficult even on a good day. My teacher, Mrs. Hayes, laid a math test face down on each of our desks. The test was fifty short multiplication problems: easy things like five times nine and eight times seven. When she said "Go" we were to turn over the test and answer all fifty problems as quickly as possible. When we finished, we were to stand next to our desks in triumph.

The objective, of course, was to be the first one to stand up. It was an admirable goal, but in the language of children, those speed tests got warped into a meaning Mrs. Hayes probably didn't intend. To us, the test meant the first one standing was the smartest person in the class and the last one standing was a retard.

I was hopeless at math. Although I understood the concepts of math easily enough, I simply could not memorize multiplication tables. Adding and subtracting were no easier and I couldn't do any of it in my head. I was forever counting things out on my fingers – even the multiplication tables – so I hated those speed tests.

All I could think about as Mrs. Hayes went around desk to desk laying the tests face down was why oh why did she pick the day I was expecting a phone call from a creepy guy to give us a test?

"Go!"

I flipped over the page and scanned it. All the other kids around me were busy marking, marking, marking. Their pencils were flying. I went down the columns and did all the times-ones because they were the easiest, but there weren't many of them. Then I did the times-twos and the times-fives.

I wasn't even halfway through when I saw Timmy McDonald push his chair back and stand up. Well, that was to be expected. Timmy McDonald always won the multiplication speed test and I didn't begrudge him for winning because math was really all Timmy seemed good for in life.

Susie West stood up next, then Linda Green. I bet that just killed Linda; she was such a know-it-all.

Four times six. I was blanking out on that one. I knew four times five was twenty, so then if I add four more the answer should be twenty-four. Or do I add six?

Johnny, Bobby, Carlos, Susie B., and Mike stood up. Caroline, Donald, Missy, and Gabe. I had a long way to go and I was spending more time concentrating about concentrating than I was on multiplication.

"Same time tomorrow, buddy," he said. He called me yesterday at 4:00. My phone would be ringing in three hours.

"I'm gonna tie you up with the phone cord," he said. "Fuck your ass."

Nine times nine. Seven times six. Eight times three. I could feel the standing class watching the remaining few of us laggards like they were watching a horse race. I had only five problems to go. I saw Mark Bakerman stand up and noticed it was only me and Justine Gonzales left. Now Justine really was a retard. She wasn't very smart because she was born in Tijuana. I couldn't let Justine beat me. I got down to my last problem, eight times seven. I figured out seven times seven earlier, so I just needed to add seven more, right? I counted off on my fingers: fifty, fifty-one, fifty-two, fifty-three, fifty-four, fifty-five, fifty-six. I saw Justine put her pencil down. I wrote fifty-six real fast and bolted to my feet. Justine, in defeat, arose slowly and looked into the faces of her victors. Her large brown eyes welled up, but she did nothing more than finger the cuff of her pink cotton sweater and gaze upon us with an expression of profound sadness.

Home again after school, I did not have a bowel movement. I did not turn on the television. I did not read a comic book. I did nothing but sit in the kitchen and stare at the almond rotary desk phone on the counter.

At 4:06 it rang.

"You okay?" said Mama.

"Yeah," I said.

"There's a package of hamburger meat in the freezer. Set it out on the counter and let it be thawing."

"Okay."

There was a pause, then Mama said, "Is there something the matter?"

"No," I said.

"Well I'll check in later," she said and hung up.

But she didn't call back. The phone didn't ring again for the rest of the afternoon. Mama came home at 5:30 and we had tacos for dinner.

***

I didn't hear from the caller again for nine days. By that time, I had learned to relax and forget and to not dread the late afternoons. On the ninth day, however, when I answered the phone on the second ring, my stomach took a wild roller coaster dip.

"Hey, buddy. Let's play a game."

Without any of the formality from the drawn-out seduction of his first call, he immediately launched into let's pretend.

"Let's pretend we're at the beach," he said. "I want to go for a swim, don't you? Let's take off our clothes and go for a swim in the ocean."

"I don't want to talk to you."

"That's not nice, Cary. That's not friendly. Boys should be nice and friendly. You know what we do to boys if they're not nice," he

129

said. "Bad things happen to little boys who aren't nice. The water's beautiful today, Cary. Let's take off our clothes and go for a swim …"

After that, the caller phoned every weekday without fail for the next two months.

***

As a special treat, Mrs. Hayes took our class to the biology department at the University of California at Espada. In our own little science class at school, we had been learning about basic anatomy and how the body worked and Mrs. Hayes thought, for some unfathomable reason, that a group of fourth graders would enjoy seeing an actual body carved up and displayed in all its resplendent gore.

Wisely, however, the university faculty declined to let twenty-five ten-year-olds in to see a cadaver dissection. Instead, a perky blond coed in a white lab coat was to give us a tour of another life sciences laboratory with a slightly lower horror quotient.

"My name's Sherry," she said as we gathered around her in the hallway. "I'm a junior pre-med student here at UCE and I'm gonna show you around a couple of the labs, okay? First of all, don't touch anything. Everything is sharp and everything is poisonous, okay? Which brings us to rule number two: don't eat anything. Again, blah-blah-blah sharp and poisonous. Rule three: lab animals. If it's alive don't pet it and don't feed it. And the same thing goes if it's dead. Last of all, you might see some gross stuff that'll make you sick, so if you're gonna throw up, do it in one of the sinks, okay? Not on the floor. Any questions?"

No one said a thing. We just stared at her with ashen faces. Mrs. Hayes, who was quite excited, asked a question, though.

"We've been learning a little about blood," she said. "Will you have anything special to show the class?"

"Oh yeah!" said Sherry with much glee. "Before you go, we'll type 'em."

None of us had any idea what Sherry meant by "type 'em." I figured that since I had seen a secretary typing a letter when we were over in the college administration building, that it must have something to do with a typewriter. Anyway, I didn't care. I didn't care about science. I didn't care if we were about to see something scary. I didn't care if the school bus crashed on our way back from the field trip.

Sherry opened the door of the lab and the kids in my class gave an almost instant chorus of "eww!" Prominently displayed before us was the flayed carcass of a cat trussed up in a metal pan with its feet sticking straight up in the air. The cat's sightless, lidless eyes stared at us in surprise; its lipless, toothy mouth gaped at us in a silent scream. Susie B. and Missy ran for the nearest sink to puke, but they didn't really need to throw up. It was just for the drama. As for me, I didn't care. It was just a dead cat. So what?

Sherry showed us several more unfortunate beasts in the process of being dissected as well as a real person who had been reduced to a dangling skeleton of bleached white bones.

"Is that real?" asked Gabe.

"Oh yeah," said Sherry. "I heard tell he was probably a four-teen-year-old Indian boy. I'm not sure though. That skeleton's about fifty years old by now."

I looked at the bones of the Indian boy and thought how odd that skeletons marked their birthdays from the date their flesh was torn away. I wondered, too, if someday my own skeleton would be hanging from a hook for all to see. The thought then changed from "if" to "how soon" that day would arrive.

The most interesting thing about our trip to the life sciences lab was how quickly the kids in my class adapted and became immune to the gross-out factor of the materials. Before we knew it, we were dispassionately gazing at the eyeball of a cow, giant beetles impaled on straight pins, and a human brain pickled in a jar of formaldehyde.

Gabe wanted to know if the brain came out of the skull of the skeleton Indian boy.

"No," said Sherry.

As our tour wound down, Mrs. Hayes brought the conversation back around to blood. "Blood comes in different types," she said, "like O, A, B and AB. Does anyone here know what their blood type is?"

Smarty-pants Linda Green was the only one who knew. She said she was O negative. "That means you're a universal donor," Mrs. Hayes said. "You can give your blood to everybody."

"Do it, Linda," said Bobby Harvey and Linda made a face at him.

Ignoring this, Mrs. Hayes asked if there were any of us who wanted to know our blood types. "I need five brave people," she said.

Gabe, Carlos, Bobby, and Timmy raised their hands and went to stand in a line by Sherry. No one else did.

Quite frankly I didn't volunteer because I didn't care to know my blood type and I was thinking about the bones of the Indian boy. I wondered if he had a caller and if that caller was the one who turned him into those bones. I pictured that boy's phone caller coming over and taking a sharp knife and slicing away the Indian boy's skin and meat. In my daydream, the Indian boy did not cry out in pain. He stood still and silent and let the phone caller carve him thinner, ever thinner, until he was nothing but the whitest of bones.

"Cary? How about you?" asked Mrs. Hayes.

I walked over to join the four boys. For a moment, I had forgotten what we were doing.

Sherry took out some glass slides, some bottles of chemicals with eye droppers and a pack of things that looked like thumb tacks. "Here's what I'm gonna do, okay?" she said. "I'm gonna take your index finger, okay? And I'm gonna give it a quick little prick with one of these pins. It's really small and it doesn't hurt at all. See, look. I'm gonna do it to myself right now." And Sherry wiped her index finger with rubbing alcohol and stuck it with one of the pins. She didn't even flinch. "Now then, when I do it to you, I'll squeeze one little drop of blood onto one of these slides and we'll see what blood type you are, okay?"

The four boys ahead of me looked apprehensive but Gabe steeled his resolve and bravely offered his finger first. Sherry wiped it with alcohol, gave it a prick and the class gasped. Gabe was silent for a moment, then with dilated pupils proudly told the class, "It didn't hurt!" and let Sherry take a drop of his blood.

He was B positive, and I thought that was interesting because it sounded so optimistic.

Bobby and Carlos had their blood typed next, after that it was down to me or Timmy McDonald. Timmy was the biggest kid in the class and looked tough because of his Marine Corps crew cut. I knew he wasn't a bully or anything and I had nothing against him, but he looked at me and in his glance I could tell he decided there was no way he was going to let a sissy like Cary Scott look braver than he was. What could I say? If he wanted to get stuck with a pin ahead of me, I certainly wasn't going to stop him.

Timmy determinedly thrust his index finger forward and Sherry gave it a swab with the alcohol.

Then Timmy McDonald fainted dead away.

Gabe and Carlos caught Timmy on the way down so he didn't hurt himself, but Sherry and Mrs. Hayes both got these horrified looks on their faces that clearly screamed "lawsuit!" Suddenly everybody was fussing over Timmy lying on the floor and I thought, "Well great, now I'll never know my blood type."

How could a tough guy like that faint? Sherry hadn't even touched him with the pin yet. How much would it have hurt?

That was what I really wanted to know: How much does it hurt? How painful is the pin? How painful is the knife when he sticks it in you? Does it hurt right away or does it hurt later on, like when you get a shot at the doctor's office?

Sherry's tray of slides and tools were sitting right there in front of me. Everybody was busy with Timmy so I went to pick up the pin to see what it would have felt like. Gabe said it was painless. My eye, however, fell on a scalpel nearby on the counter. How much does a razor knife hurt? How much does it hurt to be cut down to bones?

I picked up the scalpel and dragged the blade of the knife across the heel of my left hand.

Gabe was right. I didn't feel a thing. The pain didn't start until the small artery I severed started spurting rhythmically in little jets across the lab. I turned to face Sherry and gave a cry as I dropped the scalpel on the ground. A squirt of my blood caught the coed in the eye and splashed red all over her blond hair and white lab coat. All the girls started screaming, and even Timmy McDonald was so astonished that he sat up.

**

Since I was in the emergency room getting stitches, I missed my afternoon date with the phone caller. This made me so relieved that the thought actually crossed my mind that I should stab myself every weekday afternoon. The reality of undergoing stitches, however, put that idea right out of my head.

The trip to the hospital didn't endear me to my mother, either. Although I told her it was an accident and was sorry, Mama was less than sympathetic. She vehemently detailed for me every nickel of expense that she had personally incurred because of my thoughtless behavior. She told me how much it cost just to walk into an emergency room, how much the doctor charged, the cost of the thread, the cost of the tetanus shot, even the cost of the gasoline it took to drive us there. Thank God the teacher called Mama instead of an ambulance! And did I know how much income we lost because Mama had to take four hours off? We were now going to be poor for the rest of our lives because I needed six stitches.

Normally I would have withered under such an attack, but balanced against spending another afternoon on the phone listening to some guy describing me sucking on his wiener, the pain of minor surgery coupled with the abuse from my mother seemed worth it.

Discovering I could endure the pain of needles and knives emboldened me. On the ride home from the hospital, I made up my mind that I was not going to talk to the guy on the phone ever again. No, not ever again. All I had to do was look at my bandaged left hand to know that there was nothing he could do to hurt me worse.

The following afternoon the phone rang at 4:02.

"Where were you yesterday?"

"I don't want to talk to you," I said. "Don't call me anymore."

I hung up the phone – in fact, I put the receiver down so hard the bell in the phone gave a little ping that echoed. My heart was racing. I did it. I got rid of him. He was gone.

I waited and stared at the phone. It didn't ring again. Mama called a half hour later. I told her I was watching cartoons.

***

I enjoyed school the next day. The relief I felt at having freed myself from the phone caller along with the extra (actually positive) attention I had been receiving from my classmates because of my grisly wound left me rather euphoric all day long. This feeling of well-being and minor celebrity lasted right up until 4:08 when the telephone rang.

"Hello?"

"My baby's grown some balls, huh? My little man's got some *cojones*! We can play some different games now. Little Cary's gonna assert himself. Little Cary's gonna fight back. Are you gonna struggle, Cary? You gonna put up a fight? I like that. I like that, Cary. So what are you gonna do? Tell me what you're thinking, Cary. Swear at me, baby. Call me bad names. Tell me what you want to do to me. Are you mad at me? You want to tie me up? Come on, Cary. Yeah, baby. I want you to hold me down. Overpower me. Tie me up, Cary. Tie me up."

I only stayed on the line because I actually wished I would overpower him. I really did want to tie him up.

"Talk to me," he commanded.

"No, I hate you," I said.

"Talk to me, stud. Tell me what you're thinking."

"I want you to leave me alone."

"Let's get rough."

"No!" I said and slammed down the phone.

It rang almost immediately. Was it him or was it Mama?

"Hello?"

"Oh, baby! Come on, Cary, give me ..."

I hung up. The phone rang.

"Talk to me, Cary."

I hung up. The phone rang.

Of course it's him. I know it's him. But what if it's not? I know one of these phone rings will be my mother calling. No matter what, I still have to answer.

"Hello?"

A sigh. Breathing. "Cary ..."

I hung up. It rang again.

This time I gambled. I did not pick up the receiver on the second ring or the third. I let the phone ring fifty-seven times. It rang until I thought I would go insane. Then it went silent. There was no more.

A knock at the front door caused me to jump.

"You okay in there?" yelled Mrs. Johansson from the front porch.

"Yeah," I called back automatically. But I wasn't okay. I wasn't close to anything that even resembled okay. I considered calling Mrs. Johansson back and telling her everything, but I honestly couldn't fathom describing my present situation to an elderly woman. Even just thinking about it made me feel dirty.

Besides, maybe that was the very last call. Maybe since he knows I'm not going to answer the phone, he'll stop calling.

The phone rang again.

I gambled before that it was the pervert and not Mama, but what if I was wrong? What if that was Mama phoning the last time and I let it ring fifty-seven times? Did she then call Mrs. Johansson and have her pop next door to check on me? Is this her calling me now? If I don't answer the phone this second time, she'll kill me.

I picked up the receiver on the fourth ring. I didn't say anything. I just listened.

"I'm coming over," he said and then there was a click and a dial tone.

Coming over. He's coming over. And there's nothing I can do about it and no one I can call.

I hung up the kitchen phone and ran for the front door. It was locked, but I bolted it and put the chain on it, too. The house was completely silent except for the hum of an electric wall clock in the living room.

My best bet was to make the caller think no one was at home. I sat down on the floor of the entry hallway with my back up against the door and my knees hugged tightly to my chest and waited.

Fifteen minutes passed and I considered the possibility that he was bluffing or he didn't remember where I said I lived. Mama would be home in an hour. Maybe if he lived very far away, Mama would get here before he would. Then there's Mrs. Johansson, I thought. If a strange car pulled into our driveway, certainly she'd …

I heard the noisy rumble of something that sounded like a motorcycle pulling into our driveway. I turned around and, kneeling, I pushed open the brass mail flap in the door with my fingers and peered outside.

It was a motorcycle. And a man.

Through my horizontal peephole, I took stock of him from the ground up. He had on black boots, faded Levi's, a black leather jacket, red gloves, and a white motorcycle helmet with the visor down. I could not see his face.

So that he wouldn't catch me looking, I closed the mail flap real quick and I balled myself up in the foyer again and I remained very, very still. There was the sound of footsteps, boots, walking up to the door. Then a knock. A soft knock at first, and a voice.

"Cary? Open up, buddy. I know you're in there."

I did nothing but remain very still. He knocked again. Louder. "I brought you a present," he said. "Come see what your old pal has brought you."

I glanced up and saw the doorknob turning left to right and felt the weight of his body trying to push the door in. The locks held fast.

The doorbell rang.

"Cary?" he almost sang my name, making it sound sweet and teasing, matching the cadence of the ding-dong notes of our doorbell. There was a pause and then his voice, almost laughing, said, "Fine. Have it your way."

I heard the sound of his boots on the pavement, walking away. Then there was silence.

I was so relieved. He was gone. He was gone and I was safe. In an instant, though, it occurred to me that silence was not the best sound to be hearing at that particular moment. His motorcycle was very noisy. Why didn't I hear him drive away?

Then I thought of Mama and what would happen when she came home. She'd pull the car into the garage and come in through the kitchen. The garage door wasn't locked. Neither was the kitchen door. For that matter, the gate to the back yard was only on a latch and the sliding glass doors in the living room were …

I jumped up and ran into the kitchen to turn the lock in the door leading out to the garage. Next I skittered to the living room and stopped dead in my tracks.

The sheer draperies covering the sliding glass door to the patio were blowing softly in the afternoon breeze. Through the translucent white fabric was the clear outline of a male figure.

CHAPTER EIGHT

1974

One afternoon in late August, Mom and I were doing our usual weekend errands: a trip to the grocery store, a stop at K-mart to drop off film, a stop at the Barbara Ann Day-Old Bakery to get some hamburger buns. We were just pulling in to the line of cars at the drive-through bank teller when I noticed I had a wart on the palm of my right hand.

It was growing on the thick fleshy part of my palm at the base of my middle finger. For the past couple of weeks I assumed that I was getting a callus from the broom I used to sweep the patio, but there in the bank line I had to admit the awful truth: I had a wart.

I could feel a wave of shame wash over me. Only filthy people got warts. Hillbillies. Witches. I had always thought I was somehow superior to the kind of people who got warts. But I wasn't. The dirty, evil evidence was right there on my hand.

The good news was that the wart gave me something new to obsess about.

I had just survived three years of junior high and in a couple of weeks I was about to start high school. At the beginning of the summer, the local government had decided to gerrymander our school districts because Espada's growing Hispanic community was getting a bit too concentrated in certain pockets of town. For obviously bigoted reasons, the government thought it best to spread the Spanish-speaking children around in order to dilute their impact on "real" Americans. People like my mother were thrilled.

As for me, I didn't care one way or the other about the Mexicans – or "Chicanos" as they were now insisting on being called. The important thing for me was that I was now being forced to attend a different high school than the one most of the kids I had grown up with were headed to, simply because my house fell on the wrong side of some imaginary new line.

Hallefuckinglujah.

The last three years had been torture. You would have thought that after a couple of months, Bobby Harvey would have gotten tired of the whole boner boy routine, but no. From the seventh grade to the eighth grade and on through the ninth grade he became what can only be described as "messianic" on the topic of my penis. He spread the word far and wide so that everyone would come to know the legend of the boy in their school who once got an erection in the locker room. At the mere sight of me, he would start shouting, "Faggot. Boner boy. Pervert. Homo. Queer bait. Cary the fairy," etc. Of course, as time went on, most of the kids got tired of Bobby and simply ignored him. No teacher or student ever came to my defense, preferring to keep a sort of "there but for the grace of God" distance from me. Some of the lesser bullies, however, stayed on Bobby's good side by seeing who could verbally fag-bash Cary Scott the most. The problem was they really couldn't think up very many insults for gay kids that Bobby hadn't hurled first. The extent of their ceaseless put-downs rarely got beyond faggot, sissy, and Cary the fairy. But what the bullies lacked in creativity, they more than made up for in perseverance.

So on field trips, I sat in the front of the bus, where it was safest. At lunch, I sat alone at the table nearest the door. I spoke to no one, I looked at no one, and did my homework as I ate. Still, there were a few kids who remained somewhat civil. Gabe Gorman sometimes spoke to me in passing as if I were an actual person, and the ugly girl, Shirley Parks, now and then sent semaphores from her own tower of isolation.

Now, thanks to a stroke of civic prejudice, none of these people were going to be at my new school. With luck, I would never see Bobby Harvey again and no one in my high school class would know about my junior high shame. I could start over again and reinvent myself as a normal boy. I might even make some friends.

The problem was, I was certain that somehow I was bound to screw it all up.

Phys-Ed, locker rooms, and communal showers were still going to be mandatory at the new high school. Through extreme mental effort I had learned to tame my raging loins by practicing the multiplication tables in my head. Luckily I was still just as hopeless in math as I ever was. Multiplying anything by more than six in my head took such concentration that an atomic bomb, or even a gay orgy, could go off in the shower and I would pay it no attention. It also helped that I had become accustomed to seeing the same group of young boys naked three times a week for the last three years. It was easy to ignore what had become familiar.

And this was precisely what I had been obsessing about all summer long. Sometime in early June it occurred to me that I was going to be seeing a whole new crop of naked guys in September. In high school, some of the seniors were going to look fairly mature and I had started to realize that my erotic fantasies were tending more toward muscular, hairy daddy types than toward smooth, slender young boys. It was going to take a lot more than multiplication tables to keep me from getting another locker room erection. And if I allowed that to happen again, I might as well just leave town. I wouldn't be able to endure another three years of humiliation.

It also occurred to me that even if I started over with a whole new group of kids who knew nothing of my past, and even if I did everything right, I was now carrying the added weight of – how should I put it? – carrying added weight. Somehow, over the course of junior high, my waist measurement had overtaken my inseam and my pant size had exploded from slim to husky. I was no longer just the gay kid. I was now the fat gay kid. As I obsessed over all my potential upcoming humiliations, the wart on my hand became literally a "worry wart." In my distraction, I picked at it nonstop for days until my palm became infected and inflamed. After my little trip to the emergency room when I was ten, I stopped alerting my mother to any injury or illness that I suffered. I learned to take care of myself. I knew where the bandages were kept and I knew the proper dosage of cough syrup and aspirin for my age and weight. Mom never asked how I was, and I never freely offered any complaints. This stupid wart, however, proved to be beyond my doctoring skills. Eventually, it got so painful that I couldn't hold a pencil or a spoon any longer.

Fearing gangrene, I finally broke down and showed my hand to Mom who promptly threw a fit and yelled at me for not showing it to her sooner.

God damn it, I just couldn't win, could I?

What I didn't realize, however, was that this infected wart was going to change the course of my life.

Two days before the start of school, Mom took me back to the emergency room where an elderly doctor cleaned out the wound and used an electric tool to cauterize the wart so that it wouldn't come back. It hurt more than I can possibly describe. As he bandaged up my right hand, the doctor gave my mother instructions on how I was to care for the affected area for the next several days.

"Try to keep the wound dry until it heals," he said. "It'll probably be easier for him to take a tub bath instead of a shower to avoid getting the hand wet. Change the gauze every night before he goes to bed. I'm giving you a prescription for an antibiotic ointment, and here's a note for him to take to school. He shouldn't go to gym class for at least two weeks." The doctor then looked at me, ruffled my hair playfully, smiled and said, "No basketball for you, young fellow! You promise?"

I was so shocked and delighted all I could do was nod at him with my mouth agape. I had won the lottery.

***

My new school bus stop was two blocks away from my house. It was at an old, neglected intersection of town where the sidewalk was just hard-packed dirt and the eucalyptus trees were so ancient that their bark hung off in shaggy ribbons. To my relief, there were no other teenagers gathered there. It wasn't unusual for California kids to get a car when they turned sixteen. After that, they drove themselves to school or got a ride with friends. Needless to say, I wasn't one of those California kids. As I stood there waiting for the school bus, I realized that most likely it was going to be filled with only the tired, poor, wretched refuse of Espada. In other words: no cool kids. The very thought made me do a little pirouette of happiness – an act I immediately regretted when the bus quickly rounded the corner.

There wasn't any room to sit at the front of the bus, but there was one empty bench halfway back. With my head down, I scooted into the free seat as quickly as possible, although even I had to admit that no one was paying any attention to me. I kept my bandaged hand concealed behind my new spiral-bound notebook. If I could help it, nothing about me was going to draw the slightest notice.

Behind me, all the way to the back of the bus, there was one student per bench – all of them boys, of course – lounging sideways with feet dangling into the aisle. The boy in an Orange County Fair t-shirt directly behind me had stringy, shoulder-length blond hair and smelled faintly of hay. He was one of the kids from the rural fringes of town where people kept horses and other livestock. "Goat ropers" we called them, but I wasn't altogether sure if it was an offensive term or not since the goat ropers often referred to themselves that way. And I never heard of any of them actually owning a goat. He was talking to the boy behind him, whom I didn't dare sneak a glance at.

"Dude, Kurt Marshall totally chickened out," said the goat roper. "We waited in the parking lot for almost an hour before we went ahead without him."

"You really did it?" asked the guy behind him.

"Fuck yeah."

"Damn! You really streaked McDonald's?!"

"Yeah, but nobody could tell it was me. I mean I wore a paper bag on my head. We got in and out pretty fast."

"Dude!"

Hearing this, I felt a little charge of electricity go through me.

Streaking was the hottest craze of 1974. College students seemed to be running naked everywhere. There was a novelty song on the radio called "The Streak." Some guy had even streaked the Oscars. Picturing the goat roper dashing naked through McDonald's with a paper bag over his head gave me an instant hard-on. In a panic, I started praying to God that it would be a long ride to school. Unfortunately, it wasn't. I had to untuck my shirttails just to get off the bus.

The start of a new school year is always boring. Nothing much ever happens in class the first week, and being the new kid in school, I didn't have any old friends to catch up with. I also didn't have anyone to eat lunch with or spend free period with, but after the last couple of years, I had become accustomed to that. Gym class loomed at the end of the first day, but I wasn't overly concerned about it because I had my doctor's note. When the time for P.E. finally came, I consulted my mimeographed school map and located the entrance to the boys' locker room.

The change room at the high school had a different configuration than the one I had gotten used to in junior high. The banks of lockers were arranged around the periphery of the room while the tiled center area resembled a sort of plumbery forest with a dozen floor-to-ceiling chromium poles crowned with halos of multiple shower heads. Evidently, around each pole, a circle of young men would have to gang-shower while facing one another. It was as if the architect of the locker room had designed the place as a giant "fuck you" to privacy. And the person with the best view of all was the coach, whose glass-walled office was along the north end of the shower area.

It was to this sweaty terrarium that I presented myself to my new gym teacher, Coach McAllister. Coach was a white-haired, fire plug of a man in his early sixties. He was leaning back in his chair, scribbling something in a three-ring binder when I walked in.

"My doctor said I'm supposed to give you this," I said, proffering my note.

Coach McAllister glanced up at me, took the note and read it, then looked back up at me with a skeptical expression. I held up my bandaged hand and shrugged my shoulders. I was just starting to turn around and go home when he suddenly said, "Take a seat," and pointed to a bench outside his door. The bench was right at the end of the shower area. Anyone who sat there would be staring directly into the showers.

"For how long?" I said, trying not to sound panicked.

"Till the bell. You will be here on time every day and you'll sit there until the end of class. You understand me? If you're so injured that you can't participate in gym, then you will park your butt right there until you think your hand has healed. And if you even dream of skipping class, I will pile on so many detentions that you'll beg me to put you out on the field."

I had not considered this. I assumed that for the next two weeks I could skip gym completely. It never occurred to me that the coach would hold my doctor's note in high contempt and make me spend an hour every day sitting in the locker room. No, worse! Sitting in the locker room and staring at the other boys as they took their showers. The coach was setting me up to look like a pervert. If I had any dream that in my new school I was going to fly under the radar, I had just sabotaged that plan. Before the day was out, I was certain to be infamous.

As I took my appointed seat, the locker room started to fill with boys suiting-up for gym. Since I had left all my books in my locker, I had nothing with me to read or fix my attention on. Desperately searching my pockets, I found a folded-up mimeo from my freshman social studies class. I took it out and focused all my concentration on each blurry blue character on the page. In about ten minutes, the locker room was empty again. All the boys were out on the field and I was alone.

So far so good, but in forty-five minutes, everyone would be back to hit the showers and I was certain that my life would end.

I could not watch the boys taking showers, and I could not be seen still reading that one piece of paper – doing one, I'd seem pervy, and doing the other, I'd seem retarded. What was I going to do? I had to think of something fast.

The bandage. Of course.

I formulated an ingenious plan to wait until a few minutes before the return of the athletes and then unwrap my hand from the yards of white gauze. As everyone came back into the locker room, my scheme was to be discovered calmly re-bandaging my injured hand. This plan would kill two birds with one stone, because (1) it would keep me occupied enough so that I wouldn't seem like a perv sitting on a bench watching naked boys, and (2) it would provide an obvious answer to anyone wondering why I was sitting on the bench instead of participating in gym.

It was a great plan. In theory.

I sat in the silence of the deserted locker room, listening intently for whatever I could hear going on out on the playing field. Pretty much on cue, forty-five minutes later I made out the sound of the coach's whistle and some muffled shouting which I assumed to be the call to hit the showers. Working quickly, I tore off the adhesive tape holding the gauze on my hand in place and started unwinding myself. I worked very fast, hoping to have all the bandages removed before the first boy walked in. I went a little too fast, however. Whipping off the last of the gauze, I accidentally tore off the sterile pad covering the lesion, which, to my horror, ripped open the wound.

Blood started to seep from my palm.

With my free hand, I snatched back the now totally non-sterile pad from where it had landed by my feet on the germy gym floor. I tried to staunch the flow of blood running down my forearm, but it didn't really work. I took the tangled pile of gauze and began to wrap my hand, but the gauze started wicking the blood and became saturated. Before I knew it, I was surrounded by a dozen young men in gym shorts staring at me open-mouthed.

"Dude, what the fuck?" said a guy with shaggy brown hair and a sweat-stained t-shirt.

"Old crucifixion wound," I replied with a pained smile. (*Where did THAT come from?!* I wondered with awe. I wasn't used to saying things that were clever.)

The shaggy-haired guy paused for a second then burst out laughing and the rest of the boys around him joined in. Their response stabbed me like a knife and I felt a familiar wave of humiliation, but then I realized that they weren't laughing at me – they were laughing *with* me. I had made a joke and these boys had found it funny.

Any chance I had of enjoying this little moment of peer approval was cut short by the arrival of Coach McAllister. "What the hell happened to you?" he barked. "Stop bleeding on my floor and get to the nurse's office!"

"Where's that?" I asked.

Turning to the shaggy-haired guy, the coach said, "Cole, take him to see the nurse. And grab a roll of paper towels on the way out so he doesn't leave a goddammed bloody trail."

The guy, whose name I now assumed was Cole, gestured for me to follow him. On the way out of the locker room, he picked up a roll of scratchy brown industrial paper towels used to stock the dispenser by the sinks. He tore off a wad and gave it to me to catch the drips of blood.

As he led me across the quad, Cole casually asked, "So what really happened to your hand?"

Since I was still ashamed about having had a filthy, disgusting wart, I said, "I don't know. It just happened." To my surprise, Cole didn't question this at all.

"I thought the crucifixion thing was hilarious," he said, "because something like that happened to me when I was a kid. I stepped on a rusty nail and poked a big hole in my foot. My grandma started teasing me, saying that I had the stigmata."

"The what?"

"The wounds of Christ," he said. "We're Catholic and the Catholics believe that, you know, saints and stuff, if they're really holy, they just spontaneously erupt with the same bloody wounds that Jesus got from being on the cross."

"You stepped on a rusty nail? Ouch."

"I got lockjaw," he said. "I was sick for months."

Step on a nail and get sick for months? That's not a bad plan, I thought.

***

The next day, I went to the public library to learn everything I could about lockjaw. My stupid hand was going to keep me out of gym for only two weeks. That wasn't nearly long enough. If I could step on a rusty nail and get out of gym for months, it might be worth the effort.

It didn't take long to find the library's enormous medical dictionary. The word "lockjaw" redirected me to an entry for another disease. Lockjaw – intense muscle spasms that made your jaw clench shut – was a symptom of something called tetanus. At first glance, having my jaw muscles go into spasm didn't sound all that awful. I could probably stand that. Then I read a little further. If you got tetanus, you had to consume 4,000 to 5,000 calories a day because it wasn't just your jaw going into spasm, it was all the muscles in your body and that took a lot of energy. Hmmm. Lying in bed for months, eating massive amounts of high-calorie food didn't sound all that unpleasant, either. No gym for months and all the brownies and ice cream I could eat? Tetanus was for me!

The fantasy came to an abrupt end when I got to the part about it often being fatal.

Okay, so tetanus was out. Besides, I seemed to remember getting a tetanus shot when I went to the emergency room after I stabbed myself during that field trip to the college biology lab. Damn. And come to think of it, it probably wouldn't be easy to eat if your jaw was locked.

But what was it that Cole had said about the wounds of Christ? Staccato? Binaca? What was it called? I went over to the librarian behind the book return desk and asked her if she knew the word I was searching for.

"Stigmata," she said, and then repeated it really slowly while writing it down on a scrap of paper for me. "Looks like you're coming down with a case of it yourself," she added, nodding to my bandaged hand with a smile.

From the bookcase nearest the card catalog, I retrieved volume 18, SO-SZ, of the 1973 *World Book Encyclopedia*. I found it very enlightening.

Just as Cole had said, the stigmata were body marks that corresponded to the crucifixion wounds of Jesus. They were sores, open wounds, or sometimes even just sensations, on the hands and feet. Some people developed the sores on their wrists resembling nail holes or rope burns, some developed symbolic sword wounds in their sides, and some developed bloody scratches across their foreheads from unseen crowns of thorns. Some stigmatic wounds bled only on Thursdays and Fridays (odd, right?), and some wounds produced a sweet, perfume-like smell called the Odor of Sanctity (really? ew …). Stigmatics – that's what people who get the stigmata are called – have a lot of things in common: almost all have been members of Catholic religious orders, and almost all have been women. Well, I wasn't Catholic and I wasn't female, but a few hardy stigmatics over the centuries have defied stereotype. That being said, almost all of the non-Catholic men who have gotten the stigmata have been certifiably insane.

One thing that psychiatrists assume stigmatics have in common is a mental illness called obsessive compulsive disorder (which got me to thinking that maybe I should look that one up right away in encyclopedia volume O). Also, a lot of them probably suffered from some weird thing I'd never heard of before called anorexia nervosa, which apparently made you lose a lot of weight. Stigmatics generally don't eat. Since I had put on quite a few pounds in the last couple of years, something like anorexia nervosa actually sounded appealing to me. In fact, for my current unpleasant situation, the whole stigmatic lifestyle sounded like it was just what the doctor ordered.

Thus began, as I like to call it, "The Great Lie of 1974."

***

The next time gym class rolled around, I came prepared for my long stint on the locker room bench. I brought a couple of text books and my three-ring binder so I could do my algebra and history homework while I waited. I was also supposed to write a poem for English class. That was one particular task I was trying to avoid. I didn't like poems. I didn't understand the bizarre language of poetry. Poets used words like *ere*, *t'was*, *twixt*, and *yon*; words only good for crossword puzzles and Scrabble. How was I supposed to write something that I hated to read? I had no idea what I was going to do about the poetry assignment, so I just concentrated on completing the even-numbered problems at the end of chapter three in my algebra book.

As I worked away on my math problems, that silly novelty song by Ray Stevens, "The Streak," kept going through my mind. The tune was catchy, but beyond "streak" and "physique," I couldn't really recall any of the lyrics. Still I couldn't get the song out of my head. Plus, it made me think about streakers – and then the irony of my current situation struck me. In a few minutes, when the boys returned to hit the showers, I was going to be a sort of a reverse streaker – a clothed person among a group of naked people. I wouldn't be running, though. A streaker would zoom through the room.

"Hey, that rhymes," I thought. "Zoom through the room. Maybe I could use that for my poetry assignment."

Before I could forget the idea, I took out my notebook and quickly scribbled down the first couple of lines: "*With a crash, a splash, a zoom / A girl streaked through the boys' locker room.*"

Well, that wasn't difficult at all. In fact, it was fun. It hadn't occurred to me before that the poem might not have to be florid or serious. Maybe the teacher would accept a little verse that was humorous, or even downright stupid. As long as it rhymed, right? At the very least a funny poem would be better than no poem at all. While I had my mind on it, I decided to just keep on going. It was surprising how easy it was to continue riffing off that silly reverse-streaker idea. After working for about a half an hour, I ended up with something absolutely ridiculous:

With a crash, a splash, a zoom,
A girl streaked through the men's locker room.
Straight through the showers steaming hot.
The guys were all naked, but the girl was not.
The idea was so very strange –
To run through where the guys all change!
Her prank was grand, unplanned, and daring
(and she didn't stop herself from staring).
As she dashed past every unclothed jock,
The baseball team got quite a shock.
The pitcher screamed. The short stop ducked.
The catcher caught himself and tucked.
The outfield didn't mind at all
That she kept her eye upon the ball.
The cops might never ever caught her
If she hadn't slipped on all that water.
So now she's stuck in house arrest,
For being a streaker fully dressed.

I purposely made the main character of the poem a female because I didn't want anyone thinking that I might be writing about myself, although still harbored an uneasy feeling that, no matter how I wrote it, folks might think that anyway. Since there wasn't anything I could do about that, I decided not to think about it. Anyway, my English teacher, Miss Benito, would be the only person who would ever read it, so why worry?

I was so absorbed in my writing that I barely noticed when the guys came in off the field and started to get changed. For a moment, I had the wild idea that I should write poetry every day while I was confined to the locker room bench. No one would think I'm a perv or a homo if I was seen to be concentrating so hard on my work, right? Looking back on it later, I realized how stupid it was to think that sitting in a locker room writing poetry might somehow make me seem less gay.

***

Two weeks passed very quickly. I turned in my poetry assignment on time, but hadn't heard yet what kind of grade I got. In the rest of my classes I was mostly unremarkable – thankfully, literally so. The slightly above-average marks I had been earning had elicited comments from absolutely no one. It was all part of my quest to become invisible, to escape the notice of the students, the teachers, anyone, although I did strike up an odd sort of acquaintanceship with a heavy-set girl named Mary Figgens whom I noticed sitting alone in the cafeteria. She seemed nice, but we didn't have a lot in common.

And there was no way I was as fat as she was.

However, something *was* weighing heavily on me: the looming expiration date on the doctor's note excusing me from gym class. The following Monday, I was going to have to suit up, play sports, and shower with all the other guys. It was too horrible to imagine. Over the last couple of days, Coach McAllister had begun doing a countdown of my remaining days on the locker room bench. "Two days, Scott. Two days!" he'd say, with such an evil gleam in his eye I could tell he felt his whole purpose in life was to torture short, chubby guys, and I was going to be his next victim.

Although I desperately tried to think of some other option, the only solution I could come up with was to put the "Great Lie" into action.

On the Sunday afternoon before my first excuse-free gym class, I went out into the garage and looked around my father's abandoned workbench. There I found a hammer, a scrap of two-by-four lumber, and, from a coffee tin full of assorted screws and stuff, a huge nail about five inches long. I took the nail into the kitchen and got my mom's clockwork egg timer shaped like a hen sleeping on a nest. I started a pan of water boiling on the stove, plunked the nail in the water, and then twisted the chicken on the nest to count down ten minutes. It said in my Cub Scout handbook that boiling something for ten minutes would sterilize it. I didn't want to get an infection, and I made sure that it was a galvanized nail, not rusty at all, so I wouldn't be courting lockjaw.

After the nail had finished boiling and was once again cool to the touch, I took it back out to the garage workbench and picked up the hammer. It felt odd holding the hammer in my left hand so I gave it a few practice whacks on the two-by-four scrap to get the hang of it. The next thing I had to work out was how I was going to hold the nail steady. To do what I needed to do, it wasn't possible to hold it as I normally would between my thumb and forefinger. I soon figured out that if I rested the back of my right hand on the two-by-four and curled my fingers over my upturned palm, that I could stick the nail between my middle and ring fingers with the point of the nail resting square in the middle of my palm.

Without giving myself time to reconsider, I raised the hammer with my left hand, brought it down hard on the nail, and crucified myself.

***

My story appeared the next week on the front page of the *Espada Weekly Sun-Mirror*.

STIGMATA BOY'S A POET!

Local high schooler writes like Shakespeare, bleeds like Jesus

By Connie Purvis, Sun-Mirror staff writer
Monday, September 23, 1974

There is a miracle worker at Espada Senior High, and his name is Cary Scott.

For his first miracle, the 15-year-old freshman has managed to get the entire student body at his high school talking about poetry.

And for his second miracle, Scott has started bleeding with the wounds of Christ.

At the recent city-wide poetry competition held annually in conjunction with the Rotary Club of Espada and the local Chamber of Commerce, Scott took first prize for his untitled comic rhymefest about a fully-clothed streaker.

The poem is an amusing tale about a young woman who runs through a men's locker room while the guys are in the showers. Judges called it a clever, feminist twist on the latest streaking fad. They were surprised to find out it had been written by a boy.

Until the morning when he learned that he had won, Scott had been unaware that his English teacher, Francine Benito, 34, of Palm Acres, had submitted his poem to the competition. In fact, the news of his victory reached him in the emergency room of Our Lady of Hope Hospital where he was being treated for bleeding wounds in the palms of his hands.

Officials at the Catholic hospital are calling it a suspected case of stigmata.

According to Catholic teaching, the stigmata are the miraculous appearance of Jesus' crucifixion wounds on certain holy persons or devout believers.

Scott had been side-lined with a bleeding wound to his left hand for the past two weeks. Scott's mother, June, says that her son's right palm began bleeding yesterday, and that her son can offer no explanation for the wounds' occurrences.

Copies of the winning poem circulated quickly around the school, becoming a hot topic of conversation among most of the student body.

"His poem's funny and weird, but mostly it's funny," said ESH classmate Juanita Lopez.

"And now he's bleeding like Jesus? Far out!"

Along with a plaque from the Rotary Club, Scott was presented with a $25 gift certificate to Zody's. Upon accepting the prize, he thanked God.

There was a huge photo of me as well, in my hospital robe looking slightly dazed, holding my Rotary Club plaque in my bandaged hands. I don't know where the reporter came up with the idea that I thanked God for winning the contest. If I recall correctly, I think my actual response was, "Oh my fucking God," because I was stunned that Miss Benito would do something that awful behind my back. But that sense of violation and public exposure paled to the way I felt when I saw myself on the front page of the paper.

And who's Juanita Lopez?

I was relieved to see that the newspaper had left out, or had gotten wrong, quite a few important details. Of course my mother knew how I got the first bleeding wound. She was the one who took me to the doctor to have the wart removed. As for the second wound, I'm not sure how much she figured out or how much she even wanted to know.

I had brought the hammer down with such force that the nail had gone completely through my hand (thankfully passing between the bones) and embedded itself firmly in the block of wood. I was able to use the claw on the hammer to pull out the nail before the blood suddenly drained out of my head and I fainted. When I came to a few minutes later, I found myself face down on the garage floor with a pounding headache. As I fell, I had hit my forehead on the edge of the workbench and it had left a crooked, bloody scratch across my brow. It was almost as if I had done the job so well, my stigmata had gotten a bonus crown of thorns.

There was lots of blood everywhere, but before I could start cleaning it up, I had to bandage my hand. Thank goodness I had thought ahead to stick a fresh roll of gauze in my pocket. I wrapped up my hand as best I could and went inside the house to lie down for a while. The pain was worse than anything I had experienced in my entire life. Mom must have heard me crying when she got home from work because I looked up and she was standing in the doorway of my bedroom, just staring at me with a stony expression. Of course she must have noticed the carnage in the garage when she parked her car. There was blood on her shoes. She didn't say anything, though, except, "Come on," then walked me out to the car, and drove me to the emergency room.

On the way to the hospital, she said not one word to me.

It was only until later that I learned how the Rotary Club and the newspaper reporters tracked me down at Our Lady of Hope

Hospital. Apparently, they had first contacted Miss Benito to ask her to escort me to the award presentation, but, after learning from the principal's office that my mother had phoned to say I was in the hospital and would not be back in school for at least a week, Miss Benito directed the Rotary Club to find me there.

Another little detail that the newspapers had graciously gotten wrong was that the Rotary Club had not presented my plaque to me in the emergency room. They had delivered my prize to the psych ward where I was being held under observation. The doctor had only been speaking sarcastically to the reporter about the stigmata diagnosis. He couldn't tell *Sun-Mirror* staff writer Mrs. Connie Purvis that I was under suicide watch after suffering a complete nervous breakdown.

During my stay in the hospital, they kept those of us in my situation busy with craft therapy – for some reason it was deemed therapeutic for suicidal people to apply glaze to ceramic mugs. There was a lot of time left over for watching daytime TV, plus I had to keep a journal, and I had to speak with a psychiatrist for at least an hour every day. The psychiatric sessions were a complete waste of everyone's time. The doctor asked me a lot of questions, but there were many things that I could simply not talk about. I was too ashamed to tell him that I wasn't suicidal, and I had done all this just to get out of gym class, because he'd ask why and then I'd have to tell him about the incident in junior high when I had an erection in the locker room and was humiliated by Bobby Harvey. I'd have to tell him about researching stigmata at the library and all the advanced planning that went into crucifying my right hand. I'd have to tell him about all the food I'd been hoarding in my bedroom and how I'd started doing most of my eating in the dead of night and how I would only be able to defecate between the hours of 2 a.m. and 5 a.m. when everyone in the world was sound asleep. If I told him even one of these things, then I was afraid I would lose control and tell him that I was attracted to boys. And that was something I was just too ashamed to do.

So I stuck to the "Great Lie" and never veered from my story for one second.

Basically, I feigned a lot of ignorance about what was happening to me. I claimed to be completely unaware how the holes in my palms and the jagged scratch across my forehead came about. I had simply been praying a lot lately and these things miraculously happened to me. As I stared back at the psychiatrist in wide-eyed innocence, I could almost feel a gold-plated Oscar statuette gripped in my bandaged hand. I had no doubt that he believed every word I said.

I gave the psychiatrist extremely little information about my feelings and my past history, but still he seemed to find a lot to write down on his notepad. I really wanted to see that notepad.

At the end of my second week of hospitalization, my strange adventure into the world of miracles and mental illness got even stranger. Things took a turn for the bizarre when I received a hospital visit from a faded country singing star.

***

We lived in a very large county in a particularly fertile part of California, so it stood to reason that our annual county fair would be one of the largest and most popular in the state. Although I wasn't overly fond of prize hogs and Tilt-a-Whirls, the fair was one of the things I looked forward to each year because I loved the awful, corny shows they put on and the choice of talent they booked. The bandshell stage attracted a good deal of has-been TV stars and washed-up recording artists. The rule seemed to be that if you had ever appeared on *Hee-Haw*, your next stop on the road to obscurity was to give a concert at our county fair.

This year, fate had decreed that Kitty Belle Crawford would be the exposition's star attraction. Kitty Belle had been the hottest thing in country music during the late 1950s, with two massive number one hits, "Alabama Starlight," and "Sing, Sing, Sing Until You Cry, Cry, Cry." The swinging sixties had not been kind to her bland brand of smiling-through-the-tears ballads, however. As Billie Joe McAllister was jumping off the Tallahatchie Bridge and Mrs. Johnson was socking it to the Harper Valley

PTA, Kitty Belle's songs were sounding about as contemporary as Civil War anthems. After twenty years of being banished to county fair bandshells and Mid-western cocktail lounges she was desperately searching for a way back into the mainstream, and to be relevant once more.

In other words, she was a beehived honey in need of a gimmick – and then somebody showed her a copy of the *Espada Sun-Mirror*.

I was sitting in the common area of my ward, watching *The $10,000 Pyramid* when a nurse came to tell me that there was someone who wanted to see me. I hadn't received a visitor other than my mom the whole time I had been there (well, not counting the newspaper reporter) so I was a bit surprised to see waving to me from the doorway a tiny, middle-aged woman with the biggest hair I had ever seen.

Kitty Belle swept into the room with a rolled-up copy of the *Sun-Mirror* in her fist and rushed over to give me a big hug. With tears in her eyes, she said, "You poor, dear boy! How are you doing, darlin'?"

"Okay, I guess," I replied. I was a little confused because I didn't recognize her right away. She seemed to sense it, and after the briefest wave of disappointment passed across her face, she brightened up and went into presentation mode.

"My name is Kitty Belle Crawford and I'm a singer."

"Oh, right! Yes. Hi," I stammered.

"Oh, you don't have to pretend you know who I am. Probably the last person in your family to buy one of my records was your granddaddy. But I know *you*, Mr. Cary Scott! I've been reading all about you. You are a talented young fellow. I had my agent get a hold of a copy of that poem you wrote. I loved it! By the way, honey, how are your hands doing?"

"They're … better," I said.

"You must love Jesus and Jesus must love you, that's all I can say. There is power power power, wonder-working power in the blood of the lamb. And lamb, there is wonder-working power in your little poem. I'd like to know if you would consider selling it to me."

I had no idea how to respond to that. You mean you could sell a poem? All I could think to say was, "Huh?"

"I want to record it as a song," she said. "I've got the tune already singing in my head, and I'll record it right away if you'll sell me the rights to use your lyrics."

"No," I said.

That seemed to derail her train for a moment. It had obviously not occurred to her that I wouldn't jump at her offer, but how could I? It was mortifying that Miss Benito had entered that embarrassing poem to a contest, and it had been humiliating to learn that copies of the poem were being circulated around the school for all to read. I hadn't wanted anyone to know what I had written except for the teacher. Now that I'd got a little distance from it, I realized that the poem reeked of homo perv. And now an old lady wanted to sing it on the radio? I'm sorry, but no way.

"I don't want to sell it," I said.

Kitty Belle Crawford was not to be dissuaded, however. "I know it's a big surprise and an unbelievable opportunity, so I'll give you time to think about it," she said. "I'll come back and see you tomorrow and we'll talk it over a little more." With a huge smile, she grabbed me once more in a warm embrace then skipped brightly out the door.

Just as she promised, Kitty Belle did return the following afternoon, only this time she brought her agent with her. He was a short, balding guy with sunglasses and a lot of gold chains around his neck – and in his briefcase he carried a contract with my name on it and all of the details already drawn up. As he explained it, Kitty Belle's record label was very eager to release the poem I had written as a single as soon as possible. Since I had indicated that I didn't want to sell the lyrics outright, they were willing to offer me an advance of $500 against royalties of ten cents for each copy of sheet music or 45 rpm sold. If the song were to be included in any future LPs, I would receive five cents per album. There were lots of other details about cover versions, world rights, and public performances but it was all so confusing and overwhelming that I was too intimidated to put up any resistance.

"I have one condition, though," I said.

"What's that?" asked the agent.

"I don't want you to use my real name." Now that was clever of me! If everyone in the whole country was going to hear that poem, at least they didn't have to know that I was the guy who wrote it.

"You can have it published under a pen name, sure," he said. "What name do you want to use?"

I hadn't thought of that yet. I blurted out the first name that came to my mind. "R.B. Welch," I said. "Just the initials R and B and the last name Welch." It gave me a brief moment of pleasure to think that maybe it might make my uncle Arby happy to see his name on a song – but really, whoever notices the names of songwriters anyway? Plus, I didn't even know if Arby was alive or dead. He and my dad might have gotten killed in Vietnam.

"No problem," said the agent, and he took out a pen and wrote a quick addition to the first paragraph of the contract stating that I was to be known under the *nom de plume* of R.B. Welch.

The agent showed me where I had to initial the contract at the bottom of each page, and where I had to put my signature at the end. Since I was underage, they would have to get my mother's signature as well, and any money that I earned beyond the $500 advance would have to be put in trust for me until I turned twenty-one. Before I knew it, the deal was done.

Kitty Belle was indeed a fast worker. The song was recorded and on the radio in about a month. "Lookey, Lookey" (as she titled it) stayed at number seven on the pop charts for three weeks and was number one on the country charts for ten. That stupid song ended up equaling "The Streak" by Ray Stevens with five million copies sold. Kitty Belle Crawford was on top of the world again.

And I made a half a million dollars.

CHAPTER NINE

1992

It's couple of days before Thanksgiving, and Queen Elizabeth is on TV giving a speech. She's wearing her pearls, a shapeless green dress, and a big green hat, which looks for all the world like a bowl of guacamole, on her head. From a stack of white note cards in her hand, she reads: "1992 is not a year on which I shall look back with undiluted pleasure. In the words of one of my more sympathetic correspondents, it has turned out to be an 'Annus Horribilis'. I suspect that I am not alone in thinking it so."

The poor old thing really is having a "year of horrors." Randy Andy has split up with Fergie, Princess Anne got a divorce, Diana published an embarrassing tell-all bestseller, and Windsor Castle caught on fire. How she must be suffering.

Still, the phrase "Annus Horribilis" resonates with me. Like the Queen, I have not been having the best of all possible years. The AIDS crisis terrifies me daily, many of my belongings were destroyed in a massive earthquake in June, and I am still dealing with the emotional fallout of my mother's brief illness, death, and funeral – not to mention all the considerable expenses I've incurred for her care and subsequent disposal.

It has been twelve years since I was able to access my "Lookey, Lookey" trust fund and I've been as frugal as a Scotsman with the money so it will last as long as possible. When the money runs out, I know I am going to have to get a job or go on welfare, and I certainly don't want to do either of those things. Welfare is humiliating, and, as for a job, what am I qualified to do? I never graduated from high school and now at the age of thirty-three,

I have zero employment history. Yes, I wrote one of the biggest hits of the seventies, but the song has fallen into obscurity and the royalty checks have long since stopped. I've not earned a cent for anything else. A half a million dollars certainly sounded like a lot of money at first, but taxes ate up a big chunk of the windfall. The remainder, even when parceled out parsimoniously over the span of a dozen years, eventually ran low. Frankly, I could have made it last much longer if my mother had not decided on my twenty-first birthday that she had supported me long enough and now it was my turn to support her. She insisted that I provide her a yearly income of $30,000 and I obeyed. I started by allowing myself $15,000 a year to live on, but in the last couple of years, I've been cutting back and have made do on only $10,000, and almost all of that goes for rent. Now after paying Mom's medical and funeral bills, I'm nearly wiped out.

At least the support of my mother is now over – unless you count the monthly payments I have to make on her burial plot.

The reception on my television is not great. Now and then Queen Elizabeth looks like she is giving her Annus Horribilis speech in a snowstorm. I canceled my cable TV service months ago and have learned to live with rabbit ears on my set. The telephone had to go as well, so thank goodness there is a pay phone on the street corner. If I could have canceled the electricity and the water I would have, but lines have to be drawn somewhere if you want to continue living in modern society.

It's a Tuesday morning, my market day, and I don't have far to walk from my pink brick box of an apartment building to the Ralph's grocery store on North La Brea and Fountain. I now live in West Hollywood, which sounds glamorous to people who don't live in West Hollywood. The boarded-up storefronts I pass and the winos I circumnavigate on my way to the store tell the real story of my neighborhood. Do I feel out of place here? Not one bit.

At Ralph's, I grab a shopping cart and go on automatic pilot as I walk down the aisles. On my budget, I get to go to the grocery store one day a week and it's a real challenge because I can spend only $10 for food. Ramen noodles, five for a dollar, are a staple of my diet. I grab seven for one week's worth of dinners. I pick up the smallest jar of peanut butter they sell and a loaf of white bread. That's good for seven lunches. A box of Quaker instant oatmeal will give me six breakfasts, which means on Tuesdays I usually have to skip breakfast entirely. A quart of milk, and voila – the ten dollars are spent. I have no money left for any sort of fruit or vegetables. To keep myself from getting scurvy, in the dead of night I often steal oranges from a neighborhood tree. When avocados are in season, I have another neighbor with a bountiful tree whose harvest mysteriously diminishes, too.

As I walk home with my sad little bag of groceries, I get to thinking about the funny relationship I have with food. When I didn't need to worry about where my next meal was coming from, food was the enemy. It tempted me, it taunted me, and drove me to commit humiliating acts. You would think that being pulled out of a dumpster by the police in Taos, New Mexico, would have been a wake-up call, but it wasn't. Even after being so strict and losing a lot of weight on the Hunsacker diet, I went back to doing a lot of the same crazy things I'd done before. I would still hide food. I'd eat in secret, too ashamed to be seen putting anything in my mouth. I'd starve myself then gorge myself. At a food court, I'd order a diet drink and a salad – and then eat things other people left behind on the tables. I would consume an entire jar of Nutella, and then go jogging for three hours to burn off the shame. I entered ten marathons, ran them all, and tallied each calorie burned. Even after I was no longer fat, the avoidance, consumption, and expurgation of food controlled almost all of my daily activity. Food was exhausting.

It took extreme poverty to finally break the cycle.

Strangely enough, with all this strict rationing, food seems to have lost all its power over me. Since I'm now so broke I can stock my pantry only once a week, gorging isn't even a remote possibility. Survival trumps temptation. And with no gorging, there's no purging, so I'm spending much less time running. In fact, I've switched to doing yoga at home and no longer run at all, which is a good thing because my running shoes wore out months ago and I can't afford to replace them.

Continuing on the way home, about a block past Ralph's, I pass by one of those soulless 1960s concrete "professional" buildings that pepper Southern California. Apparently, they've got a new tenant because there's a handwritten sign taped to the glass main entrance door that says "P. Jenkins, MS, LMFT, Solution Focused Brief Therapy, Suite 107."

Brief therapy? How ridiculous.

I've been in therapy twice now – once in the psych ward after I drove a nail through my hand, and six months of regression therapy after that awful experience with Jennifer Blume at the Beverly Hilton – and as far as I can tell, one thing psychotherapists have no concept of is the word "brief." Therapy is unending. If it had been up to my last doctor, I'd still be in treatment, but after regressing me so far I swore I recalled being a zygote, the whole exercise seemed ludicrous and I stopped going. So now apparently someone is trying to turn therapy into fast food. I wonder if Dr. Brief Therapy Jenkins has a drive-thru window in the back. Hmm. I know that's just a sarcastic thought, but, quite honestly, I have to admit that I might consider going back into therapy if I could tell all my troubles to an intercom shaped like a huge fiberglass clown.

I climb the precast concrete steps to my second-floor studio apartment. The building is laid out like an economy motel – in fact, since my apartment strongly resembles a cheap hotel room, I suspect that's what it was originally designed to be. There are no interior hallways in the building; all the apartment doors open to the outside. The entrances to the second-floor units stretch out along a ribbon of balcony festooned with a wrought-iron railing. I'm located at the very end. Having an open-air passageway is nice in good weather but unpleasant in bad, especially when lugging groceries. Right now it's late November and getting a little crisp, but I've got a big, baggy sweatshirt on so it's not unbearable.

As I walk along the balcony gallery to my apartment, I notice someone has come along and stuffed flyers under every door while I was out. There's one under my door, too. As I let myself in, I stoop down and pick it up.

It's from that "Solution Focused Brief Therapy" doctor. P. Jenkins's first initial turns out to stand for Patty. Doctor Pat Diagnosis, I nickname her. I throw the flyer in the garbage.

After I put away my groceries, I make myself my usual lunch. On a plate, I place one slice of bread and carefully measure one level tablespoon of peanut butter from the jar. I spread the peanut butter in a thin even layer across the bread, and pour myself a glass of tap water.

Then I feast.

***

It's late at night and I'm sitting in bed flipping through a magazine about Hawaii. It's a big magazine, about a yard high, and all the pictures are of beaches, palm trees, and volcanoes. Bare-chested men in grass skirts touch one another gently. Some men are wearing no skirts at all. I cannot read the stories because the magazine seems to be written in some form of Hawaiian. On one page, a volcano rumbles and comes to life. Lava starts to spill down the image. I'm afraid it will set my bed on fire. Right before the molten rock comes off the page and drips onto my sheets, I fling the magazine out my bedroom door. An earthquake shakes the room and I cling to the bed for dear life.

The earthquake stops. The room goes silent. That's when I hear a soft rhythmic sound. Three slow knocks. Then another three slow knocks. Someone is knocking at the front door of my house. The front door is unlocked! I forgot to lock the door before I went to bed! I have to lock the door!

I leap out of bed and race for the foyer. As I lunge to lock the front door, I see the doorknob turning. I see the door opening slowly. I see a hand reaching in.

I push hard on the door to close it again, but the man on the other side is strong and he keeps trying to get in. I open my mouth to yell, "Go away!" but I have no voice. In terror, I try to call for help, but no matter how much effort I put into it, I cannot force a sound out of my throat. Not being able to summon help is almost more frightening than being in physical danger.

The intruder forces the door open.

I awake screaming.

***

The next morning I sleep until noon. On the nights that I have my recurring nightmare, I never seem to fall back to sleep fully until about 5:00 in the morning. By 9:00, the growing sunlight in the room actually seems to make me sleep deeper. I have no reason to get up early, so I don't bother, and stay in bed until lunchtime.

When I'm finally able to drag myself out of bed, I stumble to the bathroom and splash warm water on my face, wetting my beard stubble before I start to shave. I make it a habit now to shave first before taking my morning shower because I've learned that if I shower first, I lose interest in grooming and go about the rest of the day looking grizzled. After three days in a row, "grizzled" begins to look more like "homeless." Three days of "homeless" begins to resemble "crazy." So now I shave first thing, get it out of the way and preserve the illusion of sanity. Besides, I tried it once and I look terrible in a beard.

I've been using this one razor blade for two months now. It's so dull that shaving has become an act of torture. I realize that, even though razors are expensive, sooner or later I'm going to have to change the blade if I don't want to disfigure my face, so I give in and eject the dull cartridge into the trash.

The old blade lands on top of the flyer for Dr. Pat Diagnosis. I pull the piece of paper out of the garbage and take a closer look at it. It's actually a sort of coupon, offering two complimentary sessions of "Solution Focused Brief Therapy" with Dr. Jenkins. For the unenlightened, it describes the philosophy behind the method: "SFBT targets the desired outcome of therapy as a solution rather than focusing on the symptoms or issues that brought someone to therapy. This technique gives attention only to the present and the future desires of the client, rather than focusing on the past experiences."

Wow. I shouldn't have made fun of Brief Therapy before knowing more about it, because Brief Therapy actually sounds like something I'd be interested in. Imagine having someone help you with a problem without making you retell a lifetime of misadventure and brood over a lifetime of failure. Imagine someone not asking you to talk about your mother. Now that's the kind of therapy I'd be interested in.

The nightmares are becoming more and more frequent. They used to come every couple of months. Then they started coming once a week. Now I'm having the same dream several times a week, and it's always the same – an earthquake, a knock, a man forcing his way in, an inability to scream.

It has got to stop.

I make up my mind to book an appointment with Dr. Patty right away. Since I have no telephone, I'll have to get dressed and walk to the pay phone on the corner to do it. Getting dressed doesn't take long. I put back on the same clothes I wore yesterday. Besides, it's not as if I have a lot of clothes to choose from. I used to have nice things to wear. I bought some beautiful, brightly colored shirts when I was at the artist colony in Taos, but I was tipping the scales at nearly 300 pounds then. After I lost the first hundred pounds, I donated all my old clothes to the Salvation Army, all the while feeling very smug about my great charitable act. Ironically, because of poverty, I've lost yet another hundred pounds and the Salvation Army is the only place I can afford to shop for new clothes.

Well, for clothes that are new to me, anyway.

I pull on the jeans and t-shirt I wore to the grocery store yesterday, then clip on my red suspenders. I gave up on belts months ago after running out of notches. Suspenders seem to be the only thing I can use to keep my pants up these days. Next I pull on my heavy Cal State San Diego hooded sweatshirt that I found at the used clothing store. It's one of my favorite things to wear because when people catch sight of me in it, they assume that I went to a good college, and not that I dropped out of high school after having a nervous breakdown.

"Nervous breakdown?" Funny. That's a term people don't use anymore. I wonder what doctors nowadays would call the little break from sanity I had in high school.

I grab the flyer, go out the door, down the stairs, and I get almost to the corner where the pay phone is located before it dawns on me that I don't have a quarter for the call. I have no change at all in my pockets. Now that I think of it, it seems silly to telephone someone who is only two blocks away. I decide to just walk over to the office and book an appointment with the doctor directly. If for some reason she's in the middle of a session, God knows I have all the time in the world to sit and wait.

It turns out that I don't have to wait at all. Dr. Patty Jenkins is there and she isn't seeing anyone for the next couple of hours.

"If you've got time, we could talk right now," she offers.

This is something I had not considered. My initial impulse is to say no and come back later. I'm not prepared to have a therapy session right now. I usually like to rehearse what I'm going to talk about so that I can have some control over the process. The only thing is, I slept so badly last night that my brain isn't working fast enough and I can't think up a lie for why I can't stay and have a session.

"Uh, sure. All right, I guess."

"You want some coffee or some herbal tea before we start?"

Coffee! I haven't been able to afford coffee for the longest time. I would love a cup of coffee. Dr. Patty Jenkins, how could I ever have made fun of you? You're a goddess.

"Yeah, coffee, please," I say casually.

When handing me a mug of coffee, she pauses and looks at me shrewdly. "I'm guessing, black no sugar," she says.

"Black's fine, but I usually take milk and sugar," I say.

"Interesting."

"Why is that interesting?"

"You don't look like someone who ... oh never mind. Help yourself. There's creamer and sweeteners by the coffee maker."

I load up the coffee with as much coffee whitener and sugar as the cup can hold. I try to put as many calories as I can into the drink so it can serve as a sort of little meal for the day. The liquid goes up to the brim so I have to sip some off before going to sit down in the doctor's office.

Patty Jenkins takes a seat on one of the dozen stacking chairs arranged in a ring around a central coffee table. On the table is the requisite box of Kleenex. I take a seat directly opposite her, and she hands me a coaster for my coffee.

I'm not so sure about this. I'm not overly comfortable speaking to women about personal things, so I hope she doesn't ask me about anything sexual. I also have a feeling that she's roughly my own age, although it's hard to tell because she's a little plump, and fat people often look a bit younger than they actually are. It must be because babies are chubby, right? Fat people often resemble overgrown infants, especially when they go around wearing sweat suits and carrying bottles of water wherever they go. A bunch of big, fat, balding babies.

I silently reprimand myself for being so judgmental. I'm a terrible person. I don't even know this woman yet, and here I am thinking awful things about her. Dr. Jenkins is not wearing a sweat suit. She's in a voluminous gypsy skirt and is wearing a pullover. She doesn't look at all like a baby. She looks like every fat girl I went to high school with in the 1970s.

Dr. Jenkins tucks a strand of her long straight blond hair behind an ear, adjusts her round, red-framed glasses, and begins, "So what can I help you with?"

"I'm having a lot of nightmares. Well, one nightmare actually. I keep having it over and over again."

She wants to know the gist of the dream, so I tell her about the volcano, the earthquake, the knocking, the intruder forcing his way into my house.

Dr. Jenkins thinks about this for a moment. "Do you ever see who this intruder is?"

"No. I always wake up just when he gets in."

"So you're sure it's a man at the door."

"Oh, yeah. Absolutely."

"If you never see him, how do you know?"

"I know it's a man because I know who he is."

"Oh, really. Who is it?"

"I assume he's my stalker."

She stares at me with the blankest of expressions. I feel a little perturbed because part of me hoped that the little bombshell about me having a stalker would shock her. Instead, it seems to have no effect upon her at all. I decide to punish her a little for that.

"I really don't want to go into the whole episode. It happened when I was ten. It's all over. It said on your flyer that you focus on immediate solutions. You don't go back and rehash old traumas."

"I'm not rehashing old traumas. I asked you a simple question about your dream. I assume you're here because you want the dreams to stop."

"Yeah, of course."

"Well, let's approach it this way: think about the dream. Is there some sort of common denominator to all the symbols?"

I mull this over. "Everything in the dream is not safe. Is that it? The mountain blows up. The ground is unstable. My house is unstable. My front door does not keep me secure."

She nods. "There's a school of dream interpretation that says that you are all the symbols of your dreams. In other words, the volcano is you, the shaking house is you, the intruder forcing his way through the door is you. So the stalker thing was ages ago. Are you in an unsafe situation right now?"

"No."

"Are you thinking about harming yourself?"

"No."

"Is there someone in your life who you think will do you harm?"

"No."

"Are you certain?"

"Yeah, I'm certain. I'm all alone. There is no one in my life."

Dr. Jenkins finally expresses an emotion. She furrows her brows. "There's got to be *someone* in your life."

"Well, there isn't."

"No relatives? No friends?"

"Not really."

"Where is your family?"

"They're all gone. My mom just died. I lost contact with my dad when I was a kid. My grandparents are dead. My uncle disappeared."

"Disappeared? What do you mean?"

"He ran off with my dad when I was in first grade."

"He left with his brother?"

"No, he left with my mother's brother."

That seems to hit home with her. I am pleased. "Are you implying that your father and your uncle were romantically involved?" she asks.

I nod. Then I change the topic of conversation.

"Remember when people used to have nervous breakdowns? People have got to still be having them, but you never hear the term 'nervous breakdown' anymore. What do we call it nowadays?"

"I think we'd call it a major depressive episode now."

"I was wondering about that. It seemed to me like that term just disappeared overnight."

"You said your mother recently died. Did she have a long illness?"

"No. It was pancreatic cancer. She went pretty fast."

"Like she disappeared overnight. That must feel very unsettling."

I'm sure Dr. Jenkins could see the annoyance on my face. "I was having these nightmares long before my mom died. It's not about that."

She nods, then she just stares at me for a good long minute. It makes me uncomfortable, but I don't know what to say to break the silence. Suddenly, she breaks it for me.

"So can I ask you something?"

"Yeah," I answer with some hesitation.

"How much do you weigh?"

"I don't know."

"I don't believe that. I have a feeling you know exactly how much you weigh."

"With or without clothes?"

"Whatever."

"With pants and shirt and shoes and stuff, I don't know, about 101?"

"*About* 101? That's interesting. One hundred and one pounds is a pretty exact number. So I assume undressed, you're 'about' …"

"Ninety-eight."

"Ninety-eight pounds. So what's that about, ninety-eight pounds? Why aren't you eating? Or are you suffering from some sort of health issue I should be aware of?"

"I don't have AIDS!" I blurt out.

"I didn't ask if you had AIDS, but it's interesting you would go there. Are you sure you don't have AIDS?"

"Of course I'm sure. It would be physically impossible. I'm just poor."

Of course I can't leave her hanging after saying something like that, so I give Dr. Jenkins an abbreviated bit of backstory about my life so far. I stick to the abridged version, of course, telling her only that I wrote a poem in high school that got made into a hit song, and that the money has finally run out. "I don't eat now because I don't have any money for food," I say.

"Do you have a job?"

"I've never had a job. I never graduated high school. I've just been living off song royalties."

"How did you expect to be able to pay for these sessions?"

I say that her flyer said it was good for two free consultations, and then I admit I hadn't thought of anything beyond that. "You're supposed to be good about helping people solve immediate problems. Why don't you start by giving me a hand with that?"

There is a smart-ass tone to my voice that I immediately regret. Dr. Jenkins does not seem to be bothered by it. In fact, she plunges right in and goes to work on my most pressing needs. Whipping out a legal pad, she starts making lists. It takes her only a second to determine that I'm not receiving any form of social assistance. She tells me that if I were, then she would be able to get some government aid to pick up the cost of our sessions. "And there's no reason for you to go hungry for lack of money," she says. "I'm sure you qualify for food stamps, and there's a food bank over in Covina where you can get a bag of groceries once a week for free."

She notices the mortified look on my face. "You came here looking for help. Is there some sort of problem?"

"I can't go on welfare," I say. "It's humiliating."

"More humiliating than walking around looking like *that*?" she says harshly, holding out her upturned palm at me as if she were serving me up to myself.

Well, that's a slap in the face. I press my lips together hard but my chin quivers a bit. I can't help it.

She rips a page out of her legal pad and hands it to me. It has four agencies and their contact information written on it. "Here's your first assignment. I want you to go out right now and contact all these organizations and start getting the help that you – *as a taxpaying citizen* – are entitled to receive. There's nothing humiliating about it. It's your right. You're having nightmares because your life is a nightmare. You look like a walking corpse. Get yourself some help before you end up an actual corpse."

I am so stunned by her sudden frontal attack that I can't mount a protest. Still, there are a few practical matters standing in the way. "But I can't call these phone numbers or go to these places," I say.

"Why not?"

"I don't have any change for the pay phone or money for the bus."

Dr. Patty Jenkins takes a coin pouch out of her purse and hands me ten quarters she says she had been saving up for the laundromat. I accept them reluctantly, saying, "I'll pay you back."

"Keep the money. You can pay me back by contacting all these agencies this afternoon and then coming back for another session with me, same time tomorrow. That's not a request. It's a command."

I spend the rest of the afternoon at the county department of social services. They give me an application to fill out and assign me a case worker. It bothers me that no one I speak to expresses any sort of surprise or doubt that I'm asking for social assistance. Is Dr. Jenkins right? Do I really look like some sort of walking corpse to these people? It's enough to give a person a major depressive episode.

I go back to Dr. Jenkins the next day, same time. Today she is wearing pleated khaki pants and a big, cranberry-colored turtleneck. I'm wearing the same clothes I wore yesterday. I had thought about wearing something else, but I'm feeling a little spiteful and a little dramatic after she made me apply for welfare and food stamps. If she's going to turn me into a poor person, then I'm going to play the part of a poor person. That'll show her.

She doesn't give any indication that she gives a shit about what I'm wearing.

We start the session with my report of how things went yesterday at the aid agency. She simply nods and says, "Good." Then she asks, "So what did you dream about last night?"

"I don't know. I don't remember."

"That's progress, at least," she says. "So tell me something. The other therapists you had, what were they like?"

"I never said I've been in therapy before."

She smiles. "But you have been, haven't you?"

"How do you know?"

"You don't act like someone who's never seen a therapist. This is old hat to you, right? So tell me, what was your last experience in therapy like?"

This is dangerous stuff, but what can I say? She's going to worm it out of me one way or another, so I might as well tell her. "After what happened with the last guy, I really didn't want to go through all that again. The only reason I considered seeing you was that your flyer said you didn't dwell on the past and just worked on what's going on right now."

"I still need to know about your psychiatric history. So what happened with the last guy? How long ago was it?"

"A year and a half, two years ago," I say. "It was not long after I took a compulsive eating seminar at the Beverly Hilton."

Dr. Jenkins suppresses a smile, but I notice it anyway.

"Yeah, yeah, yeah. So I used to have an eating disorder, okay? I don't have one anymore. Just get over that. It was just that during the seminar, they led us through this regression visualization thing and I remembered an incident from my childhood that I hadn't thought about in years."

"I assume you're referring to that stalker you mentioned yesterday."

"Yeah. When I was ten, there was this guy who started telephoning me every afternoon after school when I was home by myself. It started off as a wrong number, but then he kept calling me day after day after day. He was a real sick fucker. He would make me participate in these kinky fantasy role-play phone sex games."

"He made you? If you only spoke on the phone, how could he make you do something like that?"

"He called and called and I had to answer the phone whenever it rang, because my mother used to call from work every afternoon to check on me and if I didn't answer the phone, she'd freak out. I would never know if it was her calling or him calling, so every time the phone rang, I'd have to pick up."

"But you could have hung up on him, or told your mother."

"I couldn't tell my mom. If I told her that I had told an obscene phone caller all sorts of personal stuff about us, like our address and that I was alone every afternoon, she would have murdered me. After a couple of months, I did work up the courage to start hanging up on him, but that made him mad, and eventually he came over to the house."

"And what happened?"

"Well that's why I went to see this last therapist. During the compulsive eating workshop, I remembered everything that happened to me up until the moment when the caller came over to the house. The memories up until that point were really vivid. But I could only remember what happened up to the point where the guy came to the front door. After that it was just a blank. It started driving me crazy. How could I not remember what happened next when the memories up to that point were so clear? I became convinced that I was repressing something terrible, so I looked around and found a doctor in Westwood who specialized in regression and unlocking repressed memories. His name was Dr. Humbert Morgan. Have you heard of him?"

"Actually, yes," she says, and sits up a little straighter in her seat.

"So Humbert starts putting me under hypnosis and regresses me and I remember all sorts of things I hadn't thought about in years. I remembered Dad kissing Uncle Arby. I remembered Mom sending me to Cub Scouts in drag. I remembered Granny giving me enemas. I remembered all this crazy shit I really didn't want to think about ever again. Then, after a year of sessions, Humbert regressed me to the day when the obscene phone caller came over to my house."

Dr. Jenkins says nothing. She simply stares at me. It's hard to tell, but I think I can see some sympathy in her eyes. I can't stop myself, so I keep talking. I tell her the whole story of the obscene caller from the very beginning. When I get to the part Humbert Morgan helped me to remember, I just keep on going.

"It was late in the afternoon," I say. "I was all alone in the house after school. That pervert on the phone had been calling me and calling me and I kept hanging up on him, but I still had to answer every time the phone rang in case it was Mom. Finally, I got really mad and I yelled at him and told him I hated him and told him not to call me anymore. The phone rang again and I answered it and he said, 'I'm coming over.' I got terrified. I knew he knew my name and address. I didn't know what to do. I didn't know who to call for help. I couldn't call my mom. I couldn't call the police. I couldn't call anybody. When fifteen or twenty minutes went by and nothing happened, I started to think he was just lying or had changed his mind and I was so relieved.

"That's when I heard a motorcycle pull up in our driveway. We had a brass mail flap in our front door and I went and poked it open with my fingers so I could peek out. I saw a man in a motorcycle helmet and a leather jacket, and I freaked out.

I made sure the bolt in the front door was locked and that the chain was on. Then I just sat down on the ground and waited.

"The motorcycle guy came up to the door and knocked. I just kept quiet. He called my name. He told me to open the door. He started turning the knob and pushing against the door, but the door was locked pretty tight. He rang the doorbell over and over again and kept saying my name. Then he said, 'Fine. Have it your way,' and he left.

"That's when I remembered that there were other ways to get into the house. Anybody could open the garage door and come in through the kitchen. Anybody could go through the back gate and come into the living room through the patio. I couldn't believe I was that stupid to leave those doors open. When I heard him walking away, I jumped up and ran into the kitchen and locked the door that went out to the garage. Then I raced to the living room to lock the sliding glass doors to the patio, but it was too late.

"He was already coming through the sheers.

"I was so scared I just froze, then he lunged at me and grabbed me by the arm. I struggled and yelled but I couldn't get loose. I remember we bumped into the end table beside the sofa and knocked over the bronze lamp Mom got at a swap meet. He flipped me around and put me in a headlock and I just couldn't struggle anymore.

"'Relax, relax,' he said. Then he moved us over to the couch and sat us both down with me on his lap. His right arm was still wrapped around my neck. Then with his free hand, he took off his helmet and tossed it on the carpet. He was still behind me, so I couldn't see his face. He kept me in a choke hold and began to stroke my hair and whisper in my ear. 'Calm down, Cary,' he said. 'Calm down. We're just going to have a little fun. A little fun, okay?' He was breathing in my ear. His breath smelled like cigarettes. Cigarettes and beer."

I stop. I'm seeing it all so clearly in my head. It makes my skin crawl. Dr. Jenkins senses that I want to tell it all, so she says, "Go on."

I tell her the rest of the story.

I remember that after he told me we were going to have a little fun, he relaxed his grip around my neck and lay me back on the sofa. That's when I saw his face for the first time. He looked like he was in his twenties. He had lank, blond hair that was shoulder length and a little greasy. His teeth were crooked and he had a big chip in his front tooth. He had a few days of beard stubble and his eyes were brilliant blue.

He began by sliding his hand under my t-shirt, running his fingers over one of my nipples and then around to the small of my back. Raising me up to a sitting position, he slowly pulled my shirt off over my head and then shrugged off his leather jacket and whipped off his own white t-shirt. He was very skinny. I could see the bones of his ribs. His chest was hairy, which I found kind of exciting even though I was still really scared.

While taking off his shirt, he let go of me for just a second and I made a lunge to get away from him, only I wasn't fast enough. With his knee he pinned one of my legs firmly to the couch cushion, then quickly grabbed me by the shoulders and flipped me face down and climbed on top of me.

"So you are going to make this fun for me," he said. "Cary, Cary, Cary! You've got a little fight in you!"

That's when he plunged his hand down the front of my pants and got me by the balls. His fingers started stroking my testicles and had started to grope further between my legs toward my anus.

Suddenly there was a loud "dong!" like the sound of a bell. The guy's hands stopped moving and he got really heavy on top of me. I could feel his body being rolled off of me and then heard it go "whump" on the ground.

I sat up and saw my mother standing over the sofa, holding the brass lamp in her grip like a baseball bat.

"Get in the bathroom and lock the door. Go!" she hissed.

I jumped up and did exactly what she said.

"I don't know what happened next," I say to Dr. Jenkins. "I stayed in the bathroom a long time. After a while, I heard a motorcycle start up and then drive off. The house got really quiet so I came out and saw that the living room was all put back together, the guy was gone, the motorcycle was gone, my mom's car was not in the garage."

Dr. Jenkins nods like she is not surprised one bit. "Just like nothing happened at all," she says.

"Yeah, it was weird," I say. "You know, I've thought about it and thought about it, and the only explanation I can come up with is either the guy came to and she made him leave, or …" I have a little trouble finishing the thought.

"Or what?"

"Or she killed him. She put on his helmet and jacket and drove the motorcycle somewhere, ditched the clothes and the bike in the neighborhood, walked back home, and then put him in her car and drove away to get rid of his body."

"That's quite a murder mystery," she says. She seems more exasperated than intrigued.

"Why are you looking at me like that?"

"Let me ask you something. You remembered all this during a session with Dr. Morgan, right?"

"Yeah."

"Let me guess how the session went," she says. "I'm thinking he said to you something like, 'When the man came through the curtains, did he grab you?' and you said yes and then he went, 'And did you struggle? Did he keep you from getting away somehow?' and you said yes. Am I on the right track?"

I don't know where she's going with this line of questioning, but I have to admit to her that it did sort of go that way. "It was a regression. We'd been doing stuff like that for a year. He would take me back through all these old memories step by step."

"No, what he did was implant all those old memories in you step by step. Humbert Morgan's recovered memory therapy is infamous for creating in his patients something called false memory syndrome."

"What are you saying?"

"Cary, there has been study after study which has shown that therapy using hypnosis, age regression, and sometimes even drugs to dredge up all these supposedly repressed memories, actually creates false memories in the patients' minds."

"No, this was a real memory," I insist. "I remember it as clearly as if it happened yesterday."

"I don't doubt that one bit. Those memories are in your brain. They're hard-wired now. They seem terribly real to you, but they're not. We all have memories that are inaccurate. We all misremember details of things that happened to us, but most people don't remember with epic clarity things that happened to us twenty years ago. It's not possible."

"I'm not making all this up," I say. "That guy called me almost every day! Then he came over and attacked me."

Dr. Jenkins leans forward in her chair. She takes off her round glasses and tosses them on the coffee table. "Cary, listen to me," she says. "I can guarantee you that almost everything you think you recalled about your past during your sessions with Dr. Morgan didn't actually occur. He put those memories into your head. If you want, I can copy you some of the scientific literature about false memory syndrome. You can read all about it yourself. It's a real thing, and you've got it."

"No, you're wrong."

"You think it's a coincidence that after Humbert Morgan hears that you have this gay dad who abandons you, that you suddenly remember in minute detail an elaborate scenario in which you and your mother get murderous revenge on an abusive father figure?"

"My dad wasn't like that! He wasn't a pervert. My dad and Uncle Arby were great. They never did anything like that to me. I'm telling you, the thing with the motorcycle guy was real."

"Cary! Stop it! I can't be any more blunt than this: it's all a fantasy. *None of that stuff* ever happened to you."

CHAPTER TEN

1994

At the front desk of the Hotel Olcott I ask for my mail. Angel, the concierge, looks in my slot and hands me an envelope that I've been waiting for. It's my application for Brunch Buddies. I'm excited to open it, but at the same time I dread what's inside. Still, I've made up my mind to try dating, and Brunch Buddies is as good a way as any to begin.

"Thanks, Angel," I say, pronouncing his name the English way instead of the Spanish "*On-hell*." I know enough Spanish to feel a little weird calling him that, but "Ain-jell" is what he prefers, so all of us in the building go along with it. More cherub than angel, he's short and pudgy with thick glasses and always a big smile. I'm sure at Christmastime, he makes out like a bandit with holiday tips.

I take the elevator back up to my apartment on the tenth floor. I've been in New York for six months already, but taking an elevator is still a treat for me. I enjoy many little things about living in Manhattan: elevators, certainly – especially the old-fashioned ones like we have at the Olcott, being able to walk anywhere you want to go, riding subway trains, winters with snow, buying a cup of coffee from a guy in an aluminum wagon on a street corner, going for a jog in Central Park, the anonymity of crowds, never having to worry about earthquakes. Although I've spent my whole life in the Los Angeles basin, I feel so much more at home in New York than I ever did in Southern California. Why did it take me so long to move here?

Well, money, for one thing. But now, thanks to a passing whim of Jay Leno, I have been rescued from abject poverty and can breathe easily once again. At least as long as this latest infusion of money holds out.

I let myself back into my apartment. Whereas I only suspected that my last apartment in West Hollywood had at one time been a motel, there is no doubt that in New York I am now living in an actual hotel. The Olcott on West 72nd Street was built in the 1920s and still takes some transient guests, but most of the tenants, like me, rent our rooms monthly. There are many advantages to living in an apartment hotel. For one, I didn't have to move to New York with even a stick of furniture. The room came fully furnished; it even had a TV. I'm entitled to maid service once a week, so I get fresh sheets and towels, and I don't have to scrub the toilet or the bathtub.

The only part of living in a hotel room that has taken me a little time to get used to is the rudimentary kitchen setup. Actually, my apartment has no kitchen to speak of. The management has kindly provided me with something they call a "pantry," which is basically the room's former coat closet fitted with a half-size refrigerator and a two-burner hot plate. I have a saucepan, a plate, a glass, and some cutlery. I have to use the bathroom sink to wash my dishes. Needless to say, I don't grocery shop much and I do all my cooking with my old electric kettle.

I sit down at the desk in the room and hesitate a moment before tearing open the envelope from Brunch Buddies. I had seen an ad for this gay dating service last week in a copy of the *Village Voice* that someone had left behind on the subway. There were some other ads for ways to meet guys, too, but most of them sounded creepy or kinky, or both. I couldn't imagine myself joining something called the New York Jacks, the Circle Jerks, or M.A.N. (Males au Naturel). However, meeting someone at a restaurant for brunch sounded innocent enough. At least it required clothing – unless there was some sort of urban gay subtext I was missing here.

The envelope contained a welcome letter and a multi-page application. The letter said that for a $60 fee, Brunch Buddies would provide me with the phone numbers of six other members who match what I'm looking for. I assume that conversely I would be what these other guys were looking for, too, although this isn't stated explicitly.

I glance over the application. It has fifty questions I have to answer. Not only does Brunch Buddies want to know my name, address, and phone number, I also have to state my age, height, weight, hair color, eye color, profession, ethnicity, physique, whether I smoke, drink or use drugs, and the amount of body hair I have. I have to state my levels of interest in theater, movies, music, sports, politics, and religion. Then I have to answer a whole bunch of questions about what degrees of all these criteria I will tolerate in a potential Brunch Buddy. They also want a current photo.

Where am I going to get a photo of myself? I don't own a camera and I certainly don't keep scrapbooks. There's a photo booth at Woolworth's. Maybe they'll accept that.

I fold up the application and put it back in the envelope. I'll fill it out this afternoon. At least that's what I tell myself.

***

Today I get to start a new notebook. That's always exciting. I have discovered that I write better if there is some sort of ritual involved. For instance, I only write in spiral-bound notebooks, the kind that kids use for school with the spiral on the side, not the steno pad kind with the spiral at the top. Why? Because it's now part of the ritual. Yesterday, I came to the last page of my notebook with the Bugs Bunny cover and now I'm cracking open my pristine new notebook with the Marvel Comics theme. I'm not a big comic book fan. I can recognize Spider Man and the Hulk on the cover image, but the rest of the superheroes in the montage are a mystery to me. The guy in the white tights is totally hot, though.

Another part of my writing ritual is time and location. I write every day from 10 a.m. until 2 p.m. at Café La Fortuna on West 71st Street, just around the block from my apartment. I like it here. The exposed brick walls are covered with a jumble of framed vinyl LPs and autographed photos of famous people (at least I assume they're famous – who the hell is Titta Ruffo?) The vintage ceiling is made of embossed tin and the owners play opera all day long. They say that John Lennon and Yoko Ono used to come here all the time. Now I'm the one who always comes here.

About the only thing I got from my very brief time with Dr. Patty Jenkins in West Hollywood was a well-deserved kick in the pants to stop moaning about being a fraud posing as a poet. "Oh just shut up and write!" she snapped at me. At first I was angry at her for speaking to me like that, but after all, I was doing something called "Solution Focused Brief Therapy" so what did I expect? What could be more solution focused than "Shut up and write"? Years ago, after Marla Wylie forced me to write her some song lyrics for her act, I had tried to force myself to write 100 poems. Things went well for about a week, then after poem number twelve, I quit and hadn't written anything since.

Suddenly, thanks to Marla Wylie again, I'm back on track. In the six months I've been in New York, I've filled up twelve spiral notebooks with poems, memories, and countless paragraphs of internal monologue. I just keep my pen moving and write down whatever my brain vomits out in the moment. It's all unreadable, but it feels great. Now and then, I come up with something pretty good. It's sort of like when a zinnia pops out of a weed patch.

Marla has turned about ten of my poems into songs so far, but it was that first one, "My Karma Ran Over My Dogma" that has been the most successful for her. She sang it in clubs around the country for five or six years. The melody was catchy enough that it eventually got her a recording contract. For a couple of weeks, our song even charted. Now that I've had two songs played on the radio, I have a much harder time convincing myself that I'm a fraud or a one-hit wonder. If I can do it twice, then I must have some talent for it, right?

I've lingered at Café La Fortuna later than usual today because I'm expecting a date. I'm now down to Brunch Buddy number six – my last match before I have to shell out another sixty bucks. My five previous Brunch Buddy dates have all been awkward, boring, or, in one case, a complete disaster. Three of the guys were far too old for me and two were far too young. Where are the people my own age? Am I the last thirty-five-year-old gay guy in Manhattan?

The guy I've arranged to meet this afternoon says he's in his thirties. I am now experienced enough to take this claim with a grain of salt. He might be thirty-two. He might be seventy-two. He also alleges to be of medium build, hairy-chested, and, like me, a writer. I haven't seen a picture of him, and I forgot to note whether he was Caucasian or not, but his name sounds Jewish, so it seems unlikely that I'm about to be having coffee with another black drag queen or Puerto Rican hair stylist.

When we spoke briefly on the phone, he told me that I would recognize him because he'd be wearing a blue shirt. I now realize how unhelpful that clue is. The last four men who came through the door were wearing shirts some shade of blue. Two of the guys really got my hopes up, but they weren't here for me. (In fact, they were here for each other.) And one guy passing by briefly worried me. He did look like he was Jewish and in his mid-thirties, but he was morbidly obese. I know I shouldn't be judgmental, but just looking at that fat guy gave me PTSD. Since I used to be him, I certainly didn't want to date him. Thank goodness, he wasn't here to meet me.

At last my date walks up to the table and extends his hand. "Cary Scott? Is that you?"

I am transfixed. "Hi. Howard? Uh ... have a seat."

Howard Solomon is more or less exactly as he described himself, which instantly inclines me to like him. At least he's honest. As for his appearance, Howard's not handsome exactly, but still good-looking. His face is thin and his profile is definitely Jewish (which I absolutely find attractive). He has thin lips and curly brown hair which he keeps short because it has started to recede. His blue Chambray shirt is open down to the third button so I can see his claim to chest hair is accurate, too.

I think he's dreamy.

"I'm so glad it's you," he says. "I had a little bit of a scare there for a minute. I was standing outside for a few minutes and I saw this whale of a guy go in and I thought, 'Fuck! I hope that's not Cary.'"

Although I had had the same reaction when I saw the obese man, it irks me to hear Howard being so judgmental of fat people. I used to be that fat guy, and I still feel like I am that fat guy, so it feels like Howard is judging me. Then he smiles at me and I can tell that he really is pleased that I turned out to be the one he had the date with, so I forgive him everything.

Howard orders an Italian pastry and a cappuccino. I order some more peppermint tea and ask for two slices of whole wheat toast, unbuttered, with one pack of strawberry jam. Quickly doing the math in my head, I estimate that Howard will be consuming somewhere between 720 to 800 calories, while I'm having closer to 250. He seems to have very little body fat, so I assume Howard is one of those people with a fast metabolism and he can eat anything. That's irksome, too, but that's more my problem than his.

He notices my notebook and pen and says, "It said in your profile that you were a writer. What do you write?"

"Not much," I say. "What about you?"

"I freelance. I write for a lot of magazines. Mostly trade mags, but I've had a couple of pieces in *Runners' World*, and the *Advocate*. A couple of months ago I got a job fact-checking at *New York*."

"Wow. The *New Yorker*?"

"No, *New York* Magazine."

"Oh, okay. What's fact-checking?"

Howard looks surprised at this question. "You're not in journalism?"

"No. I'm a lyricist."

"Oh, that's cool. I had no idea."

I really don't want to talk about myself, so I do my best to keep the conversation focused on Howard. "So what's fact-checking?" I ask again.

"Oh. Yeah. Whenever someone writes a magazine story, the magazine's fact-checking department first has to go over the piece word by word to make sure that everything in the story is true. The writer has to turn over all his research and interviews, and the fact-checker has to verify everything. You'd be surprised how sloppy some writers are. They take things out of context. They doctor quotes. They make statements they can't substantiate except to say it's 'common knowledge.' You have to be very careful when you're fact-checking. These guys will try to pull anything over on you. I just checked this one piece where the writer did a profile of this ghetto kid who sold drugs – and it turned out the kid didn't even exist. He was a composite character."

"What's that?"

"That's where a writer takes things that happened to two or three or four people and blends them all together to create one character. There was this one guy who actually won a Pulitzer Prize doing that. Of course they took the prize away when the truth came out."

I find out pretty quickly that it's easy to get Howard to talk about himself, so I just keep asking him leading questions and he rambles on and on, which is just fine with me. I don't have to worry about awkward silences with Howard Solomon.

He tells me that he's originally from Scranton, Pennsylvania, and has an older sister with multiple sclerosis. He moved to New York a year ago after graduating from Penn State at the ripe old age of thirty-one. Apparently he spent most of his twenties just bartending and working out, but couldn't bear the thought of living that sort of lifestyle when he was middle aged (translation: a minute over thirty), so he enrolled in journalism school. Hearing this, I definitely don't want to reveal that I never graduated high school. I pray that Howard doesn't ask me where I went to college, but it turns out to be a wasted prayer because Howard doesn't ask me anything about myself at all.

That's not exactly true. After about an hour and a half at Café La Fortuna, he does ask me if I live in the area. "Just around the block," I answer. "On 72nd Street."

"You mean in the Dakota?" he says with a mixture of awe and high expectation. He's referring to the enormous, sooty old building on the corner of 72nd Street and Central Park West where John Lennon used to live. Yoko Ono still lives there, which is odd since Lennon was gunned down on the sidewalk right in front. Also, the Dakota's famous for being the setting of the horror movie *Rosemary's Baby*. That's one creepy building.

"No," I say. "I'm a few buildings down, at the Hotel Olcott."

"You mean one of those old hotels in the middle of the block?"

"Yeah," I say hesitantly. I don't know whether to be offended or not at his characterization of where I live. Howard was obviously hoping that I was rich enough to live in the celebrity haunted house. The Dakota is wildly expensive. Is he disappointed that I might turn out to be some sort of loser who lives in a furnished hotel room? However, I soon find out where he's going with this line of thought.

"Most of the buildings on that block were built in the twenties. I'm a big Art Deco fan. If yours is one of those old Art Deco apartment buildings, I'd love to see it."

I shrug. "I don't know much about architecture," I say. "People keep calling the building 'pre-war.' I have no idea which war they're talking about, but I guess it could be Art Deco. You can come by sometime if you want."

"How about now?"

As he asks this, I feel the toe of his shoe touch the toe of my shoe. It's obvious the touch is not accidental. I feel a jolt of excitement go up my leg. My heart starts to pound. I don't know what to say, so I simply nod in answer to his question.

Out on the sidewalk in front of the café, Howard Solomon draws me toward him and gives me a long, passionate kiss right there in front of everyone. The kiss is amazing, but I feel self-conscious at such a public display of affection. How embarrassing! People will be staring. We must be creating quite a scene right here in the middle of West 71st Street.

But we're not. No one cares. Not a single New Yorker gives us a second glance.

***

I date Howard Solomon for a couple of weeks before it dawns on me that he drinks a lot. It's not a problem, really. He never gets really drunk, but he's never really sober, either. At times, I admit that I consider this to be an advantage. Especially when it comes to sex.

Yes, Howard was my first. Of course, I never want him to find that out. The afternoon of our first date, the excitement of being with a man for the first time proved a little too much for me, and I ejaculated about a minute after we got back to my room. Fortunately, Howard found this hilarious and kind of sweet, and asked to see me again the following night.

In order to prevent such an embarrassing thing happening a second time, the next afternoon I went down to a little shop in Chelsea that sold used gay books and porno mags, and I bought a 1977 copy of *The Joy of Gay Sex*. What an eye-opener that was! I had no idea how many things you could do with two penises. Also, I had no idea how many things I was going to *refuse* to do with two penises – not to mention a couple of other orifices.

Our second attempt at sex went much better – or at least lasted much longer. I'm good at following instruction manuals. Howard seemed pleased. At least he kept coming back for more.

However, tonight in bed things are taking longer than usual. Howard had a few drinks during dinner, and then he wanted to go out to a bar afterwards where he had two or three more beers. I don't drink much. Never have. I don't particularly like the taste of alcohol and I don't like the feeling of being drunk. Now the glass of white wine I had at the restaurant has given me a headache and Howard is so sleepy from all those beers that he can hardly maintain an erection. After fifteen minutes of fiddling around, we decide to give up and just cuddle and talk.

"Why don't you ever sing me any of your songs?" he asks. He's drunk, so I know I don't have to give him a serious answer.

"I'm not a singer," I reply.

"Well you could play me a tape or take me to hear someone else singing your stuff. What kind of music do you write?"

"I don't write music either. I can't even read music. I just write poems and people make them into songs."

"People like who?"

I don't want to answer the question so I hesitate before speaking. I consider saying something evasive, but I'm afraid it might not have the desired effect. Yes, I'm embarrassed about the songs I've been successful with, but if I continue to keep everything a secret, Howard is going to come to the conclusion that I've been deceiving him and that I'm not a writer at all. It's one thing to have people think you're a no-talent fraud, but being considered a liar is worse. I decide to finally come clean and tell Howard everything about my past. And the fact that he's drunk at the moment makes the decision even easier.

"There was a song on the radio last year called 'My Karma Ran Over My Dogma.' Did you ever hear that one?"

"Oh my God. I saw some bizarre woman sing that on Jay Leno. You wrote that?"

"Yeah, that was me. Marla Wylie and I were at an artist colony together in New Mexico. She's been trying to make it as a song-writer for years. Now she's a big star. In fact, Marla's appearance on Leno was the reason I was able to move to New York. She sold about a hundred thousand albums after appearing on that show."

"What else have you written?"

"Only one other thing, but it's not worth mentioning."

"How come?"

"It's just … It was a long time ago. You wouldn't know it anyway."

"Try me. I listen to everything."

"No, it's also a little embarrassing."

Howard props himself up on one elbow in bed and looks at me. "I've told you about every single story I've ever published. Even the really stupid ones. If I can tell you about the piece I wrote about my trip to the sperm bank, you can tell me the name of a song."

"'Lookey, Lookey,'" I say. "There. Are you happy now?"

"What?"

"See, I knew you never heard of it."

"The song about the girl in the shower room? By Kitty Kat something."

"Kitty Belle Crawford. You know it?"

"Oh my God. I bought that record when I was in junior high. Just thinking about that baseball team in the shower used to give me a boner. You wrote that? How old are you?"

"You know how old I am. I was fifteen when I wrote that poem … oh, my God, that was twenty years ago! Twenty years. That doesn't even seem possible."

Howard snuggles close and wraps his arms around me, then he begins to sing softly and sweetly like a lullaby: "*Lookey how she comes again, runnin' past them naked men … Woo! Woo! Woo!*"

It's so endearing I have a hard time being embarrassed. I kiss Howard on the forehead to say thank you but he's already fallen asleep.

I make a mental note to tell him in the morning that Kitty Belle wrote that asinine Woo-woo-woo chorus, not me.

***

My "Lookey, Lookey" confession ushers in a new era of full disclosure between Howard and me. For the first time in my life, I feel I have someone I can tell anything to – someone, that is, who is not in the psychiatric profession. During walks in Central Park and long post-coital conversations I tell Howard the story of my life. He doesn't judge me. He doesn't act shocked. He just wants to hear it all. He asks me so many questions that at times I feel like I'm being interviewed for something. I remind myself that he's a journalist, and it's probably just a habit of his by now.

He seems especially fascinated by my time with Dr. Humbert Morgan and the whole concept of recovered memory therapy. In fact, he's so interested in the topic that he's been doing some research into it and shares with me what he's learned.

"Memory is really interesting," he says to me as we walk down to the theater district to catch a Broadway show. "You know there's actually two kinds of memory in your brain – short term and long term? For instance, say I tell you a telephone number. You'll probably be able to repeat it back to me right away or use it to dial a phone, but if you misdial or there's some sort of interruption, you'll probably ask me to repeat the number because you've now forgotten it. The number went into your short-term memory and then it just disappeared."

I love listening to Howard's monologues and by now I'm pretty good at keeping them going. Besides, this is pretty interesting. "So how come we don't just forget everything?" I ask.

"We do forget almost everything. We forget stuff that's unimportant, and we forget stuff that's important. And once something is forgotten, there's no way of getting that memory back 100 percent. Everything we've ever experienced isn't recorded in our head like on some sort of videotape. There's a spot in the middle of your brain called the hippocampus. Memories first go into a short-term storage area in the front of your brain, then the hippocampus takes those memories – not all of them, of course, but some of them – and moves them into long-term storage spread out all over your brain."

"How could scientists even know that?"

"Well, I read this really sad story about a guy who had a stroke in his hippocampus and it left him without the ability to store any more long-term memories. He could remember a lot of stuff about his past, but he couldn't remember anything new. His life was one constant 'now.' For instance, every time his wife left the room and came back in, he'd act like he hadn't seen her in years. Poor guy."

"Poor wife," I say. "That must have been exhausting for her."

"I didn't think of that. Hey, but you know it could have worked out to her advantage. Like if she ever got fed up with him, she could just leave him and not feel any guilt. I mean, twenty minutes later the guy would've forgotten all about her anyway, right?"

"Even if he wouldn't remember it, she might still feel guilty for abandoning a brain-damaged husband. I know I'd certainly feel guilty."

"I wouldn't," says Howard. "It'd be like a Get Out of Jail Free card."

We have tickets tonight for the musical version of *Sunset Boulevard* at the Minskoff Theater. The Minskoff is one of the two or three modern theaters on Broadway. Built in the early 1970s, it feels more out-of-date than all the 100-year-old theaters that surround it. It's also bigger than most of the old Broadway houses. The auditorium holds about 1,500 seats, and since we got our tickets earlier this afternoon at the TKTS discount booth, our seats are way back in row L of the mezzanine – the furthest you can get from the stage. From that far away, Glenn Close playing Norma Desmond is about the size of my thumb, but she's so massively over-miked it's like she's right in my face. The good thing is we get a great view of the big split-screen effect when Norma Desmond's mansion lifts off the ground and we see a crowded party scene playing simultaneously directly below. The bad thing is I can't enjoy the scene because seeing Glenn Close's house rise into the air with her still in it gives me a panic attack. A house floating in the air with no solid ground below it is like something out of my nightmares.

The curtain for intermission falls right after this upsetting sight, and I say to Howard that I'd like to go outside for a minute to get some air. We follow the smokers out to the sidewalk, and as we stand there flipping through our programs, a strange little man says to us, "It's going too slow tonight."

"What do you mean?" asks Howard.

"Usually it goes a lot faster. I've seen every performance so I know."

I look up from my program. There's something not right about the guy chatting us up. He's short and dumpy with thin straight hair. He looks like he's nearly fifty, but at the same time, in his jeans and plaid shirt buttoned up to his collar, he's childlike. I wonder if he's retarded, but then I silently upbraid myself because we don't call retarded people retarded anymore.

Howard seems amused by him. "How can you afford to see every performance? These tickets cost a fortune."

"I work for Glenn Close," he says. "I do stuff for her. I get stuff that she needs. I also work for Bernadette Peters. Do you know how old Bernadette Peters is? She's about sixty! Most people don't know that. Glenn Close is about sixty-five."

Okay, that's just crazy. I look over at Howard and it's clear he realizes this little guy is nuts, too. However, Howard perversely wants to have some fun with the situation.

"How did you meet Bernadette Peters?"

"I'm a songwriter," he says.

Howard's face breaks into a mischievous grin and looks at me as if to say, "Hey, look, a songwriter just like you!" and I give him an intense stare right back as if to say, "Shut up."

"My name is Jimmy Webb," the little guy says. "I've had a lot of hit songs."

"Really? Wow," says Howard. "Like what."

"'Up, Up and Away in my Beautiful Balloon,' 'Wichita Lineman,'" he says. "I've written hundreds of songs."

"Jimmy Webb? Yeah, I've heard of you. Nice to meet you Jimmy. I'm Howard and this is Cary."

"I knew Cary Grant, too," says Jimmy. "Dyan Cannon is seventy!"

Jimmy launches into an extended monologue about all the famous people that he knows, and the more he talks, the more ridiculous his stories become. He tells us that he is particularly close to Lily Tomlin and Jane Wagner and informs us of the little-known fact that Jane was the inventor of the pop-up Kleenex box. Evidently, Patti LuPone smokes menthol cigarettes and has invested all her money in three Kentucky Fried Chicken outlets, and Chita Rivera owns a parrot. Howard is clearly loving all this and stokes Jimmy like a boiler to keep the crazy tales coming.

The second act is about to begin so we follow the smokers back into the theater. I'm glad to have an excuse to get away from crazy Jimmy, but Howard seems reluctant to let him get away. He gives Jimmy one of his business cards and asks him to call him sometime.

Once Jimmy is out of earshot, I say to Howard, "Are you nuts? Why would you give him your card?"

"I've been trying to come up with a pitch for a magazine story," he says. "I think I might have finally found something."

***

Over the next couple of weeks, things start to go wrong between Howard and me, and for the life of me I cannot figure out why. We haven't had a fight, and he hasn't done or said anything to me to suggest that he might be seeing someone else. The only thing I can think of that has changed is that he did write that magazine pitch, and apparently whatever epiphany Jimmy provided him seems to have worked because he got the go-ahead from the *Atlantic Monthly* to write an article. It's the biggest break of his journalism career, so of course he's been immersed in research and writing, but it doesn't explain why he has become more aloof with every passing day.

Over coffee at Café La Fortuna one day he says to me, "You know I looked up Jimmy Webb."

"You mean that strange little guy actually called you?"

"No. I mean I looked up the real songwriter Jimmy Webb. He lives in Encino, California, and has a wife and six kids."

"So he's not some sort of weird gopher for Broadway divas?"

"No. For a while there, I was hoping that maybe he was. That would have made a great magazine story – you know, 'Grammy-winning songwriter goes nuts and haunts Broadway.' Didn't work out that way, though. Thank God I didn't pitch the piece until after I researched the real Jimmy Webb."

"So if that wasn't the story you sold to the *Atlantic*, then what was?"

"I don't like to talk about the things I'm writing while I'm writing them," says Howard. "It's bad luck."

"Oh, okay," I say.

"But it's interesting how easy it is to verify people's stories," he says.

"What do you mean?"

"I don't know. Fantasies, lies – it's not that hard to figure out the truth. Just sayin'."

I can't tell if he means that to sound ominous, or maybe even threatening. And if he is being portentous, who is he aiming all this at? Me? I can't think of any reason why Howard would need to speak to me that way. I have noticed he's been drinking a lot lately. Maybe I should find a way to encourage him to cut back a little because he's getting creepy.

I don't have much time or opportunity to suggest anything to him, however. By the end of the week, our relationship seems to be over. I say "seems" because we don't have an official breakup. He just removes himself from my life one day. Howard doesn't phone me or return any of my calls. In fact, he even changes his phone number and gets an unlisted one. When I go over to his brownstone, I see that his name has been taken off the buzzer. Did he move? I never find out because I don't press the button. I just go home.

The message is clear: Poof! I'm forgotten. Howard's hippocampus hasn't moved me from short-term to long-term memory storage. Either that or he never existed and Howard's just a false memory I've got stuck in my brain. That last thought was a joke, of course, although it occurs to me that if someone were to ask me right now to prove that I had a boyfriend named Howard Solomon, I'd have a pretty hard time doing it.

Three months later, I'm walking down to Times Square by myself to see what's for sale at the TKTS booth, when passing by a corner newsstand, the cover of the latest *Atlantic Monthly* catches my eye. *Mis-remembrance of Things Past: False Memory Syndrome and the Dark Side of 'Recovery' by Howard Solomon.*

What?!

I buy a copy and I stand there in front of the booth just holding the magazine, staring at the cover. Did Howard use me as research for a magazine story? Is that why he was asking me all those questions about my sessions with Dr. Humbert Morgan? Is the magazine story about me? Is that why Howard cut off all contact between us?

I sit down on the curb beside the newsstand and open the magazine to Howard's article. All of my questions are answered in the first couple of paragraphs:

> In a furnished hotel room, a lonely man sits and writes the story of his life in journal after journal. He fills his

notebooks with memories of child abuse, morbid obesity, anorexia nervosa, encounters with celebrities, personal fame, great wealth, self-crucifixion, rape, and even murder.

He's thirty-five years old and has never held a job. He's never graduated high school. He's never been married or even gone on a date. His lifetime of exciting memories are real to him, but his memories are not real. They are disturbing fantasies implanted in his brain by a therapist.

He is a victim of FMS – False Memory Syndrome.

In the United States, thousands of patients are currently undergoing recovered memory therapy (RMT) to recover repressed traumas their therapists believe are the cause of numerous mental and physical illnesses. However, recent research indicates that RMT actually produces fantasies that the patient and the therapist misinterpret as memories.

RMT does not recover memories; it creates false ones.

The article then goes on to cite a couple of other cases of people who have used recovered memory therapy to find out why they are unhappy, unloved, or neurotic. As a courtesy to his subjects, Howard inserts a brief disclaimer saying that he has used pseudonyms for all of the patients profiled in this article to protect their privacy. Quickly scanning ahead, I see that when he comes back to my story, he calls me "Gary." Thanks a lot, Howard.

The next part of the article reads:

While living in the Los Angeles area, "Gary" began therapy with Dr. Humbert Morgan, a Westwood psychotherapist. Morgan is currently the object of five civil lawsuits filed by former patients who claim that Morgan helped them to falsely remember incidents ranging from childhood physical abuse to sexual abuse – and in two cases even "Satanic ritual abuse" due to relatives supposedly participating in secret Satanic cults.

But FMS lawsuits against doctors are still relatively rare. According to the False Memory Syndrome Foundation in Philadelphia, more than 800 "repressed memory lawsuits" have so far been filed – with 90% of them being civil court cases filed by daughters accusing their fathers of past crimes.

To date, the most famous of one of these cases is that of George Franklin, a Minnesota man who was convicted of murder after his adult daughter claimed to have "remembered" her father raping and killing her best friend when she was nine years old. Most of the woman's so-called recovered memories were later proved to be peppered with details from inaccurate news reports of the period.

A judge overturned Franklin's murder conviction in 1993.

And like George Franklin's daughter, under the care of Dr. Morgan, Gary also became convinced that he had a parent who had committed murder.

Through month after month of guided age regression performed under hypnosis, Gary formed the false memory of being stalked by a pedophile when he was 10 years old, and of his mother killing the attacker when she walked in upon her son's homosexual rape in progress. There is no physical or even circumstantial evidence that such an event ever occurred or that such a stalker ever existed.

Not only is Gary convinced that he is the victim of such a horrific childhood trauma, but RMT has led him to the psychotic belief that he is the lyricist responsible for the novelty pop radio hits "Lookey, Lookey" recorded by Kitty Belle Crawford in 1974 and Marla Wylie's recent hit "My Karma Ran Over My Dogma."

Both of these songs are the work of lyricist R.B. Welch – not Gary's real name. Although Crawford died of breast cancer in 1990, and Wylie was unable to be contacted for this story, public records confirm the real R.B. Welch is a prosperous 49-year-old resident of Big Sur, California and not a 35-year old high school dropout living in a New York transient hotel. It is also unlikely that a recording artist of Kitty Belle Crawford's stature would have entered into a musical collaboration with a high school sophomore in 1974.

I feel punched in the gut.

I'm not sure which astounds me more: the fact that Howard could write something so cruel and so untrue about me, or the *Atlantic* allowed it to be printed. Whatever happened to all those magazine fact-checkers Howard told me about? Did the editors verify nothing that was written in this story?

I'm no longer in the mood to go to the TKTS booth, so I get up off the curb and start back home. As I walk slowly up

Broadway, my mind is racing about the article. It's so unfair! It's so untrue! I have to write a letter to the editor and demand a retraction. I feel like yelling at somebody. Maybe I should go straight to the magazine's offices and yell at the editor. I don't know if the *Atlantic* is published in New York City, though. In fact, since it's called the *Atlantic*, it could be anywhere on the Eastern Seaboard. The address has got to be printed somewhere in the magazine. I'll look for it as soon as I get home.

But then I stop short and consider for a moment that perhaps some of the stuff that Howard wrote about me just might be true. Now that I think about it, Humbert Morgan really was a charlatan. The whole reason I stopped going to him was that I suspected he was completely full of shit. But no. I'm not psychotic. He didn't get me to remember my stalker. I had that memory before I even went to him – in fact, remembering the stalker was the whole reason I sought Dr. Morgan out.

But then again, Dr. Morgan's regressions of the event sure made those memories crystal clear and apparently memory doesn't work that way. Damn. I don't know what to believe anymore. Are my memories false? I just don't know.

So what are some things I do know? I am certain that I wrote those stupid song lyrics. I have copies of my recording contracts, so I'm clearly not like that crazy guy who's walking around telling people he's Jimmy Webb. And so what if there is another guy somewhere named R.B. Welch? For a moment there, I had gotten excited thinking that Howard had inadvertently found my uncle Arby, but then I realized Welch is not such an uncommon surname. There must be hundreds of people with the last name Welch and the first initials R and B. For all I know, Raquel Welch's middle name is Brittany and she has a house in Big Sur.

Thinking of Raquel Welch prompts me to have a very disturbing thought. One of the things I used to enjoy when I was a kid was something on TV after school every day called *The 3:30 Movie*. Monday through Friday, Channel 7 would take films, mostly box office flops from the past couple decades, and severely edit them to fit into their 3:30 to 5 p.m. time slot (with lots of room for commercials). They would do theme weeks sometimes, and invariably once a year I would see an ad in *TV Guide* saying "It's Raquel Welch Week on the 3:30 Movie!" and I'd get excited. I loved Raquel Welch movies – *Fathom, Fantastic Voyage, One Million Years BC, Bedazzled, Bandolero!* Now that I think about it, after I drove that nail though my hand, it was Raquel Welch week, and I had watched all those films on the TV in the psych ward lounge. When Kitty Belle Crawford's agent wanted me to sign the contract, I told him I wanted to use my uncle's name, R.B. Welch.

It's a weird coincidence – the kind of coincidence that might lead some people to conclude that I never had an uncle and that I had simply made up the name on the spot. But I didn't! I couldn't have. I did not.

That would be crazy, right?

CHAPTER ELEVEN

1997

For the past year, I've started spending my days at the American Museum of Natural History. I go every day that it's open. It's quiet there, especially in the dimly lit Hall of Ocean Life with its ninety-four-foot-long blue whale suspended from the ceiling. Because it's too dark to read properly in the Hall of Ocean Life, in the mornings I go to the Hall of North American Mammals and sit in front of the diorama of two mountain lions lounging on the rim of the Grand Canyon and read the *New York Times* cover to cover. I bring my lunch from home and eat it outside, sitting on the steps beneath the statue of Teddy Roosevelt near the museum's Central Park West entrance, then I wind up in the Hall of Ocean Life in the afternoon, sitting on the bench under the whale, listening to cassette tapes of Karen Carpenter on my Sony Walkman.

Once I determined that coming here was going to be a daily event, I considered buying a membership to the museum but I never carried through with it. The suggested admission price to the museum is steep, but since it's only a "suggestion," you can pay anything you want to get inside. I pay twenty-five cents. At first I was a little embarrassed to offer such a small amount, but the ticket sellers never seemed to disapprove, and once they got to know me, we didn't need to have verbal interactions any longer. I'd push a quarter at them and they'd hand me the metal badge to pin on my collar.

I started performing this daily ritual a couple of weeks after Howard's article in the *Atlantic* came out. I came to the museum to write in my notebooks because Café La Fortuna was poisoned with the memory of Howard Solomon and so I needed a new place to write.

But the problem is, I can't write anymore. Every time I write about my experiences now, I find myself second-guessing whether it's a real memory or not. And it's not just writing. This new insanity is seeping into all aspects of my day. Not only do I wonder if I was really born in California, but I also wonder if I really brushed my teeth this morning. Both memories seem equally implausible sometimes. I swear if I wasn't crazy before I had recovered memory therapy, I sure am crazy now.

This lack of confidence in the memories stored in my head has given me an obsession with verifying whether all the events in my life have actually occurred or not. I'm satisfied that a memory is real only if I can lay my hands on some solid evidence that it happened. The fact that my toothbrush is wet indicates that I must have brushed my teeth and not merely dreamed that I did so. The metal tag on my collar indicates that I really did go to the Natural History Museum and didn't stay home. The museum changes the color of the tags every day, so I can even prove that this is today's tag and not yesterday's. In the same vein, I also collect and archive receipts for every purchase I make, no matter how minor. However, when it comes to questions of things that happened in my past life, proof is not so easy to obtain.

After my mother died, I had all of her possessions – including all the items she had saved from my childhood – hauled away to the dump. I'm regretting that now. Last week, I contacted the Hall of Records in Espada, California, for a copy of my birth certificate. It hasn't arrived yet. I contacted the town hall in Brierfield, Georgia, to get my parents' birth certificates, too. I can't tell if it's dread or excitement I'm feeling about seeing those documents.

In an effort to reclaim some of my childhood treasures, I've managed to buy cassette tapes of all my old Carpenters LPs. I haven't listened to the Carpenters in decades. After I was labeled "boner boy" in junior high, the only way I could get to sleep at night was by listening to Karen Carpenter crooning on my portable record player. It's weird to think that she died of anorexia in 1983, the same year I was morbidly obese in Taos, New Mexico. But being able to find old Carpenters LPs re-released on cassette doesn't really prove that I had ever been fat, or ever been to New Mexico, or had ever experienced public humiliation after having an erection in a locker room. It just proves that Karen Carpenter used to be a singer. Last weekend at the Strand Bookstore in the Village, I found a vintage Cub Scout manual from the 1960s which also brought back a lot of old memories. Or at least I think it did. The fact that the manual exists doesn't prove that I did.

I mull over all of this as I leave the museum at the end of the day. It's ironic that the one person I never want to see again is precisely the person I now need the most – namely, a magazine fact-checker. I turn and start walking south on Columbus Avenue, thinking about Howard Solomon. What would Howard do? How would Howard fact-check my life? (And why the hell didn't he do it when he should have, the stinking motherfucker?!)

Standing on the corner, waiting for the light to change, I remember that when we were together, Howard had recently bought a home computer and was hooked up to something called the World Wide Web. He was pretty excited about how much easier it was going to make his job. On one of our dates, he had nattered on about how Yahoo was better than Archie and Veronica. It was absolute gibberish to me. I couldn't understand how comic book characters could be used to look up answers stored on computers around the world. Now I'm thinking that maybe it's a good time for me to find out.

I know of a little storefront a couple of blocks north of the museum on Columbus Avenue that sells computers, so I turn around and start walking the opposite direction. I'm trying to remember what kind of computer Howard bought. I know he thought about getting an Apple Macintosh, but it cost too much money, so he got a ... what was it? It was like a fake IBM. I forget what it was called. Like a drone or a chrome or ...

Oh. My. God.

Here I am walking along, lost in thought, trying to remember which computer Howard bought, when suddenly I find myself face to face with the guy who tried to rape me when I was ten.

Well, not all of him. Just his skeleton.

A block north of the American Museum of Natural History on Columbus Avenue at 81st Street is a very creepy store called Maxilla & Mandible, Ltd. They sell all sorts of biology lab curiosities, but mostly they are famous for selling bones: animal, human, dinosaur, whatever. The store window is a ghoulish Victorian cabinet of curiosities. Today, Maxilla & Mandible have in their window display a porcelain phrenology head from the 1800s, a nautilus shell, a reproduction of a saber-toothed tiger skull with fangs, shadow boxes of insects impaled on pins, the gaping jaws of a great white shark, earrings made of rat skulls, and the complete skeleton of the man who terrorized me and almost raped me.

How can I tell? It's the teeth. The leering skull has my stalker's teeth. The upper teeth beside his top front teeth were shorter than normal, and they slightly overlapped his front teeth which were tilted a little inward and were chipped in the middle. If it weren't for the chip between the front teeth, I might have been able to convince myself that there could be another person in the world who had my stalker's orthodontic problems, but the same crooked teeth and the same chip? It's got to be him.

Before I have time to talk myself out of it, I open the door and walk into the shop. It is the strangest place I've ever been. The store is crammed floor to ceiling with medical and scientific curiosities arranged on mahogany shelves and in glass display cases. The front window was an honest indication of what is for sale inside: anatomical charts, shrunken heads, tribal art, feathers, eggs, beads, belts, pelts, shells, and bones bones bones, any kind of bone you could think of from any kind of creature, loose in jars or fully assembled. It didn't surprise me that there were no customers inside – after all, who would want this stuff? Me, that's who.

"Can I help you?" says a man behind the counter where the shadow boxes of insects are arrayed. He's a youthful guy in his forties with wire-rimmed glasses and a touch of gray in his feathered brown hair.

"Yeah," I say. "Can you give me some information about one of the things in your front window?"

"Absolutely. Which one?"

"The big human skeleton."

"The surfer dude caught your eye?"

"What?"

"That's the nickname the medical school gave him. I picked him up on a trip to Los Angeles a couple of years ago."

"Is he real or made of plastic?"

"Oh, he's real. I've got all the paperwork on him. We make sure that all our specimens are acquired legally and ethically."

"So what can you tell me about him?"

"Surfer dude's a fully articulated human skeleton. He's in great shape. Circa 1970s. Good patination. He's got a cut calvaria and a wired jaw and a plastic costal cartilage."

"No, I mean what can you tell me about *him*?"

"Him? As in the guy he was before he was a skeleton? That's a little creepy."

"So you have no idea?"

"No. There's no way of knowing anything about who the person was. All I can tell you is where I got the bones from. It's actually an interesting story. If you can wait a minute, I'll pull the paperwork."

I tell him that I'm in no hurry at all and the shopkeeper goes into the back for a couple of minutes and returns with a manila file folder containing a couple of documents.

As he looks over the papers in his hand, the shopkeeper says, "Real human skeletons are getting harder and harder to come by these days. I pick them up wherever I can, but I get most of mine from Europe. For the longest time, almost all skeletons for sale came from India, but India outlawed the export of human bones in 1985. A really good Indian male skeleton from the seventies is worth a lot of money nowadays."

"Oh my God," I say. "When I was a kid, we took a field trip to a college biology lab and there was a skeleton there that they said came from an Indian boy. I thought they meant he was an

Apache or a Cherokee or something. So you mean he was probably an Indian from India?"

"Yeah, of course. The US government is a little sensitive
about American Indian bones. That's why they passed the Native American Graves Protection Act: Freemasons were running
amok. After India stopped exporting skeletons, China became
the big source. That's what you mostly see nowadays, Chinese
skeletons. I try to avoid them as much as possible. With China's
human rights record being what it is, I can only imagine how
they're coming up with their product, so I try to stick to Europe.
Every now and then, though, I make the odd unexpected find
here in the States."

"You said this skeleton was from California?"

"Yeah, when I was out in LA, I heard about a medical school
that was going to be closing down or merging with another
university or whatever, so I hopped over to see if they had anything interesting they'd like to get rid of and they showed me
the surfer dude."

I walk back over to the window display and examine the skeleton from the back. "There's a plate and screws holding together
the back of his head," I say. "Was he broken?"

"No, apparently his fatal injury was a knock on the head. The
folks at the medical school told me the legend was that he was
a John Doe corpse donated in the seventies. They didn't know
if he was a murder victim or an accident victim. Some students
thought he reminded them of the guys who hung out surfing in
Santa Monica and they reckoned he'd cracked his head against
the pier. But they didn't know. He could have been anybody.
After the students dissected him, they cleaned the bones and
had him mounted as a teaching tool and he became sort of a
school mascot. It's weird that you should ask about it because I
almost never get this detailed a provenance on a skeleton. The
school was still very fond of him and didn't want to sell him to
me, but he was so unique I had to have him."

I ask, "How much is he?"

"We've got him priced at $6,000."

"Wow. Okay, I'll take him."

The sales clerk stares at me, surprised. "Seriously? Great. I'll go get a box. You want the stand, too?"

"I'll need one. Does it come separate?"

"How are you paying?"

"Is cash okay?"

"Cash is great. It's a $200 stand. If you're paying by cash, the stand's on me."

I have only $100 on me at the moment, so I ask him if I can put some money down right now and come back tomorrow with the rest of the cash. For a $6,000 sale, he's more than happy to oblige.

***

Yes, I can easily get my hands on $6,000 in cold hard cash these days. Thanks to four drag queens in a purple van, I'm financially secure once again – this time perhaps for the rest of my life – and all because that stupid song "Lookey, Lookey" is the gift that keeps on giving.

About a year ago, I got a letter from a Hollywood movie studio saying they had a film in post-production which had obtained permission from Kitty Belle Crawford's estate to use her recording of "Lookey, Lookey" in one of the scenes. As co-writer of the song, they needed my permission, too, and of course I gave it. I didn't know anything about the film other than the title, *The Fabulettes*.

About six months after that, *The Fabulettes* premiered and turned out to be a monstrous box-office hit. The story wasn't even remotely original. The conceit of four New Jersey drag queens taking a road trip in a purple van was just a retread of *To Wong Foo, Thanks for Everything! Julie Newmar*, which was itself a rip-off of *Priscilla, Queen of the Desert*. What put it over the top was the film's mockumentary style and the screen debut of a young Canadian pop star who had just won the Grammy Award for Best New Artist.

For the film itself, I was paid very little money. They used about thirty seconds of my song in a montage of the drag queens lip-syncing to a campy medley of some of the most awful hits of the sixties and seventies. Really there wasn't all that much music in the film, so to pad out the content on the movie soundtrack album, they included the full version of "Lookey, Lookey." Luckily for me, the Canadian pop star performed the film's theme song – which topped the charts for several months and won the Academy Award for Best Song. *The Fabulettes* soundtrack went multi-platinum and I got 10 cents for every CD sold.

I'll leave it to you to do the math. Needless to say, it was a hell of a lot of money, not to mention the fact that it proved definitively that I'm not some crazy person. Unlike that guy haunting the stage doors of Broadway claiming to be the songwriter Jimmy Webb, I really am R.B. Welch.

Except that I'm not really. I'm still going on the assumption that I had an uncle named R.B. Welch and that I appropriated his name. The problem is I'm still having a little trouble proving that Uncle Arby actually existed and isn't just a psych ward delusion of mine caused by a mixture of psychotropic meds and an overdose of Raquel Welch movies.

I finally got a copy of my birth certificate, as well as the birth certificates of both my parents. It was comforting to see that my mom's maiden name really was Welch and that my maternal grandparents had the names that I remembered. However, birth certificates don't list siblings, so I still have no proof that I ever had an uncle. As for my father, now that I've got proof of his full name, Montgomery Burke Scott, and his date of birth, I've started a records search to see if he's alive or dead. Part of me is hoping that he died a long time ago, because frankly I have no idea what I would say to the man if I ever had the opportunity to meet him.

After I leave Maxilla & Mandible, I head to Apple Bank for Savings at 73rd and Broadway to make my big cash withdrawal to buy the skeleton. While I'm there, I take out an additional $2,000 to buy a computer. I have no idea how much a computer costs, but two grand ought to be enough to buy something I can use. It's surprising how big a wad of cash $8,000 is. I have no way to carry it home except to bend the stack of bills in half and shove it in my front jeans pocket. The bulge in my pants looks obvious and ridiculous, so I make up my mind to walk home as quickly as possible and have Angel the concierge put the money in the hotel safe for me. With luck, people on the street will think I've got a massive erection and not a wad of cash big enough to buy a used car.

When I get back to the Hotel Olcott and ask Angel to help me put the money away, he says that I've got some mail and hands me a thick envelope. At first I assume it's another plea from Brunch Buddies to entice me to join up again, but the envelope looks more like personal stationery and the address is handwritten. The postmark is from California. I turn the envelope over to see the return address written across the back flap.

It's from R.B. Welch, 36105 Palo Colorado Canyon Rd, Big Sur, CA 93920.

I thank Angel and take the elevator up to my apartment. My heart is pounding in my chest. I want to rip the letter open right now but I'm terrified. What will it say? I have a feeling it is going to either confirm the memories I have of my shitty childhood, or confirm that I'm a nutjob with a head full of manufactured fantasies. Frankly neither choice is desirable, and once I read the letter, I'm not going to be able to un-read it.

I let myself into my apartment, sit down on the bed, and stare at the envelope in my hands. It feels like there's something else inside besides sheets of paper. Something hard and a little heavy. I take my index finger and start to unseal the back flap as carefully as I can so as to not damage the return address. It's nice stationery of good, heavy quality, so the envelope opens cleanly. I take out the multi-page letter inside and see that between the sheets is a set of keys.

The writer's penmanship is beautiful, almost like calligraphy. This is not a dashed-off note; it's a testament. And it's addressed to me.

"My dearest Cary," it began …

I am your uncle Arby. It has been over fifteen years
since I last wrote to you, but it may as well have been fifty
years, or a hundred, for I suspect your mother prevented
all my letters from ever reaching you. I learned recently
that Juney has died. Although she was my sister, you can
probably guess that I was not grief-stricken at the news of
her passing. Still, she was your mother and I offer you my
sincere condolences.

I should also offer you condolences for the loss of
your father. Burke passed away four years ago of PCP,
AIDS-related pneumonia, but died happily and in peace,
surrounded by all the people he loved. All the people he loved
except for you, that is. You were the one regret he had in life.

I should go on the assumption that you know nothing
of what happened to your father after Juney threw him
out in 1965. A couple of times before that, she had walked
in on the two of us making out in your garage but she had
always chosen to look the other way. We assumed that she
was reconciled to the situation and was aware that he had
married her only because he was in love with me. I don't
know what it was that prompted her finally to snap, but we
had gotten so brazen that we shouldn't have been surprised
when she took the steps she did. After demanding that
Burke and I both leave town, she divorced your father and
had him labeled a degenerate because of his relationship
with me. A judge granted her request for the sole custody
of you and forbade Burke from ever contacting you again.
Being ripped from you broke your father's heart. As I was
not forbidden by law to have contact with you, Burke had
me write to you regularly to let you know how he was
getting along and how much he loved you, but since you
never replied, I can only guess that Juney intercepted all
my letters and destroyed them. Juney was that cruel.

Burke and I did not leave Espada. We got an apartment
in Las Colinas on the other side of town so that Burke could
keep his job. I went to art school and worked the night shift
at Denny's. After I graduated, I painted a lot and started
earning a bit of money for my work. Before long, we fell
in with the wealthy gay crowd in Palm Springs and that's
when things really started taking off for me. A gallery in

Palm Springs began representing me, and after that the sales and commissions came rolling in.

Things were not so good for your father, however. He didn't enjoy selling appliances and got more and more depressed as my income from painting grew. We had an open relationship back then – which is to say that everyone had an open relationship at that time – and Burke coped as best as he could with his lack of prospects and the loss of you by numbing himself with sex and alcohol. I am not proud to say that I acted no better.

In the mid-seventies, I managed to convince Burke to transfer his sales experience from appliances to real estate. He soon got his broker's license and things turned around for him. It was about that time that we both saw the article about you in the Espada paper. Your father was so proud of you winning that poetry contest, although I have to say we were both a bit concerned and confused about the whole stigmata thing. We had the Rotary Club send us the booklet of the winning entries and had a good laugh at your funny poem and were impressed at how clever you were. We were even more proud and excited when we started hearing your poem sung on the radio. Imagine how surprised I was when I bought a copy of the sheet music as a gift for Burke and saw my own name listed as the lyricist! It didn't take a genius to figure out what you had done, and I admit I was flattered that you had used me as a pen name. I wrote you a letter of congratulations at the time. I'm sure you never got it.

We lost track of you after that. Burke and I attended your high school graduation, but you weren't there. In fact, there was no mention of you at all. We were so disappointed.

In the years that followed, your father started working for a real estate broker up in Monterey and we moved to Big Sur. Burke's big dream, however, was for us to live in New York City. After he got sick, I thought I would make his dream come true, so as a surprise I contacted a NY agency and bought an apartment for us. I should have bought the apartment sooner. By the time I finished mailing and faxing all the paperwork, Burke was too ill to travel. He died before either of us had a chance to see the place that I had bought. Since then, I've never had the heart to visit it. It's just sitting there, empty.

A magazine writer telephoned me last week asking if I were you – that is to say, if I were the R.B. Welch who wrote "Lookey Lookey." Apparently he had written an article about you last year and wasn't able to get in touch with me at the time. He seemed very apologetic about it although I couldn't figure out why. When I explained our relationship, it sounded like he was about to cry, then he gave me your address in New York. The whole thing was very odd.

Which brings me to the reason I am writing to you.

I have recently been diagnosed with the same hereditary cardiomyopathy that my father had. My future is not looking good and I have been told I need to settle my affairs as soon as possible. I am so grateful to finally have your address and to hear that you are living your father's dream in New York. And since it was your father's dream, I would like you to have the apartment I bought for him. The keys are enclosed with this letter. I am told it's a very nice studio on West 81st Street, between Broadway and West End Avenue. I have made arrangements in my will to leave you the apartment after I am gone, but since it's just sitting there empty, there is no reason why you shouldn't enjoy it in the meantime.

I wish you had known your father better. I wish you had known me. I hope your life has been a happy one and that you know your father and I have always been proud of you.

Always, with love,
Your Uncle Arby

I read the letter over again at least two more times. I'm a mess of emotions. I don't know whether to be delighted or deeply depressed. There is so much in it to think about that I have to absorb it in stages: I have found and lost my father in a heartbeat; my mother maliciously kept me from knowing him; Howard seems ashamed of treating me so unfairly; my uncle is dying. Mom had always told me that bad hearts ran in our family. Now I know what she meant.

The thing I mostly feel is a wave of relief because Arby's letter seems to be the definitive proof that I need that my memories are real. On third reading, however, I realize that it's not. All it proves it that I really had an Uncle Arby and that he and my dad were in love. That's something at least.

I pick up the set of keys from where I'd dropped them on the bed. A tag on the key ring has the building address and apartment number on it. Instinctively, I remove the tag because if I should lose the keys or someone should steal them, I wouldn't want anyone to know what doors that they unlocked. Catching myself doing this makes me smile. Removing the address from the key ring is something a real New Yorker would do. Dad would be proud.

***

I unlock the door of the fourth floor apartment at 264 W. 81st Street and step inside for the first time. Uncle Arby was right: it is a nice condo studio in a 1970s-era building, and it certainly is empty. It's also a little dark. The unit's windows are all north-facing and look out onto the small courtyard behind the building, not onto the street. I flick the wall switch by the front door, but the lights don't come on. I go around the room and try a few more switches. None of them work. I'll have to call Con Edison tomorrow and have them turn on the power.

I hope the building's intercom works. When I went back to Maxilla & Mandible to pay for the skeleton, I arranged for them to have it delivered here to Uncle Arby's apartment this afternoon between noon and 5 p.m. I hope it comes sooner rather than later because I'd really rather not sit around here for five hours. I've brought my 200-calorie lunch and the *New York Times*, but since there's no electricity or furniture, it's going to be a little difficult to either eat or read here. Please God, I hope the toilet works.

It turns out that I don't have to wait too long. The deliveryman from Maxilla & Mandible rings the intercom a little before 1:00, and I buzz him in. He comes upstairs wheeling a dolly with a big cardboard box the size of a baby coffin.

"Where do you want this," he asks.

"Pretty much anywhere," I say.

"Are you sure you have room for it in here?" he jokes as he hands me a clipboard and a pen for my signature.

"Are there instructions inside? I don't know how to set something like this thing up."

"Don't worry. I'll give you a hand," he says. "The stand goes together with a couple of screws and then you just hang the skull from a hook."

He takes a fat Swiss Army tool from his pocket and flicks open a knife blade to slice open the box. Buried inside a nest of Styrofoam peanuts is the skeleton of my stalker lying on its side in a fetal position. It takes about ten minutes for the deliveryman to assemble the stand using the screwdriver blade on his pocket tool. Together the two of us lift the skeleton out of the box and hang him up.

My stalker and I are once more standing face to face. His smile is the smile engraved in my memory. I am now more certain than ever that he was real and what he did to me was real.

The deliveryman looks around the dim, empty room and says, "You know, when furnishing a new apartment, most people don't start with human remains. They get a sofa."

CHAPTER TWELVE

2014

I work at the museum on Thursdays. Lately, there hasn't been much for me to do there except maintenance. I haven't had to do an installation for months now, but things do continue to get dusty and the light and humidity levels have to be carefully monitored. The work is hardly onerous, but it gives me focus, as well as some purpose in life.

It's rare that I ever see anyone whenever I come to work. In the last seventeen years, I think I can count on one hand the number of times I've passed someone in the hall or ridden with someone in the elevator. That's probably because I tend to arrive in the late morning and leave in the mid-afternoon when everyone is busy elsewhere with other things. Today it's deserted as usual.

As I let myself in, I notice the third lock on the museum door has started to stick a bit so I'll need to get the locksmith back again soon. I added a second deadbolt two years ago after I read about a rash of burglaries in the neighborhood. There's never been any sign of a break-in here, but the museum's collection is valuable and you can never be too careful.

I flick on the lights and the display cases illuminate. The artifacts behind glass glow softly under LED spots. The rest of the room is lit indirectly with halogen lamps concealed in the tops of the mahogany wall units. The only sound in the museum is the hum of the HEPA air filter and the large dehumidifier.

Today is my day to carefully dust the items in the west wall display cases. It's the one job that takes me the longest to do because the west wall of the museum has no windows, so it's where the bulk of the collection is housed.

I get my cleaning supplies and step ladder from the maintenance closet then unlock the first display cabinet. Some of the items in this cabinet are extremely fragile and can hardly be touched. For instance, the McCall's printed pattern #2459 from 1961 is in tatters and on the verge of falling to pieces. The right bottom corner of the envelope has flaked away so the size and price can no longer be seen, but I know that it originally said, *50c in Canada 60c*. Except for some wrinkles and age spots, the rest of the envelope is in fairly good condition.

The illustration of the three children's Halloween costumes that the pattern creates is absolutely charming. Illustration A shows an androgynous child in a circus clown outfit. The body of the costume is a jumpsuit of high-waisted yellow trousers with blue and green patch pockets, and a bodice with long sleeves that is one-half solid green and one-half red-and-white plaid. The child wears a white hood with attached red yarn hair and little hat, and is depicted dangling a red polka-dot handkerchief from the left hand while extending his right arm straight out with a stereotypically gay limp wrist. Illustration B is of a little girl in a blond pageboy and a harlequin mask wearing the "little prince" costume. It's basically another high-waisted clown costume, but in blue and white with a big frilly collar and a conical hat topped with three pink pompoms.

This vintage pattern is in the museum because of the third illustration on the envelope. Illustration C is of a little boy in a red devil outfit. A large yellow rickrack pitchfork is appliquéd from his crotch to his chest, looking for all the world like an enormous yellow erection. The package includes the tail and cape patterns as well. The boy depicted has a black mustache and small soul-patch drawn on his face along with blue eye shadow, heavy eyeliner, and some wicked eyebrows. His pose, however, is classic Shirley Temple – tilted head, popped hip, and a flirty index finger pointed under the chin.

I give the pattern envelope a couple of gentle puffs from a can of compressed air to clear away any accumulated dust. The can of air is also good for cleaning the mounted cat skeleton that sits beside it. Before I learned about compressed air, I used to have to dust the delicate cat bones with a Q-Tip and that took forever. Now I can get my work done in a fraction of the time.

Many of the other items in the display case are much easier to dust. The jar of ipecac, the heavy beige rotary-dial phone from the 1960s, the rubber enema kit from the 1950s, the motorcycle helmet, the copies of *The Boy Who Fooled the Giant* and the *Joy of Gay Sex* aren't particularly fragile and can stand the touch of a dust cloth. The Polynesian grass skirt in the next case needs a lot of puffing with the air can, of course. At the slightest touch it sheds fronds.

Dusting just this one bank of cabinets takes about three hours normally. Over the past decade, I've amassed over 500 artifacts and almost all the smaller things are in the west wall cases. Stepping back to take a break, I look around the room and realize for the first time just how much my museum resembles the little shop Maxilla & Mandible which went out of business three years ago. Who would have guessed when I bought that first skeleton how my collection would grow?

That skeleton is still the crown jewel, the main focus of the room. He has pride of place in the corner and is lit beautifully. I stopped venting my rage at him many years ago. God knows how much abuse he has suffered from me and yet kept smiling. That's the way of bones, though. Sometimes after a shower, I look at myself in the mirror and can see my own skeleton but it doesn't smile.

And right now, I turn and catch a glimpse of my reflection in the glass door of a display case. The white-haired man staring back at me reminds me of my grandfather, pale skin draped over bones. I am three years older than he was when he passed away.

Sitting down on the floor in the middle of the room, I survey my collection and laugh to myself that I'd probably put my grandfather in the museum, too, if I could.

###